ABBY MCDONALD is the author of two other novels for young adults, *Life Swap* and *Boys, Bears and a Serious Pair of Hiking Boots*, as well as two adult novels. She graduated from Oxford University in 2006 with a degree in politics, philosophy and economics and was an entertainment critic before becoming a full-time writer. Originally from Sussex, she now lives in Los Angeles.

About *The Anti-Prom*, Abby says, "Growing up in England, I never had a prom, so have always been fascinated by the event. I set out to write about the most important night of Bliss's, Jolene's and Meg's lives … and realized that what happens *after* prom was far more exciting. Sometimes our biggest plans go wrong, but it's those unexpected detours that turn out to be the real adventure."

The Anti-Prom

ABBY McDONALD

WALKER BOOKS

First published in Great Britain 2012 by Walker Books Ltd
87 Vauxhall Walk, London SE11 5HJ

2 4 6 8 10 9 7 5 3 1

Text © 2012 by Abby McDonald
Cover photograph © Mark Lund/Getty Images

This book has been typeset in Sabon

Printed and bound in Great Britain by Clays plc, St Ives Ltd

British Library Cataloguing in Publication Data:
a catalogue record for this book is
available from the British Library

ISBN 978-1-4063-3758-7

www.walker.co.uk

For Caroline B. Cooney – for a childhood of escape and inspiration. (And all those books about "well, surviving.")

Bliss

He doesn't kiss me like that.

That's the first thing I think when I find Kaitlin Carter getting to second base with my boyfriend in the back of our rental limo.

Followed closely by, *Is she wearing any panties?*

And then, *Ew, ew, EW!*

I watch through the open door in a daze. Kaitlin is straddling Cameron's lap, kind of … grinding at him, her pinned updo thwacking against the roof in time to the rap track they have playing on the pimped-out stereo. I blink. A half hour ago, we were slow-dancing inside, my cheek resting against the crisp lapel of Cameron's tux. Now, his jacket is crumpled on the seat beside them, next to her strapless bra and the stray lipstick I came back out here to collect.

I try to leave, but for some reason, I can't look away.

She's unbuttoning his shirt now, as he gropes at every available inch of flesh. And Kaitlin's dress provides plenty of it to grope. We hit every mall in a hundred-mile radius to find these dresses, but while my mom vetoed everything slit way up my thigh and down my chest, Kaitlin walked away with a clinging pink jersey thing that could probably get her arrested in some states.

Cameron sure appreciates the easy access. As I watch, his hands creep up her thighs, pushing the fabric higher, until—

I reel back, freaked.

Make that third base.

"Omigod, Bliss, where WERE you?" Nikki pounces the minute I get back inside the country club. "The DJ totally promised to play that song we love. I've been looking everywhere for you!"

I can't find the words, but I'm lucky: Nikki is too high on prom to care. Not even pausing for breath, she drags me through the gleaming marble lobby overflowing with flowers and floating balloons. "And Kaitlin totally ditched me, too! I know you guys are, like, BFFs or whatever, but this is *prom*! You should be hanging out with us. Bliss? Hey, earth to B!" She snaps her fingers in front of my face.

"Oh, yeah, sorry." I pause. Nikki's waiting, her forehead creased in a tiny frown, and for a moment I think about telling her everything. It would be all over this place in minutes – no, wait. The way Nikki gossips, everyone would think Kaitlin had thrown an orgy with Cameron, the limo driver, *and* the pimply freshman valet before she even has time to pull that bra on again.

But just as quickly as the thought comes, I push it down again. Winding up the biggest scandal of the night is so not on my prom agenda. "I was, umm, with Cameron," I tell her, arranging my face into a perky grin. "You know, just getting some private time."

"Nice!" Nikki gives me this knowing look. "But seriously, how hot do the guys look in their tuxes? They should make them, like, mandatory uniforms."

"Right." I even manage a giggle. "Anyway, I'm here now. Let's party!"

Linking my arm through hers, I head into the thick of the crowd. It's crazy out here: five hundred kids cutting loose on the dance floor in a flashing mess of formal gear and floor-length gowns. East Midlands High has always been famous for our prom, and this year is no different. The PTA started planning way back in the fall, throwing fancy dinners and auctions to raise funds, even when they didn't need it. Half the school district is so loaded, all it takes is a couple of fat checks and a few calls and voilà! The exclusive country club is booked up for the night with uniformed waiters, armfuls of sparkling streamers, and a DJ flown in special from the East Coast by some senior's doting dad.

Tickets sell out so fast, they make it upperclassmen only, so when junior year finally came around, you can bet we were ready. I started looking for a dress in December, found the right shoes in March, and perfected my half-braided, tumbling hairstyle at the salon by the time Cameron finally asked me to go in May. It was going to be perfect.

It was supposed to be freaking perfect.

We finally reach the others, already staked out in prime position – in the center of things, like always. "Awesome!" Nikki cries as the DJ switches to a new song, some club hit with a sexy dance routine. The rest of them squeal as well, flushed and happy like this is everything we've dreamed about. Nikki turns, clutching me with glee. "Isn't this perfect?"

"So perfect!" My cheeks hurt from forcing this smile, but I pose for the flash of someone's camera, pretending like everything's just fine. And it is. Kaitlin can work her way through the whole freaking *Kama Sutra* with Cameron for all I care. This is prom. And like my mom always says, you remember prom for the rest of your life.

Four songs later, I'm still trying to dance the disturbing memories right out of my mind when Courtney grabs my arm. By now, our careful outfits are beginning to come undone: her strapless turquoise dress is slipping lower, and her hair has fallen out of its bun. I watch her lips move, not able to make out a word over the deafening thump of the music. "I can't hear you!" I yell back.

Courtney mimes something, as if she's putting on lip gloss.

"Bathroom break?" I figure her out. "OK."

Nikki grabs some of the other girls and breaks for the edge of the floor. I follow, numb. Maybe some air is what I need. I want to forget everything, but no matter how much I throw myself into the music, I still feel weirdly detached, like I'm not in my body anymore. I should be crying, heartbroken over Cameron somewhere, I know, but for some reason, the tears won't come. I just picture them together, frozen in that guilty scene. His hands, her little breathy moans.

I feel something sharp start to form behind my rib cage, a fierce knot of resentment.

"This is the best prom ever!" Brianna declares, pushing through the door into the gleaming cream bathroom. As a reigning senior, she would know, which is why Courtney and Nikki just make noises of agreement instead of asking if it's true that she spent the last one barfing in her pool house after getting drunk at the preparty. "Bliss, do you have that mascara?"

I silently hand it over. The others all crowd around the gilt-edged mirrors, carefully reapplying gloss and glitter, but I sink down onto the plush love seat in the corner, tired out.

"So, gossip," Brianna orders, gazing at her own reflection. "There's got to be something."

"I saw Patrick making out with Taryn," Nikki offers.

Brianna wrinkles her lip. "From cheerleading?"

"No, the one with red hair. Remember, she cheated on TJ last year?"

There's a chorus of delighted "Ew!" and "Skank!" and

for the first time, I wonder if they'd even take my side. It shouldn't even be a thing. I mean, Kaitlin and Cameron are the ones lying and cheating and stabbing me in the back here. But then I think of this senior girl, Melissa. She and Luke DiGeorge were like the old married couple of our group, until she found out that he'd been texting Keisha Martin behind her back. She confronted them during lunch one day: a huge showdown in front of the whole school. At first, everyone was totally scandalized and swore they had her back, but Courtney was dating Luke's cousin, and Keisha hooked everyone up with tickets to the best events through her dad, and soon enough, she was totally forgiven. In the end, Melissa just kind of drifted out of our orbit. I don't even know if she came tonight.

I watch the girls gossip, chilled by the thought of everything I could lose. I've worked too hard to get here – get *in* – to be edged out, just because my supposed friend couldn't keep her hands (or other body parts) off my boyfriend. But what am I supposed to do now: smile and let them get away with it?

The knot twists tighter.

"You guys won't believe my after-party." With a final dap of gloss, Brianna turns away from the mirror. "It's going to be epic, I swear." She notices me folded in the corner. "What's up with you, B? Is Cameron off getting wasted with the rest of the guys?"

I force another grin. "No idea! He was around here somewhere…"

Luckily, before she can ask anything else, the door

swings open. "Omigod, you will not believe who I just saw!" Another senior, Jessica, bursts in. Her hair is dyed almost white-blond, and she's straightened it into a flat sheet that hangs past her waist.

"Who? Who?" The girls crowd around.

Jessica pauses for effect and then announces, "Jolene Nelson."

I look up.

"No. Way!" They all gasp.

"Yes way!" She snatches a lip gloss wand and touches up. "I saw her lurking in one of the side rooms, and you will not believe what she's wearing. It's like, pink!"

"Pink?" Nikki sneers.

"Uh-huh. It's got ruffles and everything."

"What is she even doing here?" Brianna whines. "I thought she was suspended. Didn't she, like, set fire to one of the back buildings?"

Courtney bobs her head in agreement. "I heard they're pressing charges. She's going to go to juvie."

"I heard it was because she slept with Mr. Milton," Jessica says smugly. "Taylor told me that Nadine told her that Jolene totally seduced him, and then blackmailed him for five thousand dollars. He's like, a public school teacher, so he couldn't pay, and she ratted him out to the principal."

"The bitch!"

"What a slut."

"I can't believe she showed her face."

While the other girls rally to poor Mr. Milton's defense, I pause, an unlikely idea sparking to life. Jolene Nelson, here at prom? Part of me doesn't believe Jessica – I mean, that whole "pink ruffles" part? – but if it's true...

I leap up before I can change my mind. "I forgot!" I exclaim, reaching for my purse. "Cameron's waiting for me. The DJ's going to play our song."

"Awwww!" The looks I get are the usual mixture of simpering and sheer envy.

"See you inside!" I bolt from the room. But it's not Cameron I'm looking for.

I hurry back through the maze of glossy hallways, checking the lobby and the cloakroom and even the refreshment area for any sign of her angry glare. I don't know what I'll do if I find her. I haven't thought that far ahead. I just know that for the first time since the parking lot, I feel like myself again: like I have a mission, some freaking sense of control.

"Bliss!" A group of girls from the prom committee stops me by the portrait setup, but I just wave, avoiding the flash of their digital cameras and perfect party pouts. Even when Tristan, the undisputed hottest guy in our class, catches my eye and starts to ask "What's up?" I don't even slow for a second; I just keep searching. Finally, when I'm about ready to give it up as an urban prom legend, I open the door to one of the gloomy storage rooms.

And there she is: perched up on a cluttered shelf, smoking out of the open window. That spiky bleached hair has been gelled into something sleek and almost stylish, a pink silk dress is crumpled around her knees, and a pair of gorgeous strappy sandals lie abandoned on the dusty floor.

Jolene Nelson, the baddest girl in school.

"Do you want something?" Flicking ash out the window, she looks down at me with the trademark icy stare that's reduced freshmen to tears.

"I…" I pause, but just as I'm about to take it back and turn around, the music drifting through the open window switches to a new song. Not just any song, but ours – mine and Cameron's. The one he put on that old-school mix CD, the one playing in his car when we went on our first date. I wasn't lying to the girls in the bathroom: I asked the DJ to play it especially. I thought it would be a perfect romantic moment for us, something to look back on when I'm old and gray and sucking strained beets through a straw.

Instead, I get to remember his hands up someone else's skirt, and the color of Kaitlin's hot-pink thong panties.

I steel myself and take a couple of steps into the room. "I need your help."

JOLENE

According to my ex–algebra teacher (who, despite what everyone thinks, I didn't seduce, blackmail, and leave penniless working as a fry cook at a roadside diner in Idaho), the only real impossibilities are mathematical. You know, two plus two equaling five, or a triangle not adding up to 180 degrees. Everything else, even gravity failing or Miley Cyrus releasing a death-metal album, is just improbable—wait around long enough, and they might just come true.

I'm beginning to get what he means. Because right now:

1. I, Jolene Roseanne Nelson, am at the
   East Midlands prom.
2. Wearing a stupid pink dress.
3. And Bliss Merino is asking for my help.

Thanks a lot, Mr. Milton.

"Say it again?" Taking a slow drag, I look down from my vantage point atop the shelf of cleaning supplies. Bliss looks plastic and perfect as ever, a white floaty dress taped to her perky chest, almost glowing against the silver heels and tumble of black hair. She looks totally out of place in the messy supply closet, but then again, I can hardly judge.

Freaking ruffles.

"Will you help me?" Bliss edges closer, her face lit up in this hopeful expression, and I can feel my prospects of peace and solitude disappear right out that window with the last of my cigarette smoke.

So much for staying under the radar. A half hour more was all I was going to give this thing, and I figured I could avoid the hyper, squealing drama that long at least. But I can already hear, "You look so cute!" "No, YOU look so cute!" drifting in, and guitar from that stupid, soft-rock slow jam echoing from the ballroom.

"Help with what?" I finally ask when I get over the fact that she's actually looking me in the eye, let alone asking for a favor. "Wait, don't tell me..." I wouldn't have figured this one for a raver, but hey, I'd need to be out of my mind to tolerate her friends and their in-depth debate over the merits of Sparkle Sheen versus Juicy Glow lip gloss. "I'm not holding. Try Miles Parsons," I suggest, icy. "I saw him with some pills out on the back terrace."

"What?" Bliss looks confused. "No, that's no it!"

"Then what?" I smush out the cigarette, wondering how much of my lung capacity I've just killed. It's a crappy habit, I know, but it calms me down, and God knows I need calming in this getup. Every time I glance down, there they are: enough ruffles to smother a small child, erupting from my chest like a foul wave of pink taffeta, out to drown every ounce of credibility I've got.

"I..." Bliss takes a breath. "I want to destroy Kaitlin Carter."

"Rebellion in the social ranks, how thrilling." I roll my eyes. "So, don't sit with her at lunch. I'm sure it'll be like, OMG, the biggest scandal!"

"That's not what I mean." She shakes her pretty little head. "I'm serious. I want to tear her life apart."

I pause. It is, after all, either this or braving the main ballroom again to watch the dry-humping Olympics. Raising an eyebrow, I ask, "What happened – did she wear the same color eye shadow as you?"

Bliss folds her arms. "Nope, she's actually fooling around with my boyfriend in the back of our limo right about now."

I let out a snort of laughter. Bliss, of course, looks wounded.

"Come on." I hop down from the shelf, my feet bare on the dusty floor. "Weren't you dating that football frat dude? I weep for your loss."

"Cameron," Bliss replies, her voice thin. "And he needs to pay as well."

"OK, so she's a bitch and he's a slut." I shrug. "Tell me something I don't know." I begin to strap myself back in those heels, trying not to wince at the pain. I thought about coming in my boots, but our deal was all or nothing:

him in a cummerbund and flashy suit, me with the full *Seventeen* prom extravaganza. We laughed at the time, like it would be the biggest joke to crash their party, but I guess the joke's on me. I haven't heard from Dante in months, but I still trussed myself up like an idiot, hoping he'd come.

I make to leave, but to my surprise, Bliss blocks the door.

I glare.

"Look, I get it," she protests hurriedly, backing off. "You don't like me. And that's just fine. But I want revenge, and I can make it worth your while."

My jaw drops.

"You have *got* to be kidding me." Just when I think these girls couldn't get any more entitled. "What's next – paying someone to wipe your ass?"

"Stop, Jolene—"

"I'm not one of your little groupies." I fix her with a deathly stare. "Get one of them to do your grunt work."

I head down the hallway as fast as these perilous heels will take me. Groups of glitzy students litter every room, but I cut through the crowds, fuming at Bliss's nerve. She and the rest of that clique are all the same. I see them every day; we all do – fawning over each other's preppy designer clothes in the cafeteria, strutting down the halls like they own them. Sometimes, they even swing by the Dairy Queen, so I can serve them milkshakes and clean up the mess they always leave behind.

I used to let it slide, like everyone else. Petty social games – they're a high-school fact of life, right? That's what everyone thinks, anyway, but it's a lie. You can quit, it's simple. You just walk away. Let mindless dolls like Bliss Merino tie themselves up trying to be perfect and popular – I got the hell out. They think I'm white trash anyway, so I may as well live up to my damn name. It didn't take much, in the end: some big boots, a pair of headphones. Turn up late, fight back, carve some desks, get suspended. The rumors started up, and just like that, *they* get out of the way for *me* in the hallways. I've got four more days until graduation, two months until I start college, and most of them are smart (or scared) enough to leave me well alone until then.

Except Bliss. I'm swiping some pastry shells from the refreshment area when I hear the *tip-tap* of heels approaching. Sure enough, Bambi bounds up beside me, her white dress swishing around like she's got a personal wind machine trailing her. And who knows – on Daddy's budget, maybe she does.

"I'm sorry, I didn't think," she insists like we never stopped talking. "I don't mean it like I'm better than you. I just thought you'd want some kind of ... incentive."

I turn my back on her. Crab filling? Awesome.

"Please" – Bliss keeps at me – "would you just—"

"Jolene? Yoo-hooo, Jolene Nelson? There you are!"

I freeze. A perky-looking woman is bearing down on us, marked with the bright red pin of official chaperones. I scan the room, but it's too late. There's no escape.

"Look at you! That dress is so cute!" she gushes, enveloping me in a hug. Immediately, I choke for air, smothered by a heavy cloud of floral perfume. "When your mom said you were coming, I couldn't believe it, but here you are, looking like your old self!"

My mom? I pause, alert for danger. "Uh, hi…"

"Can I get a photo of you and your friend?" She waves a digital camera at me. "I know your mom would love some pics."

"Sure," I say weakly. "Come on, *friend*." I give Bliss a look. Luckily, those girls take classes in being a camera whore. Throwing her arms around me, she grins maniacally at the woman.

"Everybody say *prom*!" Bliss squeals.

"Fab!" The camera flashes away a couple of times, and then the woman beams. "So glad I caught you! I have to go back on patrol now. Did you know some kids are sneaking out to *get drunk*?" She drops her voice to whisper the last words.

"No!" Bliss gasps, almost sarcastic.

She nods. "You girls have fun. Be good!" And then at last, the woman sweeps away in a blur of gold beading. I let out a sigh of relief. Pure oxygen, the joy.

"Well?"

When I look up, Bliss is staring at me, smug.

"Thanks," I mumble. I didn't expect her to play along, but it's still not as if I owe her or anything.

"Don't go OTT."

"Whatever." I'm done humoring her, but just as I'm about to tell Bliss exactly where she can take her fake smiles and vast reserve of entitlement, I catch a flash of something in her expression. For a moment, the smile strains at the edge of her lips, and her eyes are full of anger. Then it's gone, and that careful mask flips back into place.

I pause, softening just a tiny bit. Anger, I know. Damn, I could write an epic novel on that. I know how it burns at you, hardening inside until you've got nothing but a metal lump in your gut that won't shift, not for anything.

At least, I didn't think there was anything...

"You really want them to go down?" I ask, suddenly curious. This is about more than just a wrecked prom, I can tell, and if Bambi here wants it bad enough, then perhaps she could be useful to me, after all.

Bliss nods, her face even again. "I said before," she answers, almost flippant. "I want revenge, and I want you to teach me how."

Yup. Tonight is definitely the night of impossibilities.

Suddenly, the room is invaded by a crowd of girls, chattering in that high-pitched whine about how freaking awesome the DJ is and how freaking cute Sam looks in his tux and how freaking uh-MAY-zing their photos will look online. They swarm around me, filling plates with tiny, calorie-free snacks and shrieking about what might get stuck in their teeth.

"Jolene?" Bliss is still pestering me, so I check my phone. Forty minutes late. There's no way Dante's going to show now. He probably doesn't even remember our deal, and even if he does ... Well, the way things went down the last time I saw him wouldn't exactly make me leap at the chance to hang out again, prom or no prom.

"And Mellie said that SHE saw this dress first, but

I was like, no way, and anyway, she has blond hair, and everyone knows blond and silver, like, so don't go, and..."

What the hell.

Checking that the coast is clear of gushing chaperones, I take a handful of stuffed mushrooms and head toward the back of the room. Just as I thought, there's a dark hallway, so the staff can bring out those fancy trays without the prized partygoers even having to glance at the help. The sign out front says NO GUESTS ALLOWED in big black lettering. I push it aside.

"Where are you going?" Bambi is still trotting after me. I don't bother to turn.

"Anywhere but here. You in?"

"Seriously?" she gasps. "Yes! I'm so in."

I lead her into the labyrinth of hallways, but once we're out of sight, I pause. "If we're going to do this, we do it my way," I warn, hands on hips. "You do what the hell I say, when I say it." Bliss nods eagerly. "And don't even think about paying me," I add, glaring. "You cover the cost of materials, and unexpected expenses, and that's it."

Her forehead wrinkles. "Unexpected...?"

I roll my eyes. "Bribes, bail, you know."

"Umm, sure."

I spot a waiter coming toward us. He's still looking down at the heavy tray of glasses, but any minute now... "Quick," I whisper, "hide!"

We duck into a side room. "Umm, I know this might be a stupid question," Bliss whispers, crammed next to me in the dark. "But why don't we just walk out the front?"

I sigh. "Because we need an alibi. You saw that woman before?" Bliss nods. "She's friends with my mom," I explain. "If anything goes wrong with this revenge plan, there are hundreds of people like her stationed all over the place, ready to report they saw us leave together."

"Hundreds." Bliss giggles, so I elbow her. She falls silent for a moment. But just a moment. "If you don't want to be here, why did you even come?"

"I'm not allowed?" I snap back.

"That's not what I said." I can feel Bliss studying me. "You're really touchy, you know that?"

"No," I drawl, sarcastic. "My therapist didn't mention it." I crack the door and peer out. The waiter has stopped about ten feet away and is chatting to another staff member. She's young and pretty, and by the adoring look on his face, we'll be here all night.

I close the door again. Bliss is still watching me. "So, why did you come?"

I exhale loudly. "You ask too many questions, you know that?"

Bliss grins. "Maybe you should give me that therapist's number."

Touché.

I check again, but our escape route is still blocked; meanwhile, Bliss is studying me with that perky head-tilt of expectation, utterly unswayed by my acerbic replies. I think I preferred it when she thought I was a loser drug-dealer.

"It was either this or boot camp," I finally declare. Like I'm going to tell her the truth.

"What?" It gets the reaction I want: Bliss widens her eyes and takes a tiny step away from me.

"This summer," I elaborate. I've already got a reputation, but there's no harm in striking some fear into her before we get things started. "I don't turn eighteen until September, so my mom said that if I didn't follow her rules again, she'd ship me off to boot camp." I give a shrug. "This place out in Arizona where they make you hike twenty miles through the desert and live on soya and psychotherapy."

"Wow," Bliss breathes.

My mom's not that hardcore yet, but I'm pushing her, I know. She's already confiscated the keys to my hard-earned junkyard car, grounded me from everything except work and school, and sworn to call the admissions board and have them rescind my acceptance if I don't stop scaring her with the smoking, late nights, skeezy boyfriends, and occasional (and completely unjustified) arrests. Tonight was an olive branch, of sorts: for one night, I'd be a normal teenage girl again. No felonies, graffiti, or fights, I promised.

Guess that's not going to work out.

Bliss peers out the doorway again. "Wait, I think he's gone!"

The coast is clear. "Stay close," I tell her, creeping back down the hallway. I can see the lights of the emergency exit winking in the distance. The promised land. "And when you hear the alarm, run."

"Alarm?" she repeats, wide-eyed, just as I pull open the door. An ear-splitting wail rings out.

I grab her skinny, corsage-wearing wrist with one hand and hike up my skirt.

"RUN!"

Meg

With one hand clutching the steering wheel, I press my cell phone to hear the message again.

"Uh, hey, Meg, it's Christopher... I'm not going to be able to make it tonight... Something, uh, came up. So, yeah, have fun without me!"

Beep.

"Uh, hey, Meg, it's Christopher..."

I let it play once more, lost in some kind of haze as I circle the country club parking lot. I've been here ten minutes, and I know Christopher's words by heart, but I still can't seem to make a decision. Up ahead, the exit is marked with grand columns and a drifting bouquet of balloons, and to my left, the main doors are polished and gleaming, inviting guests in. Stay or go, stay or go. I make another loop instead, feeling a hot tear begin to trickle down my cheek.

I wipe it away, foolish. This isn't how I imagined my first formal dance. For years, I've pored over that red leather album showing my parents at their high-school proms. The photographs are full of teased hair and netted gowns, but what I always loved was the simple happiness in their expressions: Dad, stiff in his tuxedo, goofy grin too big for his teenage face; my mom, pale and slight even back then, but lit up with a glow of giddy excitement. It's not as if I was naive enough to think it would be the same for me – after all, I'm not one of those girls tearing pages from magazines and planning their parties, gossiping over dresses and dates like the glossy elite of East Midlands High. That isn't my life, especially these days, but despite every instinct that prom would be just another lonely rite of teenage passage, I had hope. Hope that maybe when it came to my turn, I'd have just a taste of that romance, a glimpse of that glitter of dancing and fun.

I wish that for once, my instincts weren't right. Because despite the dress, the shoes, and even the son of a family friend we found as a date for me, I'm not even up the front steps and it's all falling apart.

Pull yourself together, Meg Rose Zuckerman.

My mom's voice comes suddenly, as loud as if she's sitting right here beside me. It's been three years now, but it still makes me jump a little to hear her like this. Everyone says that it's a form of comfort, the mind's way of coping, but I don't get anything as sweet as soft encouragement from my subconscious. No, when I hear her, it's the way she would talk near the end: impatient and full of dark humor.

I used to feel bad for laughing then, when she would only joke to relieve the awful tension lingering in every sterile room, but now I prefer the no-nonsense attitude.

Can't wait around for Prince Charming forever, she would always say, and I hear it again now. *You aren't the kind of girl who ever needs rescuing. It's a waste of a damn pretty dress, that's what it is.*

She's right. Swallowing back my tears, I force myself to find a free parking space and check my reflection in the mirror, carefully wiping away the smudge of mascara beneath one eye. My purse is a tiny beaded thing, twinkling black sparkles in the car light, and I grip it firmly as if it's my only protection.

You're here now. You might as well do this.

People are spilling out of the grand double doors as I approach: clusters of girls hugging on the front steps as they pose for photographs. I wait patiently to the side while they giggle and fuss over their hair, making everything perfect for those online profile pictures and albums they'll upload in the morning – if they can even wait that long.

"You got a light?"

I turn to find another straggler, lurking back from the steps in a three-piece white tux. He looks too old to be here, tall and dark-eyed, restlessly flipping a cigarette through his fingers like a magic trick.

"Umm, no. Sorry," I add, apologetic.

"Guess it's for the best." He doesn't move, looking reluctantly at the building for a long moment, as if he's trying to decide something. At least I'm not the only one in two minds about this. We stand in silence together, watching, until suddenly he shrugs. "Enjoy your night," he tells me, almost sarcastic, before he turns and walks away from the lights and laughter.

Part of me wants to follow, simply change my mind, but then I hear my name coming from the group on the steps.

"Hey, Meg, get over here!"

I stop, not quite believing it.

"Meg, hurry up!"

I start to move, but then somebody pushes past me and hurls herself at the group. It's a tiny redhead I recognize from the hallways, always tucked under the arm of her student government boyfriend. "I'm here, I'm here!" she cries, bright blue silk swishing around her legs.

"Finally!" The girls clutch one another, and the flash goes, capturing the perfect frame of friendship and delight.

I slip past them, unsteady on new heels.

Inside, I'm quickly swallowed by the crowds, rushing in a rainbow of gowns and uncharacteristically crisp shirts. For a moment, I'm caught up in their excitement, but then the groups scatter, and I'm left conspicuously alone in the middle of the marble lobby. I can feel my brief spark of determination fading already, wilting under the curious gaze of a chaperone. This was why I accepted the Christopher setup – to have some kind of shield against this awkwardness, even though having your stepmom recruit your date from her friends' ranks of teenage sons is nothing if not pathetic.

Worse still, I realize, is getting stood up by a guy you've never even met.

I take a tentative few steps down one of the empty hallways, the floor swirled with coral and gold. It's certainly pretty; the planning committee came through for that. Garlands of blue and white balloons bob gently in every corner, the huge bouquets trailing ribbons and faint floral scent. I can't help but let out a wistful sigh. It's all fit for a princess, the perfect romantic event.

And then I see him strolling toward me, his tuxedo jacket looking faintly crumpled, and his slick little bow tie askew. Tristan. I freeze. He's with the rest of his guys, of course – Danny and Kellan and Nico – and as he saunters closer, he holds his hands out, palms up, greeting the girls who emerge fresh from the bathroom behind me. I melt back against the wall to let them past. "Ladies." He dips in a funny little formal bow. "Looking lovely, I see."

They laugh at his old-fashioned tone. It's the usual suspects: Brianna and Nikki, and Kaitlin joining them too, hurrying from outside with her dress clinging dangerously to her remarkable chest. But even a potentially embarrassing wardrobe malfunction can't keep my focus from Tristan: the careless ruffle of his dark blond hair, that irritatingly charming smile. I usually only see the right corner of it from my vantage point two seats over in AP Calculus, but full-on, it's devastating.

The two groups meet in the middle of the hallway, just a few feet away from me.

"You didn't RSVP for my after-party." Brianna pouts,

reaching up to adjust Tristan's bow tie. I try to imagine just putting my hand out and touching him like that, or even touching any boy who doesn't belong to me. I can't.

"Maybe I've got other options..." He grins down at her, teasing.

"Sure you do." She laughs before turning to the others. "Remember, keep all the booze out of sight until my parents leave. And invite people if you want, but nobody ... undesirable, OK?"

At that last word, her gaze drifts over to me, still lingering in the shadow of one of those bouquets. She doesn't even think to muster a frown or sneer – no, that would imply effort, like I matter – instead, she just flicks her eyes back to the group. "Come on, let's go hit the floor."

They hustle away, pushing through the main ballroom doors so that a blast of music echoes out. And then the doors swing shut, and it goes quiet again.

I can't do this.

I know what my mom would say, but I can't help it. I'm not this girl. I hurry back through the lobby, all but tripping down the front steps as I race across the parking lot and fling myself back into the Honda. I reverse out of my space and circle toward the exit, already feeling tears well up again. They were so excited for me, fussing with my corsage and photographs on the stairs, but I can already imagine Dad's disappointed expression, and Stella swooping in to comfort me with ice cream and DVDs—

There's a flash of pale dresses in front of me, two girls

rushing into the road. My heart stops. I slam on the brakes. Silence.

Wrenching open the door, I struggle out of my seat belt and rush around the front of the car. A faint alarm is wailing somewhere, but we're all alone in the far end of the lot, next to a cluster of huge trash cans and empty boxes.

"Oh God, did I hit you?" I gasp for breath, looking in horror at the girl collapsed in a tangle of tanned limbs and white silk on the asphalt. "Oh God! I wasn't going fast, but you just came out of nowhere and—"

"It's OK!" The other girl pulls her friend up. "You didn't hit us, she tripped. That's what you get for wearing those freaking ridiculous heels," she adds with a note of disdain.

"You were the one yanking my arm!"

"Yeah, well, when I say run, I don't mean that beauty-pageant strut of yours!"

As I look back and forth between them, my panic gradually subsides. Then I realize who they are.

The girl in pink looks over, as if seeing me properly for the first time. "You go to East Midlands, right?" She frowns. "I'm Jolene."

I take a tiny step back. I know who she is. *Everybody* knows. Half the graffiti in the girls' bathroom is devoted to Jolene Nelson and her multitude of sins. And most of it has probably been scrawled there by Bliss Merino's closest friends. "Meg," I tell her, nervous. If even a couple of the stories I've heard about her are true...

"So you're here for prom?" Bliss is on her feet again

now, smiling at me without a hint of recognition. "Cute dress."

I glance down at the folds of black I thought would make all the difference. "Thanks," I mutter, embarrassed. When I tried the dress on, it made me feel ... special. Graceful. Like a waltzing starlet in all those classic movies. Now I know it's just a length of satin. "I, umm, like yours, too."

As if in response, Bliss begins to fluff out the floaty layers of her skirt and hitch the bodice back up, preening. It's an outfit made for the spotlight, dazzling even in the dusk light.

"What's that noise?" I ask, turning in the direction of the alarm. "Is there a fire or something?"

"No idea," Jolene replies quickly. She nods behind me at the Honda. "Is that yours?"

I nod again. "For tonight, anyway."

"Could we sit inside a minute? It's getting kind of cold out," she adds. As if to illustrate, she wraps her arms around herself and shivers.

Even though it's at least sixty degrees out, I agree. You don't refuse Jolene Nelson – not if you want to stay out of the emergency room, anyway. They bundle into the car and I follow slowly, still wondering what Bliss is doing with her. And how anybody managed to force Jolene into that dizzying waterfall of ruffles.

When we're all in the car, Bliss leans forward from the backseat. "So what now?"

"Now we chill," Jolene tells her, almost like an order. She flips down the mirror and begins to mess with her short, spiky hair. Bliss reaches between us and starts playing with the radio settings, searching for a new station. Jolene slaps her hand away.

"Manners!"

"Oh! Sorry!" She blinks at me, wide-eyed. "You mind if I...?"

I shake my head quickly. "No, go ahead."

She finally settles on a pop station and sits back, humming along with the song. I wait, trying to decipher what's going on. Bliss seems breathless and excited, and even Jolene keeps glancing back toward the building. She notices me watching her.

"What are you doing out here, anyway?" Her eyes narrow, assessing me. "The party started ages ago."

"I, ummm, my date couldn't make it." My voice comes out almost a whisper. It hurts to admit, especially to these two. They've probably never been left waiting more than a minute in their entire lives. Some people, you don't even dare.

"You got stood up?" Bliss exclaims, her head popping up next to me again. "That's awful."

I try to shrug, like I don't care. "It's cool. I mean, it's only prom."

The words sit, hollow between us. I want to slap myself. Who am I fooling? Only prom?

"So, what – are you going home?" Jolene is still watching me carefully, her blue eyes cool and unblinking. It's the first time I've seen them without smudges of dark liner, but they're still as unnerving as ever.

"I guess. I don't know…" My words catch in my throat, and then to my horror, I feel another tear spill over and slide down my cheek. I swipe quickly at my face, hoping they haven't noticed.

"Maybe you want to come with us?" Jolene suggests suddenly. I blink.

There's a noise of protest from the backseat, but Jolene whips her head around and fixes Bliss with a fearful stare. "We were thinking of heading to DQ," she adds. "Just getting out of here."

My heart sinks. "So, you need a ride."

"Well, yeah. But you don't have to…" Jolene shrugs, nonchalant as ever.

I waver.

For three years, I've been invisible to girls like Jolene and Bliss – drifting silently around that school; overhearing snatches of everyone else's crazy gossip, while I sneak my sandwiches in the quiet of a library carrel and daydream of one day, maybe, being a part of things. I'm not stupid; I know that they just need a chauffeur tonight, and I happened to turn up at the right time, but even so…

Bliss and Jolene *do* things. They have adventures. They don't sit, weeping in a parking lot while everyone else has the night of their lives.

It's a waste of a damn pretty dress, that's what it is.

"OK." I wipe my eyes again and start the ignition. "Let's go."

Bliss

Meg drives even slower than my *abuela*, Jolene switches the radio to some noisy punk rock station, and I get a bunch of desperate WHERE R U?? texts from Courtney, but by the time we pull into the deserted DQ parking lot, I'm buzzing with a fierce kind of energy. Bailing on prom after I spent so long planning for it is crazy, I know, but that backseat lap dance has already ruined everything. There's no point faking smiles for the rest of the night, knowing all along it's a lie. No, now's the time for pay-back, when I've still got this sharp heat in my rib cage urging me on.

Something's in motion now. There's no going back.

"I'm, umm, just going to use the restroom." Meg clambers out of the car. Her mascara is smudged, and her eyes are puffy from all that crying I pretended not to see. She waits, blinking at us.

"Sure!" I reply. What does she want, permission? "See you in there." I watch until she's inside before turning to Jolene. "So, what's the plan? When do we ditch her and get started?"

"Relax." Jolene looks amused. She slams the car shut and stomps toward the brightly lit entrance like she's heading for battle, not a soft-serve restaurant. I grab my purse and hurry after her.

"But, you've got one, right?" I'm struck with another panic. "A plan, I mean. I didn't leave the biggest party of the year just to hang out and get ice cream!"

Inside, the place is practically deserted, nothing but a depressing stretch of red-and-white tile and empty booths under too-harsh fluorescent strip lights. An overweight man sits alone by the windows, slowly scooping at a huge sundae. He stops with the spoon halfway to his mouth, staring at us and our formal dresses. I quickly turn away.

Jolene marches to the counter and calls out, "Denise, you there?"

A woman emerges, maybe forty or even older. She wipes her hands on her apron and gapes. "Oh my word. Honey, just look at you!"

"Shut up," Jolene protests, but it's softer than all her biting replies to me have been. She folds her arms over the ruffles, like that's enough to hide them. "I left some stuff in my locker. Can I grab the keys?"

"Sure thing." Denise waves her through, and Jolene disappears into the back. Right. I forgot she works here, even though I'm sure she must have served me a dozen times.

"Can I get you anything?" Denise asks, clearing up the counter. Her hair is dyed an unconvincing shade of red, and she's got a tired look around her eyes, the one my mom spends a fortune on spa treatments to smooth away.

I hover, awkward. It seems rude not to order something. "Umm, just a Diet Coke, thanks."

"I hope you girls are taking plenty of pictures." Denise beams at me. Moving to the drink machine, she begins filling a huge cup. "I remember my prom…"

"Back in the eighties, when Bon Jovi was still cool." Jolene finishes for her, reappearing with a bulky backpack. It's cheap black nylon and clashes badly with her outfit. "I know, you've been telling me all week."

"I wore a pretty blue dress, cut right to here." Denise passes me the soda with a wistful look. I open my purse, but she shakes her head. "Oh no, any friend of Jolene's…"

"Thanks, Denise." Jolene quickly drags me toward a booth in the far corner, throwing herself down like she doesn't care that she's going to leave creases in her dress. I carefully slide in after her.

"She seems nice," I offer, peeling the paper wrapping from a straw.

"What do you care?" Jolene raises an eyebrow at me, but I don't shrink away in fear. I'm back in control now, and she may be badass, but it's not like she's going to cut me with the plastic utensils or anything.

"Wow. You really are touchy." I slurp my drink.

"No, just amazed that you noticed the help," Jolene drawls, sarcastic. "I figured we were all invisible to you."

I'm about to ask how she manages to even walk with that massive chip on her shoulder, when the door swings open and a group of teenagers strolls in. I freeze.

"What?" Jolene notices my expression, following my gaze to the door. "Friends of yours?"

"Sure." I ease back so I'm hidden from view by a fake plastic plant. "Because my friends really wear generic denim and ugly-ass Ts."

Still, I can't be too careful. Brianna and the gang would flip if they knew I was even talking to Jolene, let alone plotting … something.

Jolene shakes her head. "I know you're ashamed to be seen with me and all, but you could at least try to pretend. You know, to be polite."

I sigh, still peering through the leaves. "Like your reputation wouldn't suffer if people saw you with me, looking like that."

But Jolene just shrugs. "I am who I am."

Enough with the small talk. Clearly, I'm not going to get her to loosen up any time soon, so I just switch straight to business. "What are we going to do about Cam and Kaitlin?"

"Kaitlin Carter?" Meg chooses that moment to slide into the booth. She's cleaned up her face, but her eyes are still a little red – and full of that forlorn expression from before. Digging into a cup of plain soft-serve with rainbow sprinkles, she looks back and forth between us. "What's she done?"

"Nothing, it's just … a thing." I take another sip of soda, impatient.

"She screwed Bliss's precious boyfriend," Jolene announces. "And now Bliss wants payback."

I choke on my drink. "Hey!"

"What?" Jolene shrugs, unconcerned. "Although, I don't know why you can't just walk up and bitch-slap her. Him, too." She reaches over and scoops some of Meg's ice cream with her fingertip.

"You know, there is something called discretion," I hiss. "I asked you for help because I figured you wouldn't want to get caught!"

"And?" Jolene glances over at Meg. "You won't rat us out, right?"

She blinks. "Umm, I don't know what—"

"See?" Jolene turns back to me. "No big deal."

"It's the principle!" I protest. "I can't believe you're just spilling all my secrets to some random reject. No offense," I add to Meg, because she's just the kind to take it. "Seriously," I keep complaining to Jolene, "it was bad enough telling you. More strangers knowing the intimate details of my betrayal is so not what I signed up for."

"She's not exactly part of your rich-bitch clique," Jolene points out, eating more of Meg's ice cream. Meg just sits there.

"No, but she'll probably go running to her parents the minute we do anything bad," I argue. And in this town, it would only be a matter of time before everyone knew – including my mom and dad.

"We don't know that for sure."

"Umm, I'm right here." Meg tries to interrupt, but Jolene talks over her.

"I know it's not your forte, Bliss, but think. We need a ride for this revenge scenario to work."

"So we get her to drop us at my place," I reply, bristling at her tone. "My car is in the garage."

"Right," she says with a sigh. "Your red convertible. Your inconspicuous, untraceable red convertible with the East Midlands bumper stickers."

I bite my lip. She does have a point.

I look back at Meg again: waiting silently now, swirling ice cream around her cup like we aren't talking about her right to her face. I sigh. It's clear she has nothing better to do, and she's not part of the social scene, at least, so maybe this won't get out...

"Fine," I agree, turning to Meg. "You're in."

"But in on what?" She looks nervous. "Sorry, it's just you didn't even say what this is about."

"Payback," Jolene explains, taking a slurp of my drink. "But revenge isn't a one-size-fits-all kind of thing. This Cameron guy, how long have you been dating him?"

"A couple of months," I reply, casual, like I don't even know to the day. "We got together at Nico's birthday thing."

I couldn't sleep that night after he kissed me. I stayed up, talking until dawn about how cute he was, and how long it would take for him to call. Talking with Kaitlin. I scowl. "And I've been best friends with Kaitlin since the start of sophomore year."

"Ouch." Jolene smirks. "Bet you didn't see that one coming."

"No," I say quietly. "I didn't."

"OK. So, you don't want violence, and I doubt you'll work up the nerve to destroy any of their stuff…" Jolene muses, like that's a bad thing. "Then I guess your best bet is public humiliation, and—" She stops suddenly. Denise is approaching, clearing wrappers and debris from the tables nearby.

"Can I get you girls anything?" she asks, beaming at us.

"No, thanks, Dee." Jolene smiles and waits until she's gone before continuing. "You know, this would be so much easier if you'd taken photos. Or video. Any kind of proof they've been cheating."

"Sorry, I was too busy having my heart ripped into tiny pieces." My voice comes out bitter, so I cover with a careless smile. "Not exactly a Kodak moment."

There's a pause. I can tell they're both thinking what an idiot I am; even Meg is looking at me like I should have seen this coming. But this is why I didn't tell anyone, back at prom. They would have all swooped in with their fake sympathy – and then bitched behind my back about how I must have done something wrong, how Kaitlin must be better than me. No, keeping quiet was the right thing to do. I just need to act like I'm not hurting and make sure that when news gets out, Kaitlin and Cam are so humili-ated, nobody thinks to gossip about me, too.

"You know, I bet we could get something from her

room," I suggest, thinking hard. "Kaitlin texts like, twenty-four seven. And with e-mail, video chat, it would be easy to send around." I brighten. "Like what happened to that freak Eli, you know, with that whole Gaga clip."

"I saw that." Meg finally speaks.

"*Everyone* saw it." I giggle. "We copied the entire school. I think it even made Perez Hilton."

Jolene raises an eyebrow. "That was your clique? Gee, how nice."

"Whatever." I roll my eyes. "Seriously – if you're going to goth up and do some crazy death-metal dance routine, maybe you don't want to film the whole thing. Anyway, if we can break into Kaitlin's computer, there's bound to be something scandalous to spread around."

"Break in?" Meg stops. Her brown eyes get wider, like she's just realizing what we're planning. "Nobody said we'd be doing anything illegal!"

"It's hardly even against the law," I reassure her, impatient. "I know the security for the alarm and everything."

Still, she shakes her head. "No, I can't." Reaching for her tiny beaded purse, she picks up her skirts and tries to leave, but Jolene slides around so we're sitting on either side of her in the booth. We don't move.

"You won't have to get out of the car." Jolene sighs. "Just wait for us down the block."

"Nobody would ever know you were involved. Promise." I add a beam of encouragement.

But Meg shakes her head again, determined. "Can you please move?"

Jolene slips out to let her past, and I shoot her an annoyed look.

"Relax," she mouths back, following Meg toward the exit. I gulp a final mouthful of soda and start to bolt after them. Then I remember Denise, and how tired she looked, stuck working the late shift on a Friday night. I pause to quickly clear our trash away.

When I get outside, they're standing next to Meg's car in the middle of the empty parking lot, the neon glow from the fast-food signs shining against the pale sky.

"Do you really want to say no to me?" Jolene is saying, arms folded. "I mean, I'm not asking much, but if you can't even help me out with this..." She trails off, badass once more. Pink ruffles or not, her threat is clear.

Meg tremors. "I'm sorry, but ... no."

Wow. Turning down Jolene? Maybe she does have some guts after all.

"I get it." I walk closer. Time for the good cop. "You're what, a junior?" I give her a friendly smile. Meg nods. "Exactly. We've got college applications coming up; you don't want to risk everything for someone like Kaitlin." I pause. "I mean, she's never done anything to you, has she?"

It's not much of a long shot. Kaitlin's done something to *everyone*.

Sure enough, Meg's expression hardens, just a little. "Actually—"

I don't let her finish. "I told you." I talk over her to

Jolene. "I said she's not the type. She's a good girl. I bet she's never done anything crazy like this."

Jolene tries not to smile. "You're right." She sighs. "I don't know, I just thought she would want … never mind." She shrugs, sending a ripple of pink tulle across her chest. "We'll find someone else."

"Someone with some nerve," I agree. Turning back to Meg, I give her a perky grin. "Don't worry – we're good. You can get home now."

"Right," Jolene says, hoisting her backpack over her shoulder. "We don't want you missing curfew." She starts to walk away, toward the busy highway. I follow, calling back to Meg.

"Thanks for the ride. Enjoy the rest of your night!"

I catch up with Jolene. She's already counting under her breath. "One, two, three…"

"What if she doesn't go for it?" I whisper, panicked. "These shoes are so not made for walking."

"Oh, she'll do it." Jolene flashes me a grin. "Four, five, six—"

"Wait!"

We turn around. Meg is standing there, keys in hand and a surprised look on her face, almost like she can't believe what she's saying. "I'm in."

She clears her throat and says it again, louder. Determined. "I'm in. For your plan. Tonight. I'm in."

JOLENE

I should have guessed it from the ice cream. Hot fudge sauce would have shown some promise, candy topping hints at a little spark, and even plain flavor would have been simple and determined. But rainbow sprinkles? Child's play. By the time we pull up a safe half block away from Kaitlin's house, Meg is already set to wimp out on us.

"Are you sure you have to do this?" she asks, turning the engine off. She blinks fearfully at the mini-mansions and manicured lawns rolling out around us, a quiet enclave of wealth and obedient household staff. "Just think what will happen if you get caught, all the trouble—"

"We won't get caught." I ignore her, turning to Bliss. "You ready?"

She nods, bouncing out of her seat with enthusiasm.

"Then let's go." I grab my bag and reach for the car door, but something in Meg's expression makes me think twice. I remember how I felt at the start, those early days hanging out with boys whose fingertips were always stained with spray paint, boys who could start a car just by reaching under the dashboard, boys who didn't leave the house without wire cutters and a flask. It was thrilling, sure, but I was terrified, too – that lurch of panic kicking low in my gut. I barely feel a flicker now, but back then, I would wait for sirens, always ready to bolt.

I pluck her purse from between the seats and rifle through for her slim wallet.

"Wait, what are you—"

"Security," I tell her, holding up her driver's license with a grin. "You wouldn't think of driving off and leaving us here, right? Especially not without your license. That would be very bad."

"Illegal," Bliss agrees from the backseat. Meg's face falls.

"I said I'd wait."

"And now I know for sure that you will," I tell her, slipping her license in my bag. "Now, keep watch on the driveway, and call me if you see any cars pull up, OK? I've programmed our numbers into your cell."

Meg nods. She's still resentful, but the protest is gone from her expression. Good girl.

"And keep the engine running," I add. "We might need to make a quick getaway."

* * *

Bliss is already bounding ahead of me up the sidewalk, like we're heading to a pep rally, not a break-in. "Chill, Bambi."

"Sorry." She drops back, still glowing with excitement. "Kaitlin's house is just up ... here." She falls silent as we reach a huge red-brick house at the end of the cul-de-sac. All the houses in this part of town are look-at-me large, but this one is even bigger than the rest. And occupied. Lights are on in every room, classic rock music drifts from an open window, and I can see a woman walking between rooms inside, chatting on the phone. Great.

"I thought you said they were out for the night." I turn to glare at her. I may have learned certain ... skills when it comes to getting into places I shouldn't, but that's only when there's nobody around to dial 911 and wield their desk-drawer handgun.

Bliss bites her lip. "Sorry. Does that mean it's off?"

"Nope." I sigh. "But we'll have to find a Plan B, unless you want to just walk right in ... Wait, I wasn't serious!" But Bliss is already sashaying toward the front door.

"Follow my lead and look normal," she whispers at me, smoothing down her hair.

I attempt a perky grin.

"I said normal, not psychotic."

"Whatever," I mutter, but I adjust my expression just as Bliss hits the bell. A moment later, Kaitlin's mom answers, holding the phone speaker-down against her shoulder.

"Bliss, honey, what are you doing here?" She's bronzed

and rake-thin, wearing a crisp white shirt and khakis. You know, typical relaxed Friday-night clothes. "I thought you kids would be out for hours."

"Hi, Mrs. Carter!" Bliss choruses. "We will be; don't worry. But we're having a fashion emergency. Kaitlin's bra snapped!"

"Oh no!" Mrs. Carter looks suitably horrified.

"I know!" Bliss agrees. "She can't leave the bathroom, of course, so Jo ... anna and me volunteered to come pick up a replacement."

She caught herself just in time. Even the mention of my name is enough to strike fear into the heart of every parent in town.

"Of course." Mrs. Carter waves us into the vast marble hallway, already putting the phone back to her ear. "You know where her room is."

"Sure I do!" Bliss beams again, hurrying toward the stairs. "We won't be a minute!"

I follow her up to the first floor, pausing to scope out the framed family portraits covering every wall, full of dead-eyed creepy smiles.

"How's that for fast thinking?" Bliss crows.

"We're not done yet," I remind her as she heads for the room at the far end of the hallway. I follow her inside, quickly closing the door behind us, already in attack mode. I figure we have about five minutes before Mrs. Carter comes to check; more, if she's gossiping with an old friend. That means we need to —

I stop. "Somebody lives here?"

"Yeah." Bliss flops down on the king-size bed covered in crisp white linens. "Kaitlin's kind of a neat freak."

Something of an understatement. The pale carpet is spotless, every surface is clear, and there's nothing but a mirror and a makeup box out on the dresser. I shiver at all the perfection. My room may fit in the en suite bathroom, but at least it doesn't look like a catalog shoot. "Weird. Anyway, you want to get searching?"

"Oh! Right." Bliss bounces up again and heads to the gleaming flat-screen computer in the corner. "If we're lucky, she won't... Oh, crap." She stops.

I look over her shoulder at the screen. The background is set to a big photo of Kaitlin, Bliss, and the rest of their shiny clique, but hovering in front of it is a little box demanding our password.

"Seriously?" I ask. "The girl is happy wandering around the locker room completely naked, but now she has to worry about privacy?"

Bliss shrugs. "She's always complaining about her little sister snooping around. I guess she's paranoid."

"And has something on there worth protecting," I say decisively. "Keep trying. Most people use basic stuff for their passwords: birthdays, pet names. I'll see if she's got anything stashed around here."

"OK." Bliss settles into the desk chair while I go lift the bedspread and peer underneath. It's where I keep my contraband, but apparently I have a different definition of banned substances. Instead of cigarettes, a vibrator, or even coffee (Mom swears it will stunt my growth), Kaitlin's got what looks like the entire back-catalog of *ChicK* magazines under the bed, neatly stacked according to year. Like I said: *weird*.

"Any luck?" Bliss is still clicking away.

"Not yet." I pull out every box to be sure, checking for anything remotely illicit. It's like peeking into another universe: a world of designer purses, stacked heels, and discarded makeup sets barely out of the box. MAC, NARS, Lancôme … God, she's got my entire yearly paycheck down here, gathering dust.

I move on. The bedside tables are decorated with a few photos in heavy silver frames. Kaitlin and crew at the lakeshore. Kaitlin and crew hanging out by the pool. Kaitlin and Bliss, grinning widely in matching red bikinis. They look happy, like best friends should. Suppose you never can tell.

I glance over at Bliss, wondering again why she's going through with all this effort and strategy, when she could just knee that ex of hers in the groin and be finished with it. It's what I would do. When I found out my last boyfriend had been hooking up with the door girl from Club Ninja behind my back, I made like Carrie Underwood and dug a vicious scratch into his precious car. But maybe Bliss has her reasons. Just like I have my reasons for humoring her until I can get on with my own agenda for the night.

Finished with the tables, I'm just heading to the dresser when I look up. "Holy sh – ugar!" I jump, clutching my chest. A small kid is standing in the doorway, watching us silently with big, dark eyes.

"Avery, hi!" Bliss looks panicked. "Isn't it past your bedtime?"

The girl just stares. She's sucking her thumb, dressed in a hideous lacy nightgown covered in ribbons and bows.

"What do we do? Just … ignore her?" I whisper. I've watched way too many demon spawn movies not to be freaked out by her pale skin and perfect little ringlets.

"I don't know," Bliss whispers back, so I tentatively take another few steps toward the dresser.

"What are you doing?" Avery finally takes her thumb out of her mouth.

"I'm your sister's friend, remember?" Bliss pastes on an innocent smile, the same one that reduces adults to putty. Avery isn't so easily convinced.

"Why are you looking through her stuff? She doesn't like it when I look through her stuff. Mommy says it's wrong." The kid glares at me.

"I, umm…"

"We're looking for something!" Bliss says quickly. "Kaitlin lost something very important. We're helping her find it!"

"Mommy says I'm not allowed to look." Avery takes a step back toward the hallway. She raises her voice into that high-pitched, bratty tone. "Momm—!"

In an instant, I lunge forward and grab her, clamping my hand over her mouth. She squeals, biting down on my fingers. Hard. "Owww!" I groan, struggling to stay quiet. Bliss stares at me in shock. "You want to shut the door?" I tell her, fighting to keep the kid in my arms. She quickly does it.

"What are you doing?"

"Saving your ass," I tell her, wrestling Avery into an armlock. I'm careful not to hurt her, however much she kicks and flails against me. Then she throws herself to the side, and I lose my balance. "Mneugh!" I fall hard, twisting my body at the last minute so that I hit the ground beneath her, instead of the other way around.

This is why I'm never going to breed.

"You want to maybe keep trying?" I order. Bliss looks at me as if I'm crazy, but she starts hitting keys again. Which leaves the demon spawn to me.

Gritting my teeth, I try my best to sound friendly. "Hey, kid! Kid, I'm not letting go until you keep quiet." I hold tight and eventually she stills. "Good." I exhale. "Now, we're going to make a deal here. You know what a deal is?"

She shakes her head against me.

"A deal is where you stay quiet, and I give you something. Anything you want. Do you like the sound of that?"

A pause, and then she nods. Ah, capitalism.

"OK. But if you call for your mommy, the deal's off." I slowly release her. Avery folds her little arms and glares at me, but she doesn't scream.

"I want my present."

"I'm sure you do." I pick up my bag from where I left it on the bed, nursing my poor hand. Damn, that kid's got teeth on her. "Bliss, status?"

"Nothing yet." She's rifling through desk drawers now. "I'll check if she wrote it down."

Great.

"Your present, OK. I have, umm…" I dig through my bag, flipping past the items that won't – or, rather, shouldn't – interest a preteen. But there's nothing that might win her over. No sparkly gadgets or cool little toys or anything colored pink.

"How about a Twinkie?" I hold up the package with defeat. But she snatches it from my hand and happily tears off the wrapper. Soon, she's sitting cross-legged in the corner, devouring the snack with rapturous abandon.

I raise my eyebrows at Bliss.

"Kaitlin's mom is really into health food." She shrugs. "The house is like, a sugar-free zone."

"Lucky us."

Suddenly, I hear footsteps coming up the stairs. "Quick!" I hiss, scooping Avery into my arms again. I pull her behind the door and crouch there. "Keep quiet, and I'll give you another Twinkie," I whisper, listening as the steps come closer. Avery's eyes widen, and she nods, mouth smeared with crumbs.

"Bliss, how are you doing?"

"Great, Mrs. C.!" From my huddled corner, I can see Bliss give another innocent smile. "I'm just trying to find the right one. See, it can't be dark, because then it would show through the dress, and it can't have straps, or lace, because that would totally screw up the line of the bust, and—"

"That's fine, hon." Mrs. Carter cuts off her inane

chatter. She pauses. "Where's your friend?"

"Oh, she's just in the bathroom!"

"OK. You girls make sure to keep it down. Little Avery is fast asleep."

"Of course."

The door closes, and I sigh with relief, handing Avery the other snack cake. God bless refined sugar products.

"I can't stall her forever." Bliss closes the door again and helps me up.

"I know." I nod grimly. Who knew Kaitlin would be so smart? "So what do you want to do?"

Bliss shrugs helplessly.

"Great." I sigh. "You know, this was easier for Harriet the Spy. They all just kept journals with their darkest secrets. Nice, solid things with padlocks and *keep out* scrawled across the front."

"Like Kaitlin's special secret book?"

We look around. Avery has finished the Twinkie in record speed and is licking off her fingers.

Bliss brightens. "Kaitlin has a secret book?"

Avery nods.

"Well?" I prompt. "Where is it?"

"I want another present."

I give Bliss a look. "That was my last one," I whisper.

"So what do we do?"

What I always do. When in doubt, bribe.

"Avery, hon. I don't have another Twinkie" – she opens her mouth to complain, but I quickly cut her off – "but I do have money. Well, Bliss does. Which means you can buy your own Twinkies. As many as you want!"

She pauses, furrowing her evil, demonic brow. "How much?"

"Five dollars!" I announce. Avery shakes her head. "Ten?" She shakes it again. Man, kids these days. I had to save for weeks for the latest Harry Potter when I was her age. "Twenty dollars?" I try, impatient. At least it's not my money. "That would buy you … twenty whole Twinkies."

Avery's eyes widen at the thought of all that pure, unadulterated sugar. "Yes." She nods. "Twenty."

I turn to Bliss. "You heard the kid."

"You're bribing a ten-year-old?" She looks shocked.

I roll my eyes. "Do you want the book or not?"

Reluctantly, she pulls a twenty from her bodice. And there I was thinking there was nothing but double-sided tape behind that dress.

Avery reaches for the money, but I dangle it just out of reach. "Not until you show us where it's hidden."

She heads straight for the closet.

"I thought you checked there." Bliss gives me a scathing look.

"I did," I snap back as Avery expertly clambers up the shelves and reaches into a pile of jeans. She pulls out a blue journal: leather-bound and surprisingly tasteful for the girl who dressed as a burlesque dancer for our last school fund-raiser. Our daytime school fund-raiser.

"My present!" Avery demands. I hand her the twenty; Bliss snatches the diary.

"You can't tell anyone you saw us," I say. "You'll get

in trouble for not being in bed."

She nods and then scampers away – no doubt back to her lair of doom.

"We did it!" Bliss bounces up and down with joy, but I know better than to celebrate too soon. I quickly pluck a beige strapless bra from the pile and shut the wardrobe.

"Come on. We should bail, before Meg has a breakdown and walks home."

We hurry downstairs. Mrs. Carter is in the living room, watching some Real Housewives episode on the big-screen TV, so Bliss calls through. "Thanks, Mrs. C., we're just leaving now!"

"Hang on, girls, I just want to—"

We don't wait. Bursting out the front door, we race across the lawn. The sprinklers switch on, and Bliss cries out as the cold water hits her skin. I ignore her shrieks, dragging her through the jets and down the street. I'm full of familiar adrenaline, that breathless excitement of making it out, free. From the gleeful expression on Bliss's face, she's buzzing too.

Meg's car is still loitering on the corner, thank God. I throw open the front door and pile in. "Go, go!"

"What?" Meg stares at me, panicked. "Did you get caught?"

Bliss tumbles into the backseat. "No!" She laughs. "We got it!"

I glance back at the street, just to be sure, but we're all clear. I give Meg a nod.

"Stage One is complete. Now go!"

Meg

"Didn't you hear me?" Jolene drums an impatient rhythm on the seat beside her. "I said get the hell out of here!"

I'm wound so tight with tension, I slam my foot hard on the gas, speeding away with a painful screech. Damn. I hit the brake, overcompensating with another amateur lurch. We shudder to a halt.

"The point of a getaway car is to, you know, get away!" Jolene gives me a look of utter exasperation.

I blush. I scored perfectly on my driver's test; my dad made me practice drills until I could parallel park in my sleep. Eighteen months without so much as a single ticket, but, of course, I have to fall apart now, when it actually matters, when they're depending on me.

Focus, Meg!

I force myself to take a deep breath and then finally drive away like a normal human being – even remembering the obligatory pause at the stop sign at the end of the block.

"Did they suspect anything?" I ask, glancing in the rearview mirror.

"Not at all," Jolene declares proudly. She lets out a whoop as we turn out of the quiet subdivision and head toward town, the windows down and a warm breeze whipping through the car.

"Thanks to who?" Bliss leans forward between us, her hair falling in the kind of effortless, glossy cascade it took me two hours of trying – and failing – to achieve. "Uh, my cover story was brilliant, thanks very much."

Jolene makes a noise of protest. "And who silenced the demon child with nothing but her powers of persuasion and some sugary treats?"

"And half my emergency money!" Bliss cries, indignant.

"Whatever, like you'll miss it."

I exhale a slow sigh of relief as they bicker beside me. Finally, after that agonizing wait, my nerves are beginning to ease, blossoming into a kind of fluttering excitement as I absorb their rush of laughter.

We did it!

Well, *they* did, I correct myself. You just waited down the block, flinching every time a car passed by and wondering whether the Stanford admissions people would ever overlook a misdemeanor charge.

"So where now?" I ask, excited. "Back to prom?"

"Nope." Bliss speaks up from the backseat. She's got some kind of journal, and she's flipping through the pages with a wicked smile on her face. "We're going to Brooks.

The campus is down I-32. Just make the exit out of town."

The college? "I know where it is, but why—?"

"We're going to deliver this little gem to Kaitlin's boy-friend." Bliss doesn't even wait for me to ask the question; she's already crowing over her grand plan. "Jason will freak when he finds out she's been cheating. And his room-mate hooks up with Brianna sometimes, so she'll be, like, the first to find out. If we plant it so he doesn't know it came from me, I'll be completely clear."

"Right," I say quietly. I knew the high-school hier-archies were complicated, but this level of strategy and planning is almost Machiavellian. I glance in the rearview mirror again and wonder if I'm getting in over my head.

Jolene must be thinking the same thing, because she nudges me. "I'm kind of surprised you're still with us." She gives me a long look. "Figured maybe you'd get out and walk."

"I said I was in," I repeat firmly.

"Come on, you were tempted though, right?"

I shake my head. Even if the thought did cross my mind, oh, a few dozen times, I don't want either of them to know. "We made a deal; I'm not backing out."

I feel Jolene study me for a moment as I try not to wilt under her steady gaze, then to my relief she turns to Bliss. "Let me see it," she orders, reaching back. Bliss hesitates, clutching the diary to her chest, but then Jolene snaps her fingers and Bliss relents.

"OK, but read it aloud. I want to hear everything!"

"'March twenty-sixth.'" Jolene kicks her bare feet up

on the dashboard and begins to read, mimicking Kaitlin's nasal voice. "'Brianna was bugging me all through lunch today. She wants me to fix her up with Duncan—'"

"Jason's roommate," Bliss adds.

"'—but she doesn't know he already told Jase he thinks she's only, like, a seven. He'll hook up with her, but he said she acts like such a slut.' Ugh." Jolene slams the book shut and tosses it back. "You keep delightful company, you really do."

I have to agree, but in the mirror, I see Bliss shrug. "Uh, who are you to judge? JD McGraw? That Eric guy?" Her voice is dubious. "Those guys are, like, walking felonies."

Jolene stiffens. "At least when they fight, they do it to your face."

"They would hit a girl?" Bliss's voice rises.

"No." I don't look over, but I can practically hear the eye roll in Jolene's reply. "It was a metaphor. Instead of stabbing you in the back, like your crowd does."

Immediately, I can feel the mood shift. "So I need to take the next exit ahead?" I pipe up, before they can launch into a vicious showdown.

Bliss stops, turning to me as if she'd forgotten I was even here. "Yeah, and then it's straight through for like, twenty miles."

"OK."

They fall silent as I merge onto the highway. Jolene settles back, scratching at the pink polish on her nails as she gazes out the window, while Bliss curls up in the backseat with the journal. Slowly, the stretch of used-car lots and industrial warehouses on the outskirts of town makes way for open countryside and the occasional shadow of half-built suburban developments, houses standing empty in unfinished rows. I keep a careful eye on the road and wonder yet again what strange forces brought the two of them together. Because despite Jolene's whole explanation about revenge on Kaitlin and Cameron, something just doesn't add up.

That's the thing about being invisible, I suppose: they might not know who on earth I am, but I know plenty about them. Bliss and her clique don't pause for breath during their girls' bathroom bitch-sessions when I slip in, but the moment someone else – someone real – walks through that door, there's nothing but "Shh!" and giggles and whispers until they leave. Jolene's just the same. I work a few shifts in the front office for extra credit, so I see her all the time, dragged in after they catch her smoking, or fighting, or answering back. She waits, slouching in the chairs right opposite me, but has never even looked my way.

But here they are. In my car. Together.

Jolene begins searching in the glove compartment, flipping through CDs with a noisy rattle. She looks up suddenly and catches my eye, holding it as if she's challenging me. I look away, embarrassed, but she really doesn't care; she never has.

"You know, this stuff isn't bad." She's looking at my music selection with a frown, as if she can't believe I could possibly have any taste at all.

"Oh. Thanks." I murmur a response, and then look

up to find that she's holding one of my dad's classic country mixes, not any of the vaguely-cool indie music I threw in there. With a swift movement, she slams in the CD, and suddenly, the loud guitar chords make way for a gentle bluegrass twang.

"What?" Bliss protests immediately. "Come on!"

Jolene ignores her, humming happily along to the old song.

"You like that stuff?" I venture.

"It's in my blood. Can't you tell?" She gives a wry laugh. "Born and raised with nothing else on the radio."

Her name, of course.

"I was lucky," Jolene continues, adjusting the seat so she's lounging way back – forcing Bliss to shift over to the other side. "She nearly named me Dolly. If there's one thing I can thank my dad for, it's convincing her otherwise. Can you imagine?"

I give a nervous laugh of agreement.

"Dolly?" Bliss lets out a sharp squeal, kicking the back of my seat in the process. "Who would even call their kid that?"

"Says the girl named after a freaking state of mind," Jolene snaps back.

There's silence again – the dulcet tones of Dusty or Roseanne or whoever sighing away, the momentary sharing clearly done.

I don't mind. It's enough for me just to focus on the road ahead, taking us farther away from town and that gleaming country club full of my own foolish dreams. I always love driving, getting out, away. If I've had an even worse day than usual, or I feel that loss begin to ache again, I'll take the keys and just go. Dad's surprisingly understanding, given his oft-quoted statistics about road safety, but perhaps it's Stella, murmuring in his ear about giving me space; either way, at least they let me. An hour here, a two-hour trip there – it doesn't seem like a lot, but I sometimes think it's the only thing that keeps me together anymore.

It's funny, to think I could crave more space. After all, I have nothing but distance around me all day long – a silent kind of force field hovering as I wander the faded linoleum hallways. But that's different. That kind of distance diminishes me, slowly sapping my strength away. Out here, with the radio playing loud enough to drown everything but a beat or a soaring melody, I feel most like myself. There's this one song that gets it just right, a guy singing about a dark windless night, and how a song can just surround you, punching right through your mind, pumping in your blood. Moments like that, I feel as though everything gets stripped away – school, Mom, all that endless work for grades and application essays – and there's nothing left but the core of who I am, so I can finally know myself. Like myself, even.

Eventually, as always, the road runs out, and I take the familiar exit and turn toward the college campus. I've been out to Brooks a few times before to use the library for research projects, so I save myself the embarrassment of getting lost in the crisscrossing sprawl of buildings that radiates from the old main core. Slowing to avoid the students who see jaywalking as their God-given right, I make my way to the front quad, a neat patch of grass framed by three small red-brick buildings – long since dwarfed by the new concrete sports complex and gleaming academic hubs.

"So," I say, turning off the engine while they collect purses and pull their shoes back on. "I guess I'll just wait here for you?"

Jolene nods, already reaching for the door handle. "We shouldn't be long. Which dorm is this guy in, anyway?"

"Ummm..." Bliss sounds less than certain. "I can't really remember."

"You're kidding."

But she's not. Bliss shrugs. "I've never really paid attention to the directions, I just followed Kaitlin..." She screws up her face, deep in thought. "His dorm is big, I guess, with a whole load of vending machines in the lobby. I'll know it when I see it."

"You'd better get out," Jolene says to me. "This one's completely helpless."

I look down at my floor-length black satin gown. "It's OK. I'm not really dressed for—"

"You look fine," Jolene interrupts. "Better than I do, anyway." She plucks at a ruffle with disdain. I decide not to argue, and soon we're all standing in front of the quad, surveying the campus. It's getting dark out, but there are floodlights fixed on the side of every building, and every pathway is bathed in a bright glow. "So how many dorms are in this place?" Jolene asks, a note of resignation in her voice.

"Fifteen, maybe?" I carefully hold my skirt off the dusty asphalt.

"And you really can't remember a thing?"

"Sorry!" Bliss beams at us, obviously forgetting for a moment who she's pulling her sweet and innocent act with. The smile slips. "We'll find him eventually. We'll just have to ask around."

"Or we could look him up in the student directory?" I suggest.

They both turn to me.

"You know, the online catalog of every student and their room number?" It seems obvious to me, but Bliss's face lights up as if I've just suggested a miracle.

"Genius! See, I knew you'd be great at this."

"Not so fast," I say quickly, before she gets too carried away with false praise. "It's for students only. We need somebody else to log us in."

"No problem." She grins. "Just point me in the right direction."

Bliss

Helpless. She calls me helpless, and then I can't even remember where we're going. Way to go, Bliss – striking a blow for popular-girl stereotypes everywhere.

I follow the others across campus, trying to ignore my flush of embarrassment. It's not that I'm so bad with directions – fine, maybe just a little – but the truth is, Jolene's right. I never once stopped to notice where Jason's dorm is, or how to get there. I was always with Kaitlin or one of the other girls, and they just called ahead and had one of the guys meet us by the main gates. I never saw the point in wandering aimlessly around when there were tons of cute boys willing to point the way. But what's so wrong about that? Not everyone needs to possess every ounce of human knowledge to survive. I mean, that's what Google is for.

"Where are we going, anyway?" I ask, walking faster to catch up. Meg is scurrying ahead of me, her head down and the fabric of her dress bunched up in her hands to keep it from sweeping the ground. I feel a pang for that outfit – bombshell black satin, and she's skulking down the path as if she's draped in a garbage bag. Some people don't deserve high fashion.

"The library." She nods to the concrete-and-glass building looming up ahead.

"Right." I sigh. "Figures." Girls like Meg are always programmed to detect the nearest gathering of nerds and bookworms.

I look around. It's warm out, and the campus is busy with students already in the weekend spirit as they head out for the night, joking around on the lawns and yelling to each other about plans for a pajama party or karaoke session at the bar. Even though I shouldn't be impressed by college kids anymore, I can't help but soak it all in. I always love how these older girls look so at ease with themselves, as if they have everything figured out. Jolene's that way as well – she's got this mysterious air of self-possession, like she genuinely doesn't care what anyone thinks of her. Maybe I'll get that way, too: just wake up on my eighteenth birthday with all the answers, and not even blink if Courtney "helpfully" points out that my mascara's smudged, or that she and Nikki have tickets to Jared Jameson's next show and – pause – I can come along, if I want.

I can dream.

For a moment, I wish I could just take it all back and go get a glass of punch instead of looking for that useless lipstick. Maybe now I would be giggling happily with

Kaitlin, or sneaking kisses with Cameron in the shadows of the paper streamers and balloons, oblivious. I'd be stupid and naive, sure, but at least I'd be happy. Ignorance is Bliss, right?

"We've got to do something about these dresses," Jolene mutters, climbing the front steps. She's been bitching about her ruffles all night so I barely register the comment, but then a group of gothy-looking girls gives us a long stare, and I realize that she might have a point. If someone in white face powder, a corset, and a floor-length Victoriana skirt can look at us like we're the weird ones, clearly, a change in outfits is required.

"Later," I agree reluctantly, "but stop tugging it. It makes you look even more awkward." She glares at me, but stops twitching as we file into the atrium.

It's a huge, modern building, with information desks and security barriers along the front, and then at least three vast floors of shelving, work tables, and computer stations. Even though it's Friday night, the place is packed with students clutching note pads, their eyes full of a glazed panic that can mean only one thing: finals.

"I don't know." Meg hedges. "You need to register for a reader's pass, and they're pretty strict about—"

"Come on," Jolene interrupts, tugging me quickly to the barrier farthest from the bored security guy. He's staring off into space, and the librarians all seem busy with a long line of students, so she plucks Meg's access card from her hand and swipes it through, squeezing us together past the entry in a single knot of bodies. "See? Simple." She steers us to a safe row of shelving and then raises an eyebrow at me. "Well? You said you had this next part under control."

I need to win back some credit, and fast, so I give them a superior grin. "Leave it to the expert. Just watch and learn…"

Spinning on my heel, I sashay toward the stairs, quickly thinking up my plan. Up on the first floor, it's quieter – home to only hard core study nerds, I can tell. The individual study booths are set back between the shelves, and everyone looks settled in for the night, giving off this air of total desperation.

The other girls trail behind me as I walk the length of the room, mentally crossing off the prospects as I go.

"Are we just taking a stroll for the hell of it?" Jolene mutters, dragging her shoes on the dull gray carpeting. "Or are you lost – again?"

"Shh!" I glare.

And then I spot him: the blond boy in the corner, with square black glasses and a robot printed on his gray shirt. He's squinting at his laptop, surrounded by looseleaf papers, and has a smudge of highlighter on his chin. Perfect.

"Hi." I make my approach with a big smile, not waiting for the others to follow.

The boy looks up. Up close, I can see that he's actually kind of cute, not gawky like I first thought. His hair is cut messy and short, and he's got some of those sideburns, like he should be playing in an indie rock band.

Automatically, I flip my hair and jut out one hip. "Can I ask a teeny, tiny favor?"

He gives me a vague smile. "Sorry, but I'm kind of busy…" Instead of offering to help, the boy just looks back at his laptop like I'm already dismissed.

"Oh." I hide a frown and widen my smile instead. "It won't even take a minute!" I chirp. "Well, *we* won't." I gesture at Meg and Jolene so he doesn't think I'm trying to stalk him or anything.

The boy glances past me.

"See, we're trying to track down a friend of ours, but I've completely forgotten what dorm he's in. Could you maybe look him up for us? Jason Gilbert. He's a sopho-more," I add, but the boy isn't listening. "Umm, hello?"

He looks back quickly, recovering. "Uh … sure." A pause. "What do you need again?"

"His dorm address," I explain slowly, trying not to sigh. He must be really zoned out from studying. "I think you can look it up online…"

Meg is gazing idly at a shelf of books behind me, so I beckon her over. "Meg, come here and tell…?" I wait for him to introduce himself.

He seems to snap back to life. "Scott. I'm Scott." He smiles at us. Finally.

"Tell Scott what we need," I finish, giving him another big smile. I push Meg into the chair next to him. "I'm just going to go make some copies, OK? Do you know where the nearest machine is?"

"Uh, just around the corner." He's back to looking

blank and dopey, but at least I get an answer this time.

"Thanks!" I leave them to it, hoping Meg can manage to get something useful out of him. When in doubt, delegate.

Sure enough, there's a Xerox machine waiting in the empty hallway beneath a notice board crammed with neon flyers and ads for the Students Against Unethical Vending Machines group. College kids. I fumble in my purse for quarters, but aside from gum, lip gloss, and mascara, I come up empty-handed.

"Here, I've got some." Jolene appears beside me and fetches a handful of change from her ugly backpack.

"Thanks." I flip through the diary, trying to find the pages with the most dirt to copy. "I figured it would be good to have a backup. Insurance, you know?"

She nods. "Good thinking."

"What was that?" I joke, setting it to copy. "A compliment?"

She snorts. "Yeah, well, you've lowered the bar so far, I have to applaud any rational thought at all."

I decide to rise above her digs and focus on the task at hand. The machine spits out the first few pages, so I turn to another section and set it to copy again.

"Anything good?" Jolene hops up on the table next to me, kicking her feet back and forth. I shrug.

"I didn't have time to read it all. Most of it's just petty bitching, anyway, but she talks about hooking up with Cameron, and this other guy too."

"So tonight wasn't the first time? Classy." Jolene snorts.

I give her a grim smile. Luckily, I'm still too numb from that limo lap dance to get worked up over this new revelation. So much for a single stupid mistake: Kaitlin's been planning it forever, and as for Cameron... It doesn't read like he's put up much of a fight.

I turn back to the diary and copy a new page. The more dirt, the better. Then my gaze drifts farther down the hall and my heart stops.

"Hide me," I whisper, but there's nowhere to escape, so I dive beneath the table. Jolene doesn't move. "Hide me!" I yelp, louder this time, and reach out to yank her legs, pulling her in front of me.

"What are you doing?" She sighs, but I just scoot farther back against the copier, deeper into the dust and grime and God knows what else. I shudder as my hands hit something sticky, but there's no time to complain.

"Be quiet – act like I'm not here," I whisper, watching them come closer. Five pairs of legs are approaching from the other end of the hallway: an assortment of skin-tight jeans and miniskirts stretching down to sky-high heels and ultra-fashionable boots. From under the table, I can only see the lower half of their bodies, but that's enough to know what they are.

Phi Kappas.

As they get closer, Jolene finally takes the hint and dangles her backpack in front of me, blocking whatever view they might have of my hunched, dusty body. Slowly, slowly they saunter past, while I make a mental note to take three showers when I get home.

"You can come out now." Jolene sounds amused. She doesn't help me up, just stands back and watches as I crawl out and haul myself to my feet in an undignified scramble.

"Thanks." I try to dust myself down. It doesn't look as if there's too much damage, just a suspicious smear on one leg and, yes, the remainder of some chewing gum squished against my left palm. I screw up my face and wipe it frantically with a wad of scrap paper.

When I look up, Jolene is still staring at me. "Let me guess: you stole one of their boyfriends?"

"Is my name Kaitlin?" I retort.

"Right." She grins. "I forgot, you're the virtuous one. So, what was it? I haven't seen anyone hit the ground so fast since a car backfired outside the Jay-Z show last year."

I pause. "My cousin," I explain reluctantly, reaching for my purse and applying a fresh coat of lip gloss to calm myself down. "Well, her sorority sisters, anyway, but I thought she was with them." They all look alike, those girls, with their manicures and blowouts and five-hundred-dollar purses. The Kappa gloss, Kaitlin and I always joke, even though we'll pledge in a heartbeat when our turn comes around.

Jolene frowns. "Wait, your cousin goes here? Why didn't we just ask her for help?"

I shake my head so fast, hair whips against my cheeks. "No way. She *cannot* know I'm here. She'll tell her mom, and then Aunt Estrella will call my mom, and I'll be in a world of trouble." I shudder again, this time at the prospect of Selena smugly reporting back my every mis-demeanor. It's bad enough that my mom and her sister are trapped in some cycle of constant competition, but they can't help dragging me and Selena into it, too: holding up our achievements like they're gold stars on a scoreboard. And no matter what I do, Selena always comes out on top.

"So what's the deal, you'll get in trouble for sneaking onto campus?" Jolene looks a tiny bit sympathetic.

"For starters, sure," I reply. "And then my mom will want to know everything about why I'm here, and not at prom, and what I'm doing with you..." I trail off, exhausted by the thought of all her questions.

"Right," Jolene drawls slowly, "because hanging with me is way worse than the stealing and gossiping."

I tense. "You should talk – your mom posted spies to keep watch on you, remember?"

"Vividly." Jolene sinks back against the wall as I resume copying duties. "God, what makes them think it's such wholesome teenage fun we're having at that thing? I bet kids were getting drunk and giving illicit blow-jobs back in their day, too."

"Beats me. My mom is way too involved in my social life as it is."

"Reliving her former glories?"

"More like protecting my precious reputation." I gri-mace. "Because we all know it's the most valuable thing a girl can have."

"Guess I'm screwed then."

I fall silent as the copier hums, reproducing every

scandalous page until I think it's all covered. I fold the pages into a wedge. "This is everything, I think. Except the endless angsting and weight-loss charts, I mean."

"Cool." Jolene stuffs them in her backpack as we head back toward the study area. "We're making good time, shouldn't be much longer." She looks around with a tight expression, like she can't wait to be gone.

Meg and the Scott boy are deep in discussion as we approach, tucked away in their fort of books and folders.

"*Firefly* is great, but you should try *Dollhouse*."

"I did!" Meg protests. "It was nothing but male fantasy crap. I gave up after five episodes."

Sci-fi shows? They really are geeks. "Did you get the address?" I interrupt hopefully. Meg looks up.

"Oh, yes, Westville dorm." She holds up a printout with Jason's photo and scribbled directions.

"Just turn right when you exit the library," Scott adds. "It's straight across the way. You can't miss it."

"Awesome!" I grin. "Thanks so much."

Scott nods. "Do you need any other—"

"We've got to run." I cut him off, ushering Meg out of the chair. "But you've been a lifesaver, you really have!"

I don't waste any more time; hustling the others ahead of me, I head back toward the exit.

"He was nice," Meg says, faintly wistful. "He's read all of Neil Gaiman."

"We won't hold it against him." I skip lightly down the staircase, clutching Jason's address. I glance around when we hit the main floor, but there's no sign of Selena or her Kappa girls; what they were even doing in the library on a Friday night, I'm not sure, but with my all-clear assured, I sashay toward the exit. Soon, the diary will be in Jason's hands, Kaitlin and Cam will be public enemies number one and two, and I can get back to the country club to salvage what's left of my perfect prom.

"Mission accomplished."

Jolene

"Not so fast." I shut Bliss down before she can get carried away on that tide of self-congratulation. "We've still got to sneak in the dorms and deliver it to him."

She laughs, giving me this know-it-all grin, as if I've just questioned her ability to apply eyeliner or calculate the optimal flesh-to-dress ratio. "Trust me" – she smirks – "getting three girls into that dorm on a Friday night will be, like, the easiest thing we've ever done."

I almost want us to run into trouble, just to prove her wrong, but when we make it back across the ugly campus to Jason's dorm building, the front door is propped open with a stack of textbooks, and the pimple-faced security guard doesn't even look up from his handheld game as we walk in.

"Told you so!" Bliss sings, flouncing ahead.

I take in the gray walls and vending machines and feel a swell of disappointment. God, I hate this place. After everything, I still can't believe I'm cursed to spend my college years here: a freshman in the crowd of thousands mooching between classes at an institution that doesn't make any rankings except the lower reaches of the annual "party schools" list. Too close to home, too close to everyone I wanted to leave behind.

It wasn't supposed to be like this.

The dorms at Williams are gray stone, set back from the quad and surrounded by trees and leafy pathways, like something from another time. I loved it right away. Sure, we couldn't afford the trip, but online I saw students strolling happily in the sun, broadening their minds with classes and debate, thousands of miles away from East Midlands and all the bullshit that happens in this town. It was a long shot, even the guidance counselor warned me, but I drilled SAT prep during the quiet shifts at work and polished my essays until they were clearly kick-ass, and even drove out to the city to meet alumni for coffee and talk about how college was a fresh start for me, and that my past mistakes had made me learn and grow as a person. I believed it, too, rereading that precious acceptance letter every night like it was my ticket out, to something better.

And then my failure of a father decides to break the only promise he ever made to me and suddenly it's goodbye Williams, farewell freedom. Now I'm looking at nothing but four more years commuting to this dump every day from home, working nights and weekends just to scrape tuition, like I was never worth anything more. Like I never will be.

I shake off the flash of anger and disappointment. There's no time for it now – all that will come soon enough.

"Look." Meg points to a scribbled sign taped by the elevator with a bunch of SAFE SEX stickers. PARTY – 3RD floor!!!! "Jason's in room 318," she adds, clutching the downloaded details.

"See?" Bliss beams. A group of girls hustles past, gossiping about last night's episode of *5th Avenue*, but even though they hold the elevator for us, Bliss takes off in the other direction, toward the stairs.

"More of your sorority girls?" I smirk. She doesn't reply, pushing the door open and heading downstairs toward the basement.

Stairs? As the late, great Kirsty MacColl would say: not in these shoes. I stand firm. "I get that you want to stay out of their way, but hiding out down there... That's kind of extreme, don't you think?" Watching her freak out in the library was fun, sure, but avoiding every shiny-haired rich girl in this college might take us a while.

Bliss shakes her head. "Didn't you notice what they were wearing?"

I blink. "Uh, basic college party ho attire?"

"It's a pajama party." Bliss looks at me. "Duh! And you were the one who said we needed to get out of these dresses. Ergo..." She points at the sign on the wall pointing down.

LAUNDRY.

Oh.

"Ergo?" I follow her down the concrete stairwell. I don't check to see if Meg is coming, too – she always does.

"Therefore," Bliss shoots back. "What, you think just because I have a manicure, I have to be brain-dead too?"

"You'd be the only one of your clique who isn't," I reply sweetly, pushing past her into the laundry room.

Bliss – showing her usual entitlement and lack of respect for other people's property – rummages in the dryers for clean laundry, outfitting us in an array of shorty shorts and tank tops before we hit the party. It's easy to find the right floor: music is pounding through the walls and an, ahem, amorous couple has spilled out into the stairwell, making out against the door in an enthusiastic tangle of hands and tongue.

"Move it," I bark. They shift out of our way, not missing a beat as they slam back against the wall instead, his hands gripping her ass tightly and both of them emitting a symphony of moans and grunts.

Meg is wide-eyed as we pass, and her expression doesn't change once we emerge into the main party. It's the usual college scene, the hallways packed with kids clutching beers and plastic cups – dancing, chatting, hurling themselves around with inflatable pool toys – but from the look on her face, we could have wandered into the middle of an orgy. I quickly scope out the place. Most of the bedroom doors are open and, unsurprisingly, there's no flannel or long johns in sight, just plenty of bare-chested boys in boxers, and girls wearing shrunken T-shirts, tiny shorts, and – in a few extra-slutty cases – silky nightgowns as they bounce around to the music.

"Someone better stay here and keep watch." I tug at my shorts. They're printed with tiny giraffes galloping across my butt. "In case security comes to break things up."

"Or Phi Kappa shows," Bliss adds. Taking an abandoned cup from the floor, she pushes it into my hand, finds an almost-empty beer bottle for herself, and then steals a sleep mask from somebody's door handle to arrange on the top of Meg's head. In an instant, she's transformed us from three underage girls in dumb nightwear into a trio of partygoers, perfectly blending into the crowd. I hate to admit, I'm impressed.

"I guess that means you're up," I tell Meg. I'd rather a vaguely functional Bliss as my buddy than her.

"But—" Her protest is drowned out by a pack of frattish guys whooping past, naked save a collection of Disney boxers and shaving-cream bow tics. They pile into the room next to us, only to emerge a moment later with one of the lingerie girls slung between them. She squeals and laughs but doesn't put up a fight.

"We're on our cells," I add, already backing away. "Call if you spot Jason!"

We're quickly swallowed up by the crowd, rowdy from the mix of cheap drinks and skin. Awesome. I can't shake my bitterness, just imagining how I'm going to deal with this twenty-four seven when school starts in the fall.

"You think she'll be OK?" Bliss glances back, but Meg is already out of sight. "These parties can get kind of wild."

I roll my eyes. "Relax. She's probably got 911 on speed dial. Or her daddy. Now, 318..." I start checking door numbers.

"It's down here." Bliss points the way, past a gaggle of girls in matching black lace nightgowns. I guess the pajama dress code is kind of like Halloween: just an excuse to look like a Playboy refugee for the night.

"You're sure you know where you're going?" I can't help but tease. She scowls.

"I haven't got total amnesia, you know."

I laugh at her petulant expression. "I'm just kidding. Jesus, now who's the touchy one?"

She exhales, as if forcing herself not to snap back. "Jason's the last room on the right," she says instead, adjusting her football jersey shirt so it reveals one bare shoulder. "You'd better check it out first, in case he's still there."

"Yes, ma'am." I mock-salute, leaving her camouflaged in the line for someone's keg while I do a casual stroll-by. The door's lodged half-open, and through the gap I can see a blond boy giving his hair a careful ruffle, peering at his reflection in a handheld mirror. He's wearing Simpsons boxers and nothing else, and when he's done mussing the perfect Pattinson look, he flexes a few muscles, just to reassure himself of his own hotness.

"Yo, Jason!" Another guy pushes me out of the way, slamming the door wide open. "Get out here! Eric's got a bet going we can't down ten in ten!"

Jason tosses the mirror aside. "Like hell, we can't! Those suckers can eat it."

They charge out, off to defend the honor and beer-chugging reputation of the brotherhood. I beckon Bliss over. "All clear," I tell her. "And he should be gone awhile." Or however long it takes to drink himself to the emergency room.

We slip into the room. It's messy, with dirty laundry and books littering the floor. Bliss looks around.

"Well?" I ask, impatient. "Don't you want to make the drop? Unleash destruction?"

"Uh-huh." She bites her lip. The journal is in her hands, but she doesn't make a move.

"What are you waiting for?" I frown. "I thought this was what you wanted."

"It is," Bliss says slowly. "I just … It's a big step, you know? I'd be destroying everything."

"I think they did that already," I remind her, surprised that she's wavering now, when all the hard work is already done.

Then again, maybe this is why she asked me along, to show some steel when she's set to wimp out. "Are you forgetting the whole limo thing?" I remind her meaning-fully. "Think of this as karma. Making sure she gets what she deserves."

It seems to do the job. Bliss suddenly crosses the room and deposits the journal on the nightstand. "Karma," she says, steely.

"Payback's a bitch," I agree. "Although, I've got to ask: what do you even see in these guys?"

Bliss just gives me a look.

"No, really," I insist, picking up a porn magazine between my thumb and forefinger and dangling it like evidence. "I want to know. Is it their conversational skills? Personal hygiene maybe? I'm just trying to figure this out."

"Maybe it's none of your business," Bliss snaps.

"Except you made it my business when you came looking for me," I point out. "So what's the deal – did you really care about him, or are you just mad Kaitlin stole your trophy?"

She doesn't respond, turning away to rifle through some of the papers on his desk.

"You shouldn't waste yourself on these morons." I sigh. It's beyond me how Cameron and his jock crew are even considered hot, let alone worth all this energy. "There are some decent guys around, you know. They might not have the money and the car and be, like, sooo cool, but at least they won't treat you like crap."

"What, like JD?" Bliss spins back to me, her lips set in a thin line. "And that kid who got busted for pot – what was his name, Marcus?"

I narrow my eyes. "Hey, at least I was dating those guys because I wanted to, not just because it made me look good to everyone else."

"That's for sure." She gives a mean smirk. "But can you really call it *dating* if you just go down on them in the alley behind the Loft?"

My temper flares. "Instead of what – giving head in the backseat of his SUV?" I give a bitter laugh. "You can pretend like you're so much better than me if you want, but I'm guessing you give it up just because he lights some candles and calls you baby."

She flinches.

"See?" I say, smug. "At least I fool around because I want to. You're just afraid he'll call you frigid if you don't."

I wait for another bitchy remark, some of that famous condescending sarcasm. Instead, Bliss sinks onto the edge of Jason's unmade bed, her shoulders slumped and an utterly miserable expression on her face.

Oh, boy.

"You're better off without him," I advise lightly, hoping we can skate over this part without some epic confessional session. "Anyway, you're done with him now, remember? You don't have to put up with that bullshit anymore."

"But, it's done," Bliss says quietly, tearing strips from the label of her beer bottle.

"What do you—? Oh." I stop, realizing what she means. *"That."*

"That," she echoes, looking very young. When she's all dolled up with makeup and that hair, I forget she's only what, sixteen?

I sigh. Anger can only fuel you for so long. Sooner or later, the grief is going to bleed through. Now, clearly, Bliss is succumbing to the wretched, heartbroken part of her betrayal. Great.

Crossing the room, I settle on the bed beside her and try not to think when Jason last got around to changing his graying sheets. "Are you OK?" I venture. Bliss isn't exactly high on my list of deep and meaningful confidantes, and judging by the pained look on her face, I don't figure on hers, either.

"I'm fine." She tries to brush it off with one of those fake smiles, but neither of us is convinced. "I guess," she amends, "I will be."

We sit in silence for a moment, the noise from the party drifting in through the gap in the door. The impossibilities just keep mounting, but I can't help feeling a flicker of sympathy. Jesus, what's next: me and Meg painting each other's toenails and lip-synching to Lady Gaga?

"I lost my virginity to this guy from down the street," I offer awkwardly. Girl talk isn't exactly my thing, but I need something to snap her out of this slump. "He had a goatee, a sharks' tooth necklace, and was way too old to be scamming on high-school chicks."

"Ewww." She gives a faint smile.

"Mmhmm," I agree. "And then he dumped me because I talked trash about the Dave Matthews Band. He really loved those guys."

Bliss manages a giggle. There.

"It'll get easier, I guess." She sighs, hair falling in her eyes. "I mean, I won't have such big expectations next time. It won't matter so much. That's what Kaitlin said, anyway," she adds darkly. "And she would know."

I shake my head. "It always matters. It should."

She gives me a sideways look. "JD McGraw mattered?"

"I don't sleep with everyone I date, you know."

"Oh. Sorry." Bliss at least looks a little guilty.

"It's OK." I shrug. "I thought I was supposed to, in the beginning." I shift to get more comfortable. "You know, like when you've been with a guy a while, and he starts pushing, like it's obligated."

She nods. "I thought it would bring us closer together…" She trails off. "Prove he really did care about me." Bliss gives a tight little shrug.

"Asshole." I roll my eyes. This is why I don't date high-school guys. Not that my exes are that great, either. "Well, they're going to get what they deserve now," I tell her brightly. "You've seen to that."

Bliss nods, unconvinced. "I guess…"

"Are you kidding me? Once that stuff gets out, they'll be ruined. I've seen how your group works."

She brightens, clearly spurred by their warped view of social justice. "You're right. It's over." With a reassuring look at the journal – balanced precariously on Jason's nightstand beside a mold-filled mug and a suspiciously scrunched-up T-shirt – she bounces up. Picking up the mirror from where Jason discarded it, she fluffs out her hair and adjusts her PJ outfit, as if reminding herself who she is.

"You've got my dress?" she asks, without looking up. "I need to change before we head back. And you have no idea how much it cost."

Yup. The great Bliss Merino is back.

"Right here." I pat my bulging backpack, a little relieved. Enough with the bonding.

"Then what are you waiting for?" Stalking past me, Bliss heads back out into the hallway. "Meg is probably, like, having a breakdown by now. I still can't believe you dragged her along. If anyone sees me with you both, my status will be totally wrecked."

Maybe tearful, vulnerable Bliss wasn't so bad after all...

Meg

Perhaps I was wrong, and being invisible has its advantages too. Because for five whole minutes, I'm left blissfully alone in the alcove by the stairs, unnoticed as the party shrieks and thumps around me in a riot of Victoria's Secret nightwear and trashy dance music. I watch it all with a curious mix of fascination and fear. I've never been to a college party before. To tell the truth, I've barely been to high-school parties, either – at least, not the kind where kids drink and flirt and fall against walls making out with each other as if there's nobody else around. No, back when I still had an approximation of a social life, my experiences were always on the safe, sedate side: juvenile slumber parties, or birthday gatherings where we would all go bowling or to the movies or something, like we did when we were in fifth grade. I suppose I'm all grown-up now, because here, the Jell-O comes in shot glasses, and the only punch I've seen is the one being guzzled from red plastic cups by enthusiastic frat boys.

Something tells me it's not plain old lemonade.

"Hey!" A stocky guy in neon boxers suddenly catches sight of me, lurching closer with a beer in his hand. He must be nineteen or twenty and looms over me. "You're that chick from my chem lab!"

"No." I try to edge backward, but I'm already against the wall. I give him a polite smile. "I think you're confused."

"No way." He shakes his head vigorously, sloshing sticky liquid over my bare legs. "You sit in the back, remember? And one time, you lent me your notes. That was cool of you." He grins, taking in my outfit.

"Really," I say again, painfully aware of his eyes zeroing in on my chest, barely covered by a tiny pink tank top with SNUGGLY emblazoned across the chest in sparkly gemstones. "It's not me."

"How'd you do on the final?" he asks, unconcerned with the fact that we've never actually met before. "Killer, right? I studied so hard, but I still blew it."

"Mmhmm." I make a noncommittal noise, looking around for an escape. What's taking Jolene and Bliss so long? "Killer. Sure. Can I just...?" I gesture to get past him, but the boy doesn't move; he just sort of leans against the wall, blocking me in.

"Peterson is such a dick," he sneers. "I was ten minutes late handing in this paper one time, and he gave me an F." He pauses, distracted by a passing group of girls in silky negligees. I take my chance and quickly duck under his arm.

"See you in class!" I back quickly into the crowd.

It's hot and noisy in the hallway, and I push my way through the riot of bodies, trying to avoid any more spilled drinks or leering guys. There's a bathroom just ahead, so I duck into the gray-tiled room, jostling for space by the long row of sinks as I do my best to dab the beer off my legs.

"You saw Elliot, right? In the onesie? That guy is totally ridiculous."

Beside me, two girls are reapplying lip gloss, dressed in matching athletic T-shirts and men's boxers. Their drinks are perched on the narrow ledge by the mirror, next to tiny purses overflowing with makeup and keys.

Her friend giggles, ruffling her bangs. "Ridiculously cute, you mean."

"Ewww! Seriously?" The girl snorts. "You'd have to, like, unbutton it, like a baby!"

They fall into hysterics as I finish cleaning myself up. It's not too bad, at least: if I were wearing normal pajamas, they'd be soaked through by now, but as it is, I'm just left with sticky skin and the waft of beer around me. Score one for the indecent short-shorts, I decide. Not that I'll be rushing out to buy myself a pair any time soon.

"Excuse me." There's a quiet voice behind me, and I turn to find a petite girl clutching a shower bucket waiting patiently for the sinks.

"Oh, sorry." I back away, letting her through. She sets out her toothbrush and mouthwash on the ledge and begins to cleanse and tone her face in methodical swipes with a cotton ball. Her pajamas are, I realize, real: flannel printed with tiny musical notes, with fuzzy pink slippers.

"Or he could keep it on!" The party girls are still falling over themselves, clutching each other at the idea of Elliot and his hilarious outfit. "And just undo the crotch! It, like, pops open!"

The other girl's eyes meet mine in the mirror, and for a moment we share a look of sheer exasperation as the pair collects their things and stumbles out, back to the party. The girl reaches for her floss.

"How will you get any sleep?" I venture, curious.

"Earplugs," she replies, her voice resigned.

"Oh."

More girls bustle into the bathroom, brimming over with laughter and gossip, but she ignores them all, curiously detached from the chaos. I watch, my sympathy fading into something else, a new kind of chill. For a moment I wonder if this will be me in two years' time: still on the outskirts of everything, still alone, while the party whirls on around me. I've been thinking of college like it's my own green light on the horizon, but watching this girl now, it strikes me for the first time that it may never end; that the location may change, but my life could remain exactly the same.

Something I read once pops into my mind like a warning. *You never grow out of high school.*

I shiver.

. . .

When I get back to the lounge, the party is even louder. I perch on the edge of a couch in the common room area to wait. All eyes are fixed on a group of girls grinding in the middle of the room, but I keep a careful watch on the exits, cell phone in my hand, poised to make the call to Jolene and Bliss if I catch sight of Jason or – worse still – security. I can't even imagine what my dad would say if I was dragged home at midnight from a college party wearing … *this*.

"Meg?"

It takes me a second to realize someone's saying my name, but still, I don't look over. Who here would even know who I am?

"Uh, Meg? It's me, Scott. From the library?"

I whip my head around so quickly, I almost tumble right off the couch.

"Whoa." Scott laughs, putting out a hand to steady me. "You OK there?"

"Yes, fine," I say breathlessly. He's dressed in the same outfit from before: the graphic print T-shirt and a pair of black skinny cords, but in the midst of all the ridiculous costumes, he suddenly looks like a beacon of sanity. "Hi." I try to recover, hoisting myself back up on the couch arm. "How's it going?"

"Stressed, hectic." He gives a rueful grin, straightening his hipster glasses. "Figured I'd take a break from the all-nighter, try to relax for an hour or so."

"Good plan," I agree. "Although, I don't know how relaxing you'll find it here…" I pause, wondering if I sound like a loser, but he laughs.

"Yeah, maybe not." Scott glances around, but unlike the other guys in the room, he turns his back on the floor show and looks down at me with what I can almost convince myself is genuine interest. "So, how about you – did you find that guy you were looking for?"

"Jason? Not yet. That's where the others are. Looking for him, I mean." I cross my arms over my chest, trying to cover the low-cut neckline. I thought I felt self-conscious in my prom dress, but this much, much worse. Does he think these clothes are mine? And that I'm wearing them by choice?

"Cool." Scott nods slowly. There's a pause as he studies me. "You know, I was thinking, after you left – it's weird that I haven't seen you around. It's a big campus, but you usually run into everyone at least once. What are you, a freshman?"

I feel a pulse of embarrassment. "I, umm, I don't actually go here. I'm in high school," I admit, my voice small.

"Really?" He doesn't seem fazed by the news, but I'm sure he's just humoring me. "So what brings you all out here?"

"It's a long story." I don't want to bore him with the immature details, so I give a vague shrug instead. "It's mainly their thing; I'm just the designated driver for the night."

Scott chuckles. "I know that one. My sister's always calling me up, begging for a ride. Last week I wound up with a car full of fourteen-year-olds, driving to the city for some mall tour autograph signing." He gives a rueful grin. "I'm counting the days until she gets her license."

I exhale, starting to relax. "So you're from around here?"

"Over in Adamstown," he says, naming a town another hour away. I nod. "It's kind of nice, being so close to home. But that probably sounds lame." Scott sticks his hands in his pockets, as if he's the embarrassed one now.

"Oh, no." I shake my head vigorously. "I understand. I'm trying to figure out where to apply now, but the schools I want are all so far away. Part of me likes the idea," I add shyly, "of just starting over somewhere on the other side of the country. But, then reality sets in…" I remember the girl from the bathroom, and her careful isolation.

"I know what you mean." Scott grins. "Even starting here was overwhelming, at first, but I think you adapt to it. Like you grow to fit the space."

"I hope so." It's a nice thought, but I've been drifting around in a school of hundreds for years now, with no sign that I'll blossom to meet the environment. Perhaps my evolutionary instincts are faulty, despite the fact that I score perfect As in all my science classes.

"Hey, can I get you a drink?" Scott asks suddenly, and I remember that we're in the middle of a party, surrounded by other people. For a moment, I'd forgotten.

"Sure." I hop down from the couch and follow him into the crowd.

"There's beer, if you want…" He falls back, resting a hand lightly on my back as he guides me through the mess of people and noise.

"Oh. No, I'm driving. And even if I wasn't … I mean, I don't ever drink…" I trail off, feeling like a child all over again. I can't help it; most of the kids here are clearly underage, but I've had my dad quoting statistics about alcohol poisoning and drunk drivers ever since I was in junior high.

"Then I guess we'll give the punch a miss." He nods at where two jock guys are ladling peach liquid from a huge plastic bowl. Empty bottles of juice and vodka are abandoned nearby, and the whole corner is giving off a potent smell.

I laugh. "Yeah, maybe not."

We keep going, meandering past open bedroom doors and clusters of partygoers. "So what are you, like, straight-edge?" Scott asks, ducking to avoid a giant inflatable crocodile being tossed around the hall.

"No, just sensible," I joke, but it comes out flat. I cough. "Are you?"

He shakes his head. "I tried it out for a while; some of my friends were into that scene, back in high school, but – I don't know, I wasn't really into the rules side of it. Having such a fixed ideology, you know? I prefer just to do my own thing." We come to a split in the corridor and he stops, deciding between the two hallways in front of us. "What do you think?" He grins, teasing. "Should we leave some string to find our way back?"

I smile. "I saw a girl with some floss back there… It's your call."

"Hmmm … eeeny, meeny, miny, go." He points to the

left, and we set off, deeper into the complex. I wonder if Jolene and Bliss are around here somewhere. They can't have bailed altogether yet; I'm the one with the keys.

"Ah, here we go." Scott finds a vending machine and digs in his pocket for change.

"Here." I begin to unzip my purse, but he's already feeding the coins in.

"No, I've got this." He grins. "So, are you a Coke girl, or a Sprite?"

"Dr Pepper, actually," I decide.

"Really?" He draws the word out, still almost teasing. "See, you never can tell from a first impression."

The machine hums and rattles for a moment, but with no result. Scott fakes looking around, furtive, before thumping the side with his fist. A can rolls into the dispenser; he presents it to me with a little bow.

"Thanks." I'm overcome with a moment of déjà vu, remembering Tristan making his own little bow to the girls back at prom. The prom I'm missing completely.

"So what happened with the dress?" Scott asks, as if reading my mind. He takes his own drink and pops the cap, leaning against the vending machine as he waits for my reply.

"It's a costume party." I shrug, as if that's explanation enough, but – painfully aware of the pink sparkles adorning my body – I can't help adding, "Bliss insisted."

"The bossy one?"

I nod, even though to me, she and Jolene are equally determined.

"Shame." Scott gives me a slow sort of grin. "I thought it looked great. I mean, you did."

I freeze, feeling a low blush begin to spread across my face. "Umm, thanks," I manage, staring at the floor. "It's ... prom. At least, it was."

"Oh, that's right," Scott nods, still utterly at ease. "My sister doesn't shut up about it. She can't wait for hers – she's only fourteen," he explains with an affectionate kind of grin.

"Oh," I murmur, not wanting to admit that I'm only sixteen. No wonder he's being so sweet – I clearly bring out the big brother in him.

Suddenly, a shrill voice ricochets down the hallway: "Where did you get that shirt?"

A girl with long, dark hair is approaching, wearing one of those almost-indecent black negligee outfits. Her expression is grim, and I take a step back in fear as she gets closer.

"You heard me," she demands, raking her eyes over me. "Where did you get that shirt? And those socks!"

"Umm," I stutter, thrown by the fearsome combination of gleaming hair and tiny, tanned thighs. "I don't, I mean..."

She lunges forward and snatches at the tank top, inspecting the label sewn by the lower hem. "It's mine!" The girl's glossed lips drop open. "What the hell?" Whipping around, she yells down the hall to a cluster of gleaming-haired, golden-skinned doppelgängers. "I was right; it's mine!"

They begin to advance.

"Wait a second." Scott moves in front of me, forcing the girl to back off, just a little. "How can you even tell? You probably both just bought it from the same store. Look at all your friends!"

She crosses her arms and glares at us. "Sure, you can get the shirt anywhere, but Cory had it custom designed for my birthday!"

On some level I register disbelief that anyone could choose to have *snuggly* emblazoned across her chest, let alone as a special gift. But that thought is quickly dwarfed by fear as her friends line up behind her in solidarity. A silk-clad firing squad, armed with bare skin and kohl-lined stares.

I gulp.

"Look, I'm sure we can sort this out." Scott is still trying to reason with them, his tall body and soothing voice the only thing standing between me and ... what, I'm not exactly sure. Death by mascara?

"Meg!" Someone yanks my arm from behind me, and I turn to find Bliss and Jolene coming from the other direction. "Where have you been? You were supposed to stay out front!"

"I know, but..." I swivel back and forth between them and the ranks of angry college girls. "I ran into Scott, and then—"

"She's wearing my jersey! The one Eric gave me!" A blond backup girl suddenly gasps, pointing at Bliss, who is, sure enough, wearing the jersey with E LAWTON on the front.

"And those are so my giraffe shorts," another adds. "I just put them in the laundry tonight."

"See, I told you!" the original accuser crows triumphantly. "Who are they, anyway?" She narrows her eyes at us. "Do you even go here?"

"What do we do?" I ask Jolene, who is surveying the area with a practiced eye. Scott is still blocking their way, but I'm not sure how long the girls will stay back – especially now that there is even more evidence against us.

"Plan B," Jolene announces.

"Which is?" I barely have time to ask before she grabs my hand and takes off, racing back toward the stairwell with Bliss following us close behind.

"But—" My protest is lost as we dash through the crowd. As I look back, I catch a glimpse of six very angry party girls in hot pursuit; behind them, Scott is left by the vending machine, clutching the can of Dr Pepper with a confused look on his face. I want to tell him I'm sorry, but there isn't time.

Then the door slams shut behind us, and we're gone.

Bliss

I can't believe I told her that.

By the time we stop for gas about ten miles out of town, I've thought up at least a dozen ways Jolene could ruin my life – starting with a casual comment to anyone at school, and ending with anonymous blog entries all over the East Midlands network sites, telling the world that, yes, I slept with Cameron, but it wasn't good enough to stop him from cheating. I climb out of the backseat, shaken. What was I thinking? Like it's not already dangerous enough with her knowing about Kaitlin and Cameron and this whole diary thing, now I have to go and spill the biggest secret I have.

Double standards, right? Everyone assumes you're

doing it, but the moment anyone says so, it's the biggest scandal. Gossip like this – my mom always reminds me – you don't live down.

Jolene is already smoking a cigarette, mooching a safe distance from the gas pumps while Meg fills up the car. I remember her awkward sympathy back in the dorm room and feel a fresh wave of embarrassment. She must think I'm pathetic, breaking down like that, but I can't help it. She was talking like Cameron had only been a shiny new accessory to me, as if I hadn't cared at all. But I did.

I do.

"You need to get anything?" Jolene wanders over, already toying with another cigarette. "When I have a bad breakup, I reach for the ice cream. And candy." She gives a wry grin. "Once you eat yourself into a sugar coma, things don't seem so bad."

I shake my head slowly. "No. Thanks."

She gives me a sympathetic kind of smile. "C'mon, what's a few calories when your asshole ex-boyfriend is fooling around?"

I stiffen. "I said no. But can I get my dress back? I can't show up back at prom wearing *this*."

"Forgive me," she drawls, sarcastic. "I forgot about your dress codes." Jolene pulls a handful of dry-clean-only silk out of her bag and tosses it over to me like it's some kind of rag.

"Careful!" I yelp, snatching it before it can touch the ground. "Jesus. Do you know what would happen if this got ruined?"

"You'd have to charge another?" Jolene seems amused, but there's nothing funny about my mom and her "my family came to this country with only the clothes on their backs so show some respect for your possessions" speech, even if she does deliver it in a designer outfit with our maid on the other line.

"I'll be inside," I tell Jolene instead, stalking away.

"Don't be long!" Meg calls after me. "I'm going to miss my curfew."

Of course she is.

The place is empty when I get inside, just long aisles of junk food and auto supplies waiting under harsh neon strip lights. A teenage boy slouches behind the register, flipping through a car magazine while he chews on a strip of packaged jerky.

"Hey." I manage a grin. "Do you have a bathroom?"

"Customers only." He sighs. Then he looks up. "Uh, s-sure," he stutters, blinking at my bare legs. "Out back, just over—"

"Thanks!" I'm already scooting to the back of the store when my cell rings. It's Nikki.

"Where are you?" she demands as soon as I pick up. "I've called, like, a hundred times."

I can hear chatter and laughter in the background, and the fierce thump of music. The fun they're having without me.

"Sorry," I exclaim brightly, pushing into the stall. It's scattered with wet toilet paper, grafitti scrawled on every wall, and a foul smell coming from the corner. Awesome.

"Fashion emergency," I say, trying not to touch anything. Or breathe. "My, uh, bra snapped."

"No way! You poor thing." There's a pause, and then I hear the echo of her retelling the others. "No, she had to go home. Uh-huh, I know!"

"I'm on my way back now," I say loudly, starting to peel off the football jersey. "I'll be, like, five minutes."

"No, that's why I called – we're on our way to Brianna's."

"Already?" I stop. "But it's not even midnight." My heart sinks.

"Uh-huh." Nikki is still distracted. "See you there!"

I hang up, suddenly feeling very alone. While we've been running around playing dress-up and sneaking Kaitlin's diary, I've missed everything. My whole prom, over. They're partying in a limo, while I'm stuck in a dirty gas station bathroom far away from all the action.

Was it even worth it?

I was expecting it to be a victory. All night, ever since I found them together, I've been focused so hard on making Kaitlin and Cameron pay, like that will make everything OK somehow. If I can prove it, if I expose her for the lying, cheating, backstabbing bitch she really is, if we do it without any blame touching me – then I'll be fine. I'll win. But standing there in Jason's room, delivering the evidence that would see them crash and burn, I felt nothing.

No, not nothing. I felt the same as when I saw him kissing her. Lost, like everything has slipped out of order and I don't know how to get it all back again. Best friend, boyfriend, the whole social scene – I worked so hard to get everything perfect, the way high school is supposed to be. And now I'm left with this ache in my chest, knowing that it was all a lie, and I was dumb enough to believe them.

"Bliss, get a move on!" Jolene hammers on the door.

I swallow. "OK, OK," I yell back, quickly shimmying back into my dress. Unlocking the door, I take a gasp of almost-fresh air. "There, I'm done."

Jolene pushes past me, not even waiting for me to close the door before she strips off her pajama set and pulls the pink ruffles back on.

"I thought you hated that thing," I say quietly, checking my reflection in the soap-smeared glass.

"I do," she says, "but it'll cause way more questions if I go home without it."

There's a timid knock, and then Meg pokes her head in too. "Is there room for me?"

"Can't you wait—" I start to say, but Jolene waves her in.

"Zip me up. Please."

We shift over, crammed in the tiny room while Meg complains about the smell and fusses with the catch on the back of Jolene's dress. I ignore them, trying to pull myself back together. That dorm-room confessional was just a mistake, I tell myself, some kind of hormonal glitch in sanity. The sooner I'm back with Courtney and the crew, the sooner I'll stop feeling so strange.

"You can drop me at Brianna's, up in Cedar Heights," I instruct Meg, fluffing out my hair. I still look flawless, at least. And I've learned by now, that's all that matters.

"The after-party," she says, wistful.

"Yup. They're on their way already, and I can't miss anything else, not after bailing on the main event. So, can you guys get a move on?" I look over to find Jolene mussing up her hair and Meg twisting uselessly under the weight of her dress. "I'll be outside."

I've read all the tabloids on the magazine stand, so I wander the aisles, idly poking at the packs of Doritos and sugar-rush snacks that I can never in a million years eat. Not unless I want Brianna offering to lend me a workout DVD. Again. I sigh, wondering what they'll all say when I get to the party. Will Cameron and Kaitlin act guilty and ashamed, or will they be sneaking off every half hour to dry hump behind the pool house? I don't know which would be worse.

"Hey, *señorita*. Can I get that ass to go?"

I look up. A couple of men dressed in dirty jeans and trucker hats are unloading six-packs from the cooler nearby. They've got goatees and tattoos and look like the kind of guys who blast heavy metal from their truck and holler dumb-ass racist comments at you on the sidewalk.

I turn away.

"Aww, don't be like that." The one with his gut bulging against his shirt saunters closer. "We're not so scary, are we, Chuck?"

His friend chuckles. "Nah, we're regular gentlemen."

I take a couple of steps back, but I'm boxed in the corner by the refrigerator cabinets. Gut Guy gives me a leer.

"You're pretty dressed up tonight, huh? Heading to a *fiesta*?"

I look around, but the boy at the register is still slouched over his magazines, and there's nobody else in the store. I shiver.

"Uh-huh." I give a vague murmur, trying to look enthralled by the row of processed potato products, but the men don't shift; they just loiter behind me, filling the space.

"I could do with some fun." The man laughs. "We should come along."

I finally turn, giving an icy look as I move to pass them. I've been around guys like them before – guys who think it's some kind of compliment to rake their eyes all over you. Usually, I can handle them, but tonight, something's not working because they block my path.

"Don't go running off so soon. We were just gettin' to know each other."

"No, thanks." I take a step to the side. He mirrors me. I fold my arms. "Prom," I offer, hoping they'll back off once they know my age. "I'm going to junior prom."

He's undeterred. "Oh, yeah?" He grins. "So, you want a dance?"

Before I can move, he grabs me around my waist.

"I've got to go." I try to pull away, but he's laughing, stepping in a clumsy slow dance while I'm crushed against him close enough to smell the cheap deodorant and tobacco. "Get off me!" I protest, pushing uselessly against him. His friend is whooping, and for a terrible minute I'm trapped.

"Stop flirting, and get your ass out here!" I hear Jolene's yell and manage to twist around, sending her a desperate look. Right away, her face changes, getting harder and full of steel.

"C'mon, we're going." She doesn't hesitate, just sends the guys a deadly glare as she elbows into our corner and takes firm hold of my wrist. "Say good-bye to the nice men, Bliss."

But Gut Guy doesn't loosen his grip on me.

"Hey! Here's your partner." He laughs to his friend. "Double date. That's more like it."

The other man reaches for Jolene, but she makes some kind of movement with her leg and suddenly he's bent double, cursing loudly.

"You bitch!"

"Like I said, time to go." Jolene glares at Gut Guy with such ferocity, he backs off, hands up in surrender.

"Hey, we were just playing."

"Yeah, well, play with yourself in the future." Jolene shoves me backward into the open aisle, planting herself between me and his meaty hands. "You should be used to that."

My heart is racing. Any minute now, they're going to fight back, I just know it, and Jolene's angry stare will be no match for their weight and height and willingness to, you know, hurt us.

"Jolene," I whisper, tugging at the back of her ruffles, "let's just go."

"Not until you get an apology." She folds her arms.

"I don't need one," I protest. The guy she kicked is still rubbing his shin, looking at us with a murderous glint in his eyes. "It was just ... a mistake, OK? We were just hanging out. No need for anyone to apologize. Right?"

To my intense relief, Jolene seems to reassess. "Fine," she spits reluctantly. "We're done. But you guys better keep your fucking hands to yourselves."

I yank her away, still full of fear, but Jolene doesn't hurry at all – she just saunters slowly outside as if we've been chatting about the weather or whatever, not facing down two full-grown sleazy men.

"Thanks," I breathe, glancing back toward the store. What has to be the guys' truck is parked right out front, a Confederate flag draped in the back window. I shudder. "They were drunk, I think. They wouldn't back off."

Jolene just gives me another of those looks. She pauses in the middle of the parking lot, halfway to where Meg is waiting patiently in the car. "You shouldn't let men put their hands on you like that."

"I didn't really have a choice!" I protest.

She rolls her eyes. "Here." Unzipping a side pocket in her backpack, she brings out a tiny canister and a round thing that looks like a key fob. "Pepper spray, rape alarm." She holds up each in turn and then offers them to me. I shake my head.

"I'm fine, I just—"

"Think you can get your way just by asking nice?" Jolene rolls her eyes. "The real world doesn't work that way, Bambi. Take them."

It's an order, so I do.

"Thanks." I stuff them into my purse next to the photocopies, thrown by how *nice* she's being. I mean sure, the excuse to inflict physical pain on some random dude was probably a big motivator, but still, she just saved my ass.

Jolene smiles. "Now you owe me two favors."

"I do?"

"Yup." She grins wider. "So you're not going straight to that after-party. You're going to help me out with something first."

I look at her, wary. "What kind of something?"

"Just a thing." Jolene presses her lips tightly together, and I realize with a sinking feeling that the smiles are just sugar-coating. Whatever this thing is, it's trouble. "You probably won't even have to get out of the car," she adds, still acting casual. "Just keep Meg from bolting, and I'll take care of the rest."

"It's late." I try to argue, worn out. "Can't we do this some other time? Meg's already past her curfew." I could care less about Meg's overprotective parents, but I've still got the party ahead of me, and all the fake smiles and gossip I'll have to throw around to make it look like nothing's wrong.

"Meg called her parents already." Jolene interrupts my plans. "She said she was having so much fun, they let her stay out longer. So, that's no problem."

I sigh. "Jolene..."

Her face shifts. "I need to do this," she says, quiet but forceful. "You're not the only one who wants payback."

We face off under the bright neon signs, and for a second, she looks the way I felt. Angry. Determined. Heartbroken.

"OK." I agree at last, not even wanting to imagine who would dare cross her. "But you'd better not get me arrested. I'm armed now, remember?"

JOLENE

With Bliss on board, Meg is outnumbered. She barely puts up a protest at our slight diversion, and before long, we've pulled up just around the corner from my target. It's another exclusive development, with wide streets that back onto the golf course and white picket fences at every turn. Suburban bliss.

"Wait here," I tell them, easing out of the car. "I won't be long."

"But—"

"Relax." I give Meg a careless grin. "It's my dad's place. I'm just picking something up."

She relaxes, as if that's all the reassurance she needs. It shouldn't be.

I've only been to the house once before, but I remember everything. It was a baby shower for the twins a few years back, full of women with shiny hair and tailored silk dresses who widened their eyes every time I sullenly introduced myself as his other child. The Blonde held court, beaming in the middle of the room with a fat belly, while Dad fussed with caterer's platters, making sure everything looked just right.

I left after twenty minutes. I couldn't take the perfection anymore.

Tonight, the house is gleaming with a fresh coat of paint, the lawn trim and lush despite the early summer heat. I slip around the wide, two-car garage out back and find wrought-iron garden furniture arranged on the immaculate paved patio and a blue-tiled pool nestled behind a child-proof gate.

He always did land on his feet.

The tree is by the far end of the house, gnarled and easy to climb, with branches stretching all the way to the first-floor bathroom window. I clamber up in a flash, the bark scraping my bare legs, but I barely notice the pain. I reach an arm through the open window, find the catch, release it, and just like that, I'm inside.

We only found out last month, when the first tuition demand came through. You'd think I would have seen it coming by now, after all the other times he's let me down, but no – this one thing, I actually believed he'd deliver. Stupid. He was too much of a coward to even tell me to my face; he had to call to explain that the college fund he'd been waving around for years like some get-out-of-alimony-free card didn't exist anymore. The markets took a tumble. His business expansion needed funds. He's got his own family to support these days, and can I not be so angry, please; I'll be eighteen soon, and he has no legal obligation to support me anymore.

Not that he ever did.

I hop down from the window seat and land in a crouch, low to the floor. For a moment, I wait for any footsteps or voices from the stairs. But there are none. If I know that babysitter, she'll be too busy taking advantage of the surround-sound entertainment system, the stocked fridge, and her boyfriend to come check on the kids until a half hour before they're due home.

I'm already barefoot, so I don't make a sound as I creep out onto the landing. Light from downstairs soaks me in a dim glow, and I pause a moment, absorbing the plush surroundings. It's like Kaitlin's house all over again, another world of thick carpeting and gilt-edged picture frames on heavy wallpaper. The staircase is centered and the hallway wraps around, overlooking the foyer below. Marble floor, polished banisters.

Even though I swore I would be all business, quick in and out, I catch sight of a family portrait on the wall and feel my heart clench. It's taken on a spotless beach somewhere, and he's grinning, a kid in one arm and the other wrapped around the Blonde, looking perky and perfect with the other child on her hip. They're wearing matching sun visors and his-and-hers pastel polo shirts, and everything about them screams preppy rich bliss.

When he was my dad, he wore stretched-out Knicks shirts and wasted twenty bucks a week on lottery tickets.

Vacations were swimming at the community pool, and sweaty road trips to the lake to fend off mosquitoes and splash around in the crowded water. Popsicles were a treat; diner key lime pie the ultimate indulgence. I took it all for granted as a kid, but when you get older you see behind the cracks: the revolving wad of credit cards, my mom's military policing of the grocery store cart, the hushed fights and tense look on her face every time the mail came. See, being poor isn't just about the stuff you can't have; it's a low note of insecurity that echoes in the background of everything you ever do, that sick fear that there won't be enough, that you'll never have enough.

I blink at the photos, paralyzed, until some morbid curiosity in me twists, and I find myself padding silently down the hall to the door with rainbows and fluffy clouds painted in bright brushstrokes.

The twins.

Carefully, I push the door ajar, step into the room, and pull the door closed behind me. My eyes adjust to the dimness. The curtains are drawn, but there's the pale glow of a night-light in the corner, with some kind of revolving case that casts star shapes up onto the ceiling above the matching miniature twin beds.

I edge closer.

Asleep, they're angelic – even I can admit that. Two years old now, with blond ringlets, adorable cotton pajamas, pudgy little hands clutching the luxury plushy animals our father now imports. One has sailboats on the bedding and the other, tiny cowboys.

I got an invite to their last birthday party – the Blonde saw to that – but I couldn't do it. I went to the Polaroid Kids show instead, drank too much whiskey, and made out with a third-rate drummer in the parking lot with their names echoing in my head. Camilla and Stephan. Classy names, both of them. Her doing, again I'm sure, but why shouldn't they be? These kids are set for a life of prep schools and privilege, birthday cars and whatever college they damn well choose. And if Daddy screws it up and fails all over again, as I know without a single doubt that he will, then her trust fund will prop them up all the same. They'll never know the bitterness of my life, and as much as I get that they're innocent – that they didn't choose this for me – I can't help but feel a hot wave of resentment as I stand over their sleeping bodies.

I hate them.

It's pure, and sharp, and the intensity of it scares me, but my hatred fills the room, spinning out like those little stars until I can barely breathe. I don't exist to him anymore, not now that there's this new life for him to enjoy. Up here, with his shiny golden family, he can pretend like he wasn't a deadbeat failure, like he didn't let us down and screw around, and then finally just cut loose and bail.

I don't matter to him, not enough.

Backing out of the room, I close the door behind me and head for the master suite. More family portraits line the room, perfect in their gilded frames, and I have to stop myself from looking – from getting sucked into their glossy little world. I check every room in turn – faster, more frantic – but I still don't find what I'm looking for. It's not downstairs either, I know that much, but he couldn't have sold it, not after the petty, selfish effort he went through to keep it in the divorce.

Even now, I can't believe he cared so much. Visitation access? He didn't ask, but when it came to that painting, he spared no effort: hitting us with threatening letters and lawyer fees until Mom just gave in to get him off our backs. It's not even valuable yet; that's the crazy part – just a swirled abstract thing he got suckered into buying from some gallery in the city instead of replacing the boiler that year. But he swore that one day, this guy would be the next Rothko, and we'd all be set, like that counted as a solid investment plan.

Now, I'm almost glad he fought so hard for it. See, hurting someone is simple in the end. Find what they love, and take it from them.

If I can find the damn thing.

I stand in the study, my breath coming fast. I need that thing as focus, to keep me from thinking of all the other damage I could do, the ways I could hurt him. But now I'm left shaking in the shadows of this life he's built – three miles and a world away from the existence my mom and I scraped out of thrift-store clothes and late shifts and coupons. My hands are clenched, pressing fierce half-moon prints into my palm, and it takes every bit of self-restraint I have not to hurl every bookcase from the wall, to smash the picture frames into shrapnel, to burn his fucking house down.

I take a breath.

Think, Jolene. Where would he keep it?

And then my eyes find the keys and folders left on his

heavy antique desk and I realize: there is one more place.

Moving quickly, I sweep the heavy key ring into my bag and flip through the thick leather journal. It's stuffed with dates and meetings, notes about shipping data and new marketing teams. My new, improved father. God, I bet he loves it: the respected, productive life of an entrepreneur. But I know not everything can have changed; he was always bad with numbers, and sure enough, there's a page at the back with a neat list of scribbled codes. *Card PIN, Penny – cell,* and then, finally, *Alarm – office.*

Jackpot.

It feels like I've been up here a lifetime, but the same R and B seduction song is still playing from downstairs when I hoist myself out the window and scramble down the tree. Under five minutes, and I'm out clean. I guess hanging around all those bad influences taught me some things, at least.

"Oh, thank God!" Meg is looking severely panicked when I slide into the passenger seat. "What were you doing in there? You said it was your dad's place!"

"It is." I shrug, slamming the door closed behind me. After creeping around so carefully, the sound jolts right through me.

Meg stares, wide-eyed. "But you didn't ring the bell."

"I went around back," I snap. "Now, do you want to get moving?"

I'm edgy, wired in my seat. I need to get away from this house, from the gleaming perfection of it all. I need to make him pay.

Meg gives me another anxious look, but she doesn't press. Starting the ignition, she carefully drives away.

"So are we done yet?" Bliss speaks up. She's still lounging in the backseat, clearly bored. "Because it's midnight already. I'm going to miss the party too if we don't get back soon."

"Patience, grasshopper." I force myself to sound casual, trying to pull it all back under control. "But I do need your phone for a sec."

"What for?" I can hear the reluctance in her voice. Phones are practically an extension of those girls – it's like I asked to borrow her arm.

"Does it matter?"

There's a sigh, and then she passes it forward. It's small, but equipped with a Web browser and a bunch of useless apps – and covered with diamanté gem stickers in silver and pink. Classy. With a few clicks, I find a map program and use my hastily scribbled address to figure out the way to his office. Just having something to do helps calm the itch in my veins, gives me some direction.

"OK, you need to take a right up ahead and get on Pinewood Avenue," I tell Meg, glancing up from the tiny screen.

"But Brianna's house is this way."

"I know." I shrug, still aiming for nonchalance. "I just need to make another stop first."

"Noooo!" Bliss wails. "No more stops. Or just, drop me off first. I'm done."

I whip my head around. "You're done when I say you are. You owe me, remember? Or do you want me to call

Kaitlin and let her know what we've been up to?" I hold up her phone and start scrolling through the contacts list. "Jared, Jenny, Joel, Kait—"

"OK, OK!" She gives me a murderous look. "I'll wait. But can Meg maybe drive any faster? At this rate, we'll be stuck out here all night."

I turn back to Meg. "She does have a point..."

Meg takes a breath. "This is the limit," she says firmly, "and besides, I don't even know where we're going."

"Elmwood Business Park," I reply, casual. "Now can we go faster?"

"What's there?" She frowns instead.

I sigh. "Just something I need to pick up. It wasn't at the house, so..."

"But it's the middle of the night; everything's closed," Meg argues.

"That's kind of the point."

"You're going to break in?"

Meg slams on the brakes and we lurch to a halt on the dark, residential street. Sure, it's only from about twenty miles an hour, but I'm still thrown forward against my seat belt.

"Ouch!" Bliss yelps from the back. "Meg!"

I peel the strap from my chest. That precious control is slipping fast. "Are we seriously going to go through this every time I tell you what to do?" I demand. "Because your innocent thing is getting old."

"It's not innocent to want to stay out of jail!" Meg cries.

Bliss leans forward. "Yeah, I kind of have to agree."

I grit my teeth. "Can you both just relax a minute? Nobody said anything about jail." I retrieve the key ring from my bag and dangle it in front of them. "See. I'm not breaking anything. And I have the alarm code, too. Nothing to worry about."

Meg just purses her lips disapprovingly. "Right, nothing. Except motion sensors, and CCTV, and security patrols..."

"Don't be such a baby," I argue, but her words ring alarmingly true. Sure, the keys and code will get me in without any problems, but she's right: a complex like that will have security cameras all over the place. I may have skills, but invisibility isn't one of them.

I think hard. There's no way I'm quitting yet, not after everything. So there's surveillance? That just means I need something extra.

"What would you do?" I ask Meg.

"What?"

"You're smart, right? Straight As, I bet. So how would you get around CCTV? I'm serious," I add. "Finesse has never been my thing."

Bliss snorts from the backseat. "You don't say."

I quell her with a look. "Come on, Meg, think."

"You're not supposed to get around security – that's the point." She sounds offended that I'd even ask her to consider breaking the rules.

"Bliss?" I turn. This is what it's come to: asking Bambi for criminal input. But desperate times...

She rolls her eyes. "Uh, no. Unless you've got some

magic wand to wave around, you're screwed. And I'm still missing my party." Bliss folds her arms, sulking, but something in her words triggers a spark. An old memory of late night, and hushed laughter, and the pair of us playing tag out on the damp fifty-yard line, the stadium rising, empty around us, as Dante crushed me into the ground.

Don't worry about security, he'd told me. Eli had fixed it.

I groan.

"What now?" Bliss whines.

"New stop," I tell them, already resigning myself to the indignities ahead. Sure, Eli Graff may be the undisputed geek criminal – and inadvertent YouTube hit – of East Midlands, but that doesn't mean he won't make me beg. "We need to go to the Loft, on Second Street."

"Are you going to break in there, too?" Meg asks, still petulant.

"No." I sigh. "I need to see a guy about a thing."

"How specific."

"The longer you argue, the longer you're stuck with me." I give her a look that could melt steel, and sure enough, she puts the car back in drive.

As we drive away, I rest my forehead against the cool glass. It's another detour, but I don't care. All this will be worth it in the end, when I get that painting, when my father knows what it's like to lose even a fraction of what he's taken from me.

Meg

I don't complain when Jolene changes our destination yet again and orders me back toward downtown; I can only pray that whatever new task is sending us there distracts her from the most definitely illegal activities she's planning. Revenge stunts are one thing, but I can tell from her tense expression that we're veering into darker territory.

"I think this is it." I pull over, peering through the windshield at the old warehouse. It's lit up inside, with cars parked all around and people hanging outside in groups. I recognize some from school: the pierced goth kids and alternative crowds who wouldn't be seen dead at prom.

"Ew," Bliss says, scrunching up her face at the view. "I'm staying in the car."

"Fine with me." Jolene pauses to try and pat the ruffles into submission, but they won't be denied. She makes a face and reaches for the door regardless. "But you'd better not bail."

I watch her stride across the parking lot, her dress bright among the ripped denim and dark leather around. She's halfway to the stairs when a guy breaks away from his friends and saunters to intercept. She stops dead.

"Who's that?" Bliss asks, bobbing forward for a better look.

"I don't know." As I look harder, I realize that it's the guy from outside prom, the one who asked me for a light. But the white tux is gone, and he's dressed in a beat-up leather jacket now, his slicked-back hair disheveled.

Jolene plants her hands on her hips and shifts into a defensive stance.

"She doesn't look happy to see him," Bliss notes before bouncing out of the car. "Come on. This is going to be good – I can tell."

I pause, uncertain, but then she hurries after Jolene and I'm left alone in the car on the side of the dark street. Quickly, I lock up and follow.

"What are you doing here?" Jolene is sizing the guy up as we approach. "College doesn't finish for weeks."

Bliss puts out a hand, stopping me from going any closer. "What do you think, is he an ex?" she whispers, loitering just within earshot. I shrug.

The guy gives her a crooked smile, his eyes drifting from head to toe. "Nice dress."

Jolene folds her arms. "It's prom, remember? *Some-one* said it would be fun."

"So what are you doing out here, then?"

I watch him, curious. He's younger than I thought, maybe only eighteen or nineteen, but there's a casual self-possession in the way he stands that makes me think he can handle Jolene. He glances past, to where we're standing. "Hey." His eyes widen a little in recognition when he sees me. "I'm Dante."

"Hey," Bliss coos back, fluttering him a little wave, while I blush, embarrassed to be caught eavesdropping. Jolene fixes us with a fierce glare, but clearly, we're the least of her problems. She turns back to him.

"It's none of your business what I'm doing. At least, is hasn't been for the last year." Jolene is trying to sound glib, but I hear something shake in her voice, just a faint quaver, but it says everything her glare and angry body language won't.

Dante must have heard it, too, because his grin slips.

"You thought we could just slide on by that little fact?" Jolene adds, "No *Hey Jolene, how have you been?* or, *What's going on with you?* or even, *Happy Birthday, by the way.*" Those last words, she practically spits at him, furious.

Bliss turns her head back and forth. "We should have brought popcorn."

"Shhh!" I murmur as they face off, neither moving out of the other's way. All night, Jolene has struck me as utterly invincible, but now, I can finally see someone real underneath all the swagger. Someone like me.

"I thought that's what you wanted." When it comes,

Dante's reply is quiet. "You said you never wanted to see me again."

Jolene shakes her head. "You took me by surprise. I needed to process it all!"

"Process?" Dante repeats, his voice rising with disbelief. "You threw me out of a moving vehicle!"

"It was going five miles an hour," Jolene counters. "And what did you expect? Just changing everything on me. I didn't see it coming, I didn't know you felt that way."

"You knew," Dante answers flatly. "And you made it real clear that you didn't feel the same."

"So what?" Jolene gives an angry shrug. "You head off to college and don't speak to me again? I figured our friendship was more than you just wanting to screw me, but hey, guess I was wrong about that."

I see him wince, but before he can reply, Jolene holds her hands up. "You know what? It doesn't matter. It's done." She exhales, giving a sharp little shrug. "And now I've got things to take care of, so you just do ... whatever the hell you want. I don't care."

She turns on her heel and stalks toward the building. Dante looks over at us.

"She hasn't changed a bit." He gives a wry smile, but there's something wistful in his voice. "Anyway, I'd better..." He nods toward the building and then goes to follow Jolene, his pace casual but full of purpose.

"Wow." Bliss waits until they're both inside before turning to me gleefully. "Drama! What do you think went down?"

"I don't know..." Now that they're gone, it feels wrong to be picking over their relationship in the dark of the parking lot, like we're nothing but vultures swooping for gossip. "It's not really any of our business."

Bliss sighs, clearly disappointed. "You saw that look in her eyes though, right? He's dead to her."

I'm not convinced, but I don't want to get drawn into an argument about the nuances of Jolene's private life, not when we're surrounded by a crowd of pierced, tattooed kids. I nod instead, heading back to the car to wait.

"What's taking her so long?" Bliss asks impatiently not even three minutes later. She's laid claim to the front seat in Jolene's absence, propping her bare feet on the dashboard and wriggling her French-manicured toes. "I bet they're making out in there. Or worse."

"I don't know what she's doing, and I really don't want to," I reply, trying not to feel anxious. "Plausible deniability, remember?"

Bliss looks at me. "Relax; she's a big girl. She can take care of herself. And if she doesn't, I'm sure Dante will." She gives a salacious grin. "He's hot, you have to admit."

I give another vague shrug. "Sure. Hot. If you like that kind of thing."

"Tall, brooding, handsome – who wouldn't?"

To be entirely honest, I don't. Dante seems nice enough, but there's an edge about him, as if he could do anything; some girls would say that's exciting, but I've never been one to pine over bad boys. No, that honor has always gone to guys so far out of my league, they can barely even see me. Like Tristan. Or ... Scott.

I catch myself midthought, blushing in the dark. At the party, I was too busy feeling awkward and self-conscious to even focus on him, but now that things have slowed, I can't help but remember how sweet he was, trying to defend me against the raging sorority girls. And how I just bailed, without even saying good-bye. Not that he even cares, I remind myself. He was probably just relieved that his charity project for the night made such a swift exit.

"I'm hungry." Bliss sighs beside me. "Brianna better have catering. Like the mini-puffs she did for her New Year's party – they were amazing." She looks ravenous at the thought of it.

There's nothing I can say to that. I remember the party, though – or at least, the furious gossip that dominated the next week at East Midlands. Two new reigning power couples were formed, another split up, and Nikki Hopington did a dance routine to Rihanna that got mass e-mailed to every student in school. Just your typical, average teenage party. With catering, illicit alcohol, and a professional band.

Bliss flicks the radio on, impatiently switching stations. "What's your deal, anyway?" She asks it almost like an accusation. "You've barely said a word all night."

"I haven't needed to," I reply quietly.

She stops. "What's that supposed to mean?"

"Nothing." I pause before venturing, "Just, you haven't really said a thing to me, either."

I shouldn't have said that. I drum my fingertips lightly on the steering wheel, keeping my eyes fixed on the stairs for Jolene, but I can feel Bliss watching me.

"I haven't seen you in school," she says eventually. "When did you move to town?"

"About fifteen years ago." My voice has a note of sarcasm in it; I can't help myself. "We were in History together, ninth grade," I explain shortly. "And study hall, all last year. And for the past eight months, we've had Miss Bowers for Wednesday afternoon PE classes. I was on your volleyball team."

"Oh."

There's silence.

"You spilled grape juice on me in the cafeteria line last month," I add softly. "Kaitlin said it looked like I had my period. You all laughed."

"What are you, like, keeping track?" Bliss sounds defensive.

"No. I just pay attention to the people around me."

She stiffens. "And I don't?"

I'm on dangerous ground here. I backtrack. "I never said that."

"No," Bliss says quietly. "You don't say much of anything. You just skulk around, keeping out of the way and pretending like you're above us all. 'No, we *can't* take Kaitlin's diary,'" she mimics, "'We *can't* go to a college party. That would be *wrong.*'"

I don't respond. What's the use? She's back in her superior clique mode, as if she owns the place. Never mind that any sane person would think twice about getting tangled up in trouble; no, when I say so, it's because I'm pathetic.

"See?" she says, sounding amused. "I bet you're doing it right now, thinking how mean I'm being, and how much better you are than me."

"What do you want me to do?" I ask, tired. "Start crying? Insult you right back?" I shrug. "What's the point, anyway?"

"The point is, you need to start sticking up for yourself." Bliss begins to twist her hair around one finger. "You'll never get anywhere like this."

"Thanks, but I don't need your advice," I reply, fighting to stay calm. I hate that I get emotional so easily – already, I can feel the telltale heat of tears welling up in the back of my throat, my skin flushed and prickling. "I'm fine."

"Fine?" Bliss snorts. "Sure, being a total outcast is fine."

I break. "Why do you have to be such a bitch?"

There's silence, and then she looks at me with a curious smile on her freshly glossed lips. "That's better."

I blink. "What do you mean?"

Bliss sighs, clearly exasperated. "I mean, fight back, for once in your life. God, don't you get sick of it? Always doing whatever you're told. No wonder I don't remember you; it's like I'm looking at a black hole or something – you just suck all the fun and energy out of a room!"

"I..." I start to reply, but my survival instincts are

screaming the same as usual. Retreat. Hide. Wait for this all to go away. "At least I'm not shallow and self-absorbed like you," I manage, still holding back tears.

"There you go again." Bliss shakes her head, sending ringlets bouncing around her face. "Little Miss Perfect. Did it ever strike you that maybe the reason you don't have any friends isn't that we're all bitches, but that you're just … boring?"

I look away, but that doesn't seem to matter to her.

"I mean, sure, I might not talk to you in school, but give me one good reason why I should," Bliss continues, sounding self-righteous. "I didn't just wake up one morning with friends and plans every weekend. I worked for it. You've got to make an effort, Meg. No one will just hand you everything for free."

I pray for her to finish, but it seems like she's just warming up.

"It's not that you're even weird." Bliss gives me a critical look. "I mean, you're kind of nerdy, but look at Callie Stephans, or that Tom guy who keeps scoring perfect 800s on all the SAT prep – they manage to have functioning social lives, so why can't you?" She sighs, as if I'm exhausting her with my uselessness. "You could be fine, if you'd just stand up and *try*."

That gets me. I feel the tears again, hot in my throat.

"Just join a few clubs," she suggests, as if I've never thought of that before. "Or try out for teams. Well, maybe not sports." She corrects herself. "But you've got to be good at *something*, and—"

"Shut up." I can hear my voice break and hate myself for it, but not as much as I hate her right now. "This is my car, and I get to make the rules, so you just shut the hell up!"

Bliss just gives me this pitying look. "OK." She shrugs. "Fine. I'll go find Jolene."

I wait until she's inside before I let myself cry. She sounded as if she was almost trying to help me in her own twisted way, but to me, it's so much worse than a sneer. Bitching, I can ignore; I just tell myself that it's all a stupid lie. This sincerity is something worse.

Something true.

Bliss

I walk away from Meg feeling like a totally worthless human being. I didn't mean to make her cry like that; I didn't even mean to get so personal. I just wanted to give her a few social pointers, but something about the way she looked at me set me on edge – that resigned, victim expression in her eyes, like she's curling up and waiting for it all to be over. The thing is, it's never over; that's what she doesn't get. We have to fight for everything – status, popularity, whatever – and Meg might think I don't understand what it's like for her, but I do. I orbited on the edge of Brianna's clique all through junior high, getting invites as an afterthought, tagging along after the others at lunch and to the mall even though they didn't really care if I came or not. I was the new kid then, the outsider, but I didn't give up like Meg. I decided I was going to belong, and I didn't quit until I was right there in the middle of everything.

At least, I used to be. Before tonight.

Inside, the Loft is dark and noisy, with a grungy band onstage wailing about misery and alienation, and people mooching around, trying to look like they're not having any fun. I've never been here before. This is freak central, a place for all the alt kids to drink bad coffee and plot against consumerist society, or whatever. No need for IDs or, you know, actual social skills – just torn-up couches and the sound of third-rate emo screeching from the sound system. I grimace, heading deeper in search of Jolene.

"Inside, I die, for you, tonight!"

A group of teenage boys is blocking my way, chanting along with the chorus. I try to edge through them, but they're lurching around in a tight knot, and soon, I'm surrounded.

"Excuse me?"

They don't move.

"Hello?" I try again with my elbows out, but they're moshing, oblivious. Then one of them hurtles into me, crunching his ugly-ass boots on my bare toes. "Hey!" I yelp. And with Jolene's pep talk fresh in my mind, I shove him back. Hard.

He knocks back against the next guy, who flails around until they both go crashing to the floor.

"What the hell?" He swears. "Crazy bitch!"

I leave them in a pile of bad hair dye and inner pain and head deeper into the crowd, hoping to just slip through and find Jolene without any drama. But everywhere I look, there's nothing but suspicious stares and flat-out hostile glaring. A couple of pierced, rainbow-haired girls even start to move in my direction before I turn on my heel and flee. Why couldn't Jolene need to stop somewhere normal? I'm used to being able to own whatever room I walk into, but I don't think it's just the fact I'm subverting their precious dress code that's making me Most Hated around here. They know me, and clearly, I'm not welcome.

Finally, I spot Jolene down the back corridor, just inside a dim office. Dante waits in the doorway, a few steps away.

"There you are!" I head toward her, relieved. "This place is so lame. Can we get out of here—" I stop. A skinny boy is lounging at the desk inside, dressed – surprise – all in black with tiny loops pierced down the outside of one ear and a swoop of bleached hair falling over his forehead.

I feel a flicker of unease.

"Bliss Merino." Eli sizes me up, already starting to smirk. "Wouldn't have thought this was your scene."

"Because you know me so well." I roll my eyes, but inside, I feel ... well, not exactly *guilt*. I mean, Brianna was technically the one who hit *send* on that video forward, alerting the entire school to his drag queen lip-synch act. And who films themselves doing that kind of stuff unless deep down, they have some subconscious desire for everyone to see it? So he got mercilessly bullied, dropped out, and became the joke of the entire Internet... It's not *all* my fault.

But from the look in Eli's eyes, I'm guessing he doesn't agree.

"Well?" I turn to Jolene. "Can we get out of here already?"

"Not yet." She keeps her gaze fixed on Eli, unmoving. "I need something first."

Eli shrugs. "And I've already told you: no."

"I only need it an hour, maybe less!" Jolene looks strangely desperate. "Come on, Eli, what's your problem?"

"My problem?" Eli leans back on his chair. He's freakishly pale, like he never goes outside, and not even in a cute chiseled vampire way. "What do you think will happen when you get caught? They'll take one look at the hardware and come right to me. You think I want the police crawling all over this place?" He gestures around. It's not exactly a secret lair, just piles of comic books and some peeling Marvel posters on the wall, but who knows? Maybe he has other, more illegal stuff stashed away behind the Star Wars action figures.

"I'm not going to get caught," Jolene insists, her face flushed. "I told you – I have everything to get me in there. I just need to disable the security feed."

"Sorry." Eli shrugs, sounding anything but. "No deal. This is proprietary tech, I've got to put my business first."

Jolene swears. Her hands are clenched in tight fists by her sides, and for a moment I wonder if she's going to snap and start trashing the place, but then she spins on her heel.

"Jolene—" Dante tries to stop her.

"Get the hell out of my way." Jolene shakes him off, not even looking in my direction before disappearing out into the dim hallway.

"What's going on?" I look around for answers. Jolene is freaking me out now – not so much vengeful and determined as slowly cracking up.

"She's just PMSing," Eli says smoothly.

Dante shakes his head, unreadable. "Don't worry about it."

"It's kind of late for that," I exclaim, but both of them refuse to meet my eyes. They idle there, not saying a word, as if whatever's going on here has nothing to do with me. "I'll go find her," I say. They shrug, like they're synchronized freaking swimmers or something.

Boys.

Jolene's in the narrow storeroom, tearing into a pack of candy, when I approach.

"Hey," I start cautiously, checking if she's still ready to explode, but Jolene just sags against the ugly Formica counter top.

"Hi." She exhales, worn out, so I figure it's safe to come closer.

"Does Eli run this place or something?" I ask, trying to figure out his power trip.

She nods, gnawing on a hunk of red licorice. "He graduated early. Took his SATs and got the hell out."

"To this?" I look around. "Isn't the entire point of leaving high school to go someplace better?"

She gives me this ghost of a smile. "Are you kidding? He sits around all day playing Xbox and taking money from freshman Mountain Dew addicts. It's like heaven."

"Sure it is." There's a pause, the noise of that terrible band drifting loud from the main room.

I wait for a second, trying to figure out what to do next. Meg's out crying in the car, Jolene's fixated on getting this thing from Eli, and I'm no closer to my after-party and general normalcy. Perfect. For a moment I think about just calling a cab and bailing on this whole mess, but the idea doesn't last long. Even I'm not that low, and something tells me Jolene likes to hold a grudge.

"So…" I reach over and take a thin ribbon of licorice, peeling off an even thinner strand to nibble. "What's this thing all about?"

Jolene looks at me for a second and then relents. "He's got this device that can jam transmission signals. Video feeds, radios, even cell phones if you set the right frequencies."

"And?"

"And I need it," she says simply.

I nod, beginning to understand. "To get into your dad's office."

"Yup. It's kind of the electronic version of an invisibility cloak. In and out, no trace left behind."

"Hmmm." I twist the strip around my finger, watching the blood pool in the tip. "It's a lot of effort, just to steal something."

"Says the girl who had us dressed like a Victoria's Secret catalog, like, an hour ago," Jolene snaps back.

"Fair point." I watch her, curious. "What did he do? Your dad, I mean."

I expect her to clam up and get defensive, but instead, Jolene just exhales again. "He took something from me – the thing I wanted more than anything. So, I'm going to do the same." She pauses. "At least, I was going to."

"It's not money, or anything like that?" I ask, struck with sudden panic.

"No. It's ... a painting," she admits, her voice quiet. "Just a stupid painting." But I can tell it means way more than she's letting on, because her lower lip begins to tremble. She turns quickly and begins to rifle through the fridge, like she's still pretending this is no big deal, but the careless act isn't fooling me anymore.

This matters to her.

The strange and secret desires of Jolene Nelson should be the least of my problems, but despite all the glares, sarcasm, and general hostility she's thrown my way tonight, I can't help but feel some weird debt. She helped me out with my revenge, so aren't I honor-bound to help out with hers? Besides: if I deal with this, she won't ever tell about Cameron.

Sometimes, I hate my conscience.

"OK." I decide quickly, figuring I'd better get moving if I'm ever going to see that after-party. "I'll deal with Eli. You ... just relax."

"I'm fine," Jolene mutters, glaring. "It's just ... all this, and Dante showing up, and—"

"No problem!" I back away. "It's late, and we're all tired. Find some caffeine!"

•   •   •

"So what's it going to take?" I burst into Eli's office without any warning, sizing him up over the three different computers he's got lined up on the desk. He gives me a blank look. "For the gadget thing Jolene wants?"

Eli begins to smirk.

"A hundred bucks?" I offer, even though I have no idea where I'd get the money at this time of night. This isn't exactly the kind of area I want to stroll around in search of an ATM. He doesn't look impressed, so I try again. "One fifty?"

"No deal." Eli leans back, clasping his hands behind his head. The red light behind him glows through his bleached hair, making it look as if he's got a creepy halo. "You can't just buy your way out of everything, you know."

Taking a deep breath, I give him one of my most charming grins, "C'mon, Eli... Don't be like this. We really need your help." I tilt my head down and then look up through my eyelashes, leaning over the desk a little. "There must be *something*."

He looks me up and down, eyes lingering on my chest. "Maybe a couple of things..."

"Eww!" I cut him off before he can say anything else. "Not *that*. Seriously?"

"Depends how bad you want this thing."

I shudder at just the thought of his pale, clammy hands on me. "I promise you, nobody will *ever* want *anything* that bad."

It's the wrong thing to say: right away, Eli's face goes

hard, and he narrows his eyes. "Yeah, it's been kind of hard to get a girlfriend recently. They just google me and bam! Suddenly, they're busy."

"Hey, at least you're famous," I offer, trying to show him the bright side. "Some people kill for that kind of exposure. I mean, Licia Devlin's been doing YouTubes of herself singing forever, but all she gets is creepy guys sending her naked photos. People all over the world know who you are."

"I didn't want it!" Eli scowls. "It was a stupid freaking dare, and now there's no way I'm ever going to live it down, thanks to you and your stupid friends. Do you realize what you did to me?"

I pause. "Look, I'm sorry, OK?" I admit, reluctant. "But it's not like I can fix it now. What do you expect me to do – wipe the Internet blank or something?"

"No..." Eli looks at me funny for a second, and then his thin lips spread into a truly evil grin. "But maybe it's time you found out what it's like to be a total joke, in front of everybody."

I stop. "Wait, what?"

Eli laughs, almost to himself. "Yup. This is going to be good. Come on." He rounds the desk and gestures for me to go ahead of him. I don't move.

"I'm not going anywhere with you."

"Then you don't get this." He takes a slim black gadget from his pocket and dangles it in front of me. "See, I figured out the price, what it's going to take for you to earn it."

"Asking nicely?" I suggest, already getting a sinking

feeling in my stomach. "Pretty please, with a cherry on top?"

"Nope." Eli has a smug expression in his eyes. Smug, and definitely cruel. "You're going to grace us with a public performance. Maybe even a song."

"No. Way." I back away at the thought.

"Aww, c'mon. Kind of fitting, don't you think? Eye for an eye, and all that." Eli is still smirking, like he somehow knows exactly how much I don't want to get up on that stage. There's a reason nobody has ever heard me sing in public, and it's directly related to a little something called my dignity. "But, hey, if you don't want to, then my original offer still stands."

"What, you mean...?"

He looks at my chest again. "A date. With, you know, benefits."

"Hell, no." I think fast. "Come on, Eli, there's got to be something else." Something that won't make me need to scrub my skin off, or require therapy after.

"Nope, that's it." The smile slips, and Eli looks at me, totally serious. "I'm done wasting my time with this. Either you pick one, or we're done here. Your call."

I gulp. There's no way in hell I'm renting myself out, and failure isn't an option if I want to get back to normal prom fun anytime soon, which leaves...

"Can I at least pick the song?"

I'm already regretting this when Eli interrupts the band and drags me to the edge of the stage. "Hey, listen up, everyone! We've got an extra-special performance tonight."

I look out at the crowd. There are maybe a hundred or more scowling kids, all looking supremely unimpressed that we've interrupted their night. My stomach gives a nauseous lurch. Right now, seven minutes in heaven with Eli is looking way more attractive.

"Eli—" I start to panic, but he's talking to the band, tapping microphones and checking wires. I feel a hand on my arm and turn to find Jolene.

"What are you doing?" She looks around. "We were going to be discreet, remember?"

My whole chest is closing off as I realize exactly what I'm about to do. "Eli … the deal … I have to…" I flap my hands uselessly.

Jolene grips my shoulders firmly. "Focus, Bliss! What's going on?"

"He's making me perform!" I finally get a full lung of air. "For the gadget thing. It's his idea of, I don't know, sadism and torture!"

Jolene brightens. "That's great!"

"No, it's not! I can't sing!" Jolene rolls her eyes, thinking I'm just being dramatic. "No, really," I insist, losing all sensation in my legs now. Any minute, I'm going to break out in some kind of rash. "I'm like, tone deaf. I can't carry a single note!"

Jolene shakes her head. "You'll manage. It's only a couple of minutes, and if we pick the right song … something that's mostly talking, OK?" She bundles me back to the middle of the stage, where Eli is waiting with a mic.

"Here she is, everyone," he announces to the crowd.

"Our star performer, Bliss Merino!"

"Give me just a second," I hiss desperately as a spotlight flashes on. "I need to find the music, and—"

"Already taken care of." He gives me a firm push into the middle of the space. "I chose a real classic. You're going to love it."

Oh God.

I try and remember how to breathe, surrounded by a mass of bored, hostile strangers. I can see it in their eyes, they hate me already – there's no way I'll ever be able to live this down. And then, when I think this can't get any worse, the music starts. Three familiar chords that are burned into the brain of every teenager who has been remotely conscious for the last five years. "Hit Me Up." The most annoying pop song known to man, even the singer needed auto-tune to get through it alive.

This is what hell feels like.

"Woohoo, go Bliss!" Eli yells, loving every minute of my pain. The first lyrics appear on-screen behind me but I turn to Jolene, looking for a last-ditch escape.

Instead, she stares at me, eyes wide. "Please," she mouths. That's when I know for sure I'm doomed. Jolene would rather die than even admit for a moment that she doesn't have things under control, and here she is, begging me for help.

I grip the mic, say a prayer, and turn to my audience.

"Ooh, baby, I want you so bad."

JOLENE

I've got to hand it to Bliss – the girl does nothing halfway. She may be tone deaf and unable to hit a single decent note, but she throws everything into that performance, prancing across the stage area and pouting like this is all just a big joke, and anyone who thinks otherwise isn't in on the plan.

"Hit me up, don't stop, I've got to get what you've got," I sing quietly as we head toward the exit. That terrible melody is already carved deep into my brain, but I'm too wired to care. Because I've got it: gripped tightly in my hand, the last thing standing between me and that painting. A little black box of technological magic. *"Tonight, make it right—"*

"Please stop." Bliss shudders. She trips out onto the fire escape, gasping for air. "That song is going to haunt me forever!"

"But it worked."

"Mmmhmm." Bliss sinks to the ground, perching on the edge of the metal staircase. She rummages in her bag and pulls out her lip gloss, swiping it back and forth over her lips as if it's some sort of meditative gesture. Slowly, her breathing returns to normal.

I pause. For the first time, I realize that the panic and terror before weren't just drama queen hysterics; Bliss is actually scared to death of singing. But she did it anyway. For ... me?

"That was amazing," I tell her, confused but grateful. "Thank you. I don't know what to say."

"That you'll never tell another soul what I just did?"

"I think it's kind of late for that." She looks up at me, eyes wide. "There were some camera phones waving around in there." I grimace. "And, knowing Eli, he's got the whole thing taped."

Bliss lets out a whimper.

"But, it's fine," I promise quickly. "You were hamming it up so much, you can just say it was a dare. Part of some scavenger hunt or something."

She doesn't look convinced.

"Nice show you put on there." A voice from behind makes me jump. I turn to find Dante leaning in the doorway, grinning at Bliss. "I mean it – that was awesome. Next stop: Vegas."

"Can you not do that?" I snap.

"Do what?"

"Lurk."

His gaze slides over to me. "You said you didn't want me getting in your way."

"I meant *at all*." I shift under his stare, self-conscious. For all my ice-queen act, this dress is a big flashing neon sign saying I showed up, that I remembered our plans. "Don't you have anything better to do?"

"Nope." Dante meets my eyes, unruffled. I always used to like his calmness, how nothing would ever shake that nonchalance. It made me feel safe when everything else was whirling in a riot, like the world could fall to pieces but he'd still be there to keep me centered, keep me from going too far. I've lost count of the times he's pulled me back from making stupid mistakes with that look, the one that says, "I've got you."

Now I know that look is a lie, I wish he'd break a sweat, just once. Just for me.

"Let's get going," I tell Bliss, turning my back on Dante and the way the shadows cut across his face. "I promise, I'll have you at Brianna's soon."

She nods, slowly getting up. "Thanks."

Dante follows us down to the parking lot, whistling some song I don't recognize. I force myself not to turn, or even acknowledge his existence, but I can feel him behind me with every step. "Where are you heading?" he asks when we reach the car. Meg clicks off the central locking, looking miserable behind the wheel.

"None of your damn business," I answer at the same time that Bliss says, "Her dad's office."

"Bliss." I give her a murderous look, but she just shrugs.

"What? Maybe he can help."

"I don't want his help. I don't want anything from him," I lie, hurling myself into the front seat.

It's too much. My dad, and Dante, and college, and Meg and Bliss. I can't deal with them all at once. I don't have the space.

"Are you OK?" Meg asks quietly.

"Sure," I lie again. "Sorry we took so long."

She nods, starting the ignition.

"Wait for Bliss," I remind her. Meg scowls, hitting the horn in a sharp gesture. A moment later, Bliss slides in.

"I thought you were going to leave without me!" She's breathless.

"Maybe we should have," Meg murmurs through gritted teeth. She checks her mirror and then pulls away with an angry screech, faster than she's driven all night. I don't ask what's wrong – I can't find it in me to care. All I can do is lean my head to the window, the glass cool against my cheek as we speed back through town. I turn the remote over in my hands, tracing every smooth surface and pointed edge as I pull myself back under control.

"So, how do you know Dante?" Bliss finally asks from the backseat.

The streets rush by, dark and blurred. I close my eyes. "He's just a boy I used to know."

The industrial park is dark and deserted, and even I feel a flicker of unease as we roll to a stop, half a block away. The streets around here are full of warehouses and wire fencing; no warm houses or neat front yards to help me pretend this is just a crazy teen stunt we're pulling. No, here there are only flickering streetlights and dirty concrete, and the low feeling in my stomach that this is somehow a mistake.

"You both stay here." I decide suddenly. I'd planned to drag at least Bliss along for backup, but she's put herself on the line already for me tonight. I'd rather not reward her with a misdemeanor charge. "I'll check in on my cell and call if I need any help."

"You're sure?" Bliss looks fearfully around. "I mean, you're sure you want to do this?"

It's not so much a question of wanting to do this, as needing to get it done. I give her a smile, full of false confidence. "Are you kidding? It'll be fun."

She frowns. "Then, good luck, I guess."

"Luck is for losers." I switch on Eli's remote, setting it to jam any surveillance. "This is all about skill."

I grab my backpack and jog quickly toward the buildings, keeping to the shadows and out of sight. As much as I can, at least. I wish I were dressed better for this – some black clothes, boots I can run in – but maybe this is a good thing. You can't claim innocence when you're caught trespassing looking like a cat burglar.

McKenna Imports is on the far side of the lot, a modern, glass-fronted building with plush animals frolicking in every window and a cutesy cat logo above the door. Stuffed animals. I'd never have figured they were a booming market, but clearly, there are plenty of people willing to pay a hundred bucks for a giant pink bunny rabbit, if this place is any indication. I peer through the window and see dark reception area, full of potted plants and sleek couches. No sign of life.

There are two security cameras trained straight on the door, but I don't have time to second-guess Eli. I pull out the key ring I swiped from the office back at the house, trying each in turn until both locks are open. I step cautiously inside. There's no sound of sirens, so I cross straight to the alarm panel on the side wall, blinking red at me. *62–34–62.*

Nothing.

I enter the numbers again, trying not to panic, but the system doesn't disarm. *62–34–62.*

Oh, crap.

A warning beep starts up. I've probably got another thirty seconds or so before it dials up the security company, then starts wailing so loud that every cop in the neighborhood will hear. Heart racing, I keep hitting the numbers, not even wanting to think about bailing before—

"You have to press *star* for it to register." An arm reaches across me, inputs the numbers, and then hits the last button. The beeping stops, and the light turns green.

I exhale.

"Details, Jolene. What am I always telling you?"

"I don't know." I turn to him, pulse still speeding in my veins. "You don't tell me much of anything these days."

Dante doesn't respond. He looks older than I've been remembering him: a faint shadow of stubble on his jaw, broader in the shoulders. Smarter, too, like he's finally grown out of those grungy T-shirts and beat-up sneakers I used to tease him about.

God, I've missed him.

"Are you going to help, or are you going to stand around bitching?" I manage to sound casual, pulling a slim flashlight from my bag and closing the door behind me. He must have followed us from the Loft in that beat-up Camaro.

"I'm here, aren't I?"

I ignore the soft resignation in his tone. Switching on the flashlight, I sweep it across the room. "It should be in his office, in the back maybe."

"The Lorenzo?"

Of course he'd know what I'm here for. I don't answer, crossing behind the reception desk and heading deeper into the building. The beam of light swings out in front of me, cutting through the dark and landing on neat rows of stuffed animals lining the hallway.

"Creepy." Dante sounds amused, pausing to pick up a three-foot elephant. He wiggles it at me. "Your dad knows that half his customers are guys with weird fetishes, right?"

I keep walking, checking every room as we pass.

"Furries, I think they call them," he muses, tossing the toy up in the air. "Or is that the people who like to dress up in bear suits? Maybe it's plushies. Either way, his product isn't getting tucked in at night with the kids, if you know what I mean."

I don't even break a smile at his joking – that would be

too easy. He might think that we're OK now – that he can just come back and throw some of that charm around, and I'll forgive him, but he's wrong. It doesn't work that way.

I reach the end of the hallway and a door marked with a fancy metal animal plaque. The blinds are down, but I know this is the place; I just know it. I grab for the door, but it's locked. I try each key in turn, but nothing works. I slam against it in frustration.

"Hey, calm down." Dante reaches to stop me, but I step back, already looking around for other options. We're deep enough in the building that I risk turning on the light, flooding us with harsh fluorescent from the strip above.

"Do you think there's an air vent going in?"

"Not unless you're starring in an action movie," he jokes in reply. "And I don't know if those ruffles will fit…"

"Fine then." I hoist a fire extinguisher down from the far wall and take a few practice swings toward the glass partition. Dante lets out a strangled yell and snatches it from my hands.

"What the hell are you doing?"

"Getting in." He stares at me as if I'm insane. "You could do something, you know," I add, bitter. "Instead of following me around and lurking in the shadows. Can't you bust the door down?"

"Bust it?" Dante takes a sharp breath, like he's trying to keep control. "What do you say we just get out of here," he says instead. "I've got Xbox back at the house; we can go kill a few thousand zombies and drive my mom crazy, the way we used to."

I feel an ache at the reminder, but it's not enough to shake me. "I have to do this."

"No, you don't."

I glare back. "Since when do you care what the hell I do?"

I'm expecting a fight, but Dante simply looks at me, his jaw set.

"You're right," he says eventually. "I can't do this anymore." He stares for a moment and then turns to leave. Because he's so damn good at it.

"Fine."

He stops.

"Fine?" Dante gives a twisted kind of laugh. "Jolene, we're a lot of things, but we're not fine."

"And whose fault is that?" I whirl on him, anger hot in my chest. "Who just up and left without a single word? Don't you dare make like this is my fault!" I'm shaking, a year's worth of insecurity and anger pumping through me. All those months seeing his silent icon up on my chat window, before I broke and deleted him for good. All those months expecting him to call, and the bitter disappointment every time it wasn't him on the other end of the line.

And all because of a stupid kiss I didn't see coming.

"Did you care so much I turned you down?" I yell. "Did our friendship mean that little to you?"

There's silence in the hallway, lights glaring overhead.

"You think it was about that?" Dante stares at me, a curious expression on his face. "You think I cut you out over…? Jolene." He stops, like he can't even find the words.

"Then what?" I demand. "What did I do that was so bad, you couldn't even send a damn e-mail? We were friends! You were everything!"

I catch my own words too late. Trust me to only realize what I've got when he's gone, to ache for a boy I came so close to having. "Look, you don't want to be here. You've made that clear," I add, before he can register what I said. "Why did you even come?"

"Because someone's got to keep you from screwing up your entire life." Dante flings the words at me, accusing.

I gape.

"Jesus, Jolene, what the hell are you doing?" He gestures around angrily. "Breaking and entering – this is a felony. You're not a minor anymore – you'll get real time for sure!"

"My dad won't press charges," I shoot back. "And where do you even get off playing law-abiding citizen? I was right there with you for those stunts we used to pull."

"I remember. What do you think I was doing all that time?" He's mad now, for real: fists clenched by his sides and those dark eyes blazing. "Watching out, making sure you didn't get caught, trying everything to keep you away from the real trouble."

I blink. "What are you talking about?"

"You think I would have been pulling that crap without you?" He looks at me with a strange mix of exasperation and pity. "Sure, it was fun in the beginning, but we're not kids anymore. I was trying to keep you safe."

"So why did you shut me out?" I demand, spiteful. "Why did you start ignoring me like that? Did you want me to fall?"

"I wanted you to grow the hell up!" Dante yells suddenly. "You think I should have stayed, thrown my life away on you, on *this*?" He gestures around at the dark building on somebody else's property. "I'm not some pretty white girl who can bat her eyelashes and get away with community service. Hell, I'm more likely to wind up in prison than ever get through college!"

I feel guilt slap me, hard. "You never said." My voice shakes.

"I know." He gives me this faint smile that almost breaks my heart. "I tried, so many times, but then..." Dante shrugs. "I can't say no to you, Jolene. I just had to make it so you couldn't ask me at all."

I catch my breath, trying to understand, to rearrange all my memories to see this new version of things.

"I thought maybe, if I wasn't around..." Dante starts. "If you had to deal with it all on your own... But you haven't changed at all, have you? You're still so self-destructive, you don't care who you hurt."

"I'm not hurting anyone." I clench my jaw, my fists, my everything to keep it together.

"Oh, yeah?" Dante gives me a faded smile, and for a terrible moment, I can see myself from his perspective. Falling apart at the seams.

"It's my life," I manage to say, hating him. "I can do what the hell I want with it."

Dante's face changes. "But don't you see – this is your shot now, your chance to get out, and you're risking it all for *what*? Some meaningless payback that won't change a thing."

I shake my head. "You don't know what he did."

"I know he doesn't love you." Dante says it low and clear. "At least, not the way you need. I know he left, and let you down, but how is that ever going to change? You think you'll hurt him, but you're the only one getting hurt here."

My mouth drops open. I'm coming apart; I can feel it – every word splintering into me until I don't know how I'm still standing. It's too much; I knew it was. It's all too much.

"Jolene." His voice softens and he pulls me closer. For a brief second, I'm in his arms, like I belong there. "You don't have to do this," he murmurs, holding me tight. "Every time he lets you down, you can just let go. Don't—"

"Stop!" I break, pushing him away. "What the hell do you even care? I never asked you to do this, I never wanted you to save me!"

My words are sharp and fierce, echoing in the empty building.

Dante looks at me for a long moment. "No. No, I guess you didn't."

Something in his tone slices right through me.

"Go," I say, because it's just about all I can manage. "I'll do this on my own."

"Jolene…" His voice trails away.

We used to make plans together, laying out by the river

on the far side of town. We plotted our escape there, tossing old soda cans into the water and imagining the world beyond state lines. New York. LA. Austin. Any town with a decent record store and a roller derby would suit us fine. But he's gone now, living his life without a second damn thought to those hazy dreams. And me? I'm never getting out.

"Go." I pick up the fire extinguisher and aim it for the glass with everything I have.

It smashes so loud, I don't hear him leave.

Meg

We wait.

Of course we wait. Sometimes it feels like I spend my entire life waiting – in hospital waiting rooms and hard plastic chairs, the shadows of the library carrels. There's a skill to it, I've found. You have to empty your mind and slip into a kind of haze; let the time drift by while you wait for something to change.

I exhale, gazing restlessly at the digital clock on my dashboard – the numbers flipping over with infinite slowness. I would have been better heading straight home from prom to accept Dad's and Stella's awkward sympathy. At least then, there would have been brownies.

"I'm, um, sorry." Bliss's voice comes from the backseat, hesitant. "About what I said before."

I don't turn.

"It's fine," I say, even though it's anything but. "No big deal."

"Yes, but—"

"I said it was fine." My voice is sharp, and even Bliss can take the hint. She falls silent, leaving me to stare into the neon-lit dark. The things she said to me back at the Loft have been echoing ever since, and even though I try to push it all away as petty bitching, I can't.

Because what if she's right?

The thought is more terrifying to me than the deserted warehouses and black, empty street. Some days, the only thing that makes life bearable is the knowledge that I'm graduating next year. An end to this silence, to being constantly ignored – my chance to start again. But if Bliss is right, then it's not simply circumstance that's making me miserable. Part of it is me.

I see lights behind us.

"Get down," I say, ducking down behind the wheel. Bliss is already lounging low in the backseat, but she scrunches even farther as the car draws closer.

"Who is it?" Bliss asks, twisting around to get a clearer look.

"How would I know?" I peer over the dashboard as the vehicle passes us by: a white car with blue insignia printed on the side. It begins to slow. "It's security." Fear twists in my stomach. "This place must have a dedicated patrol."

Bliss swears. "But which building?"

"I can't tell." The car turns lazily into the industrial park, the same block that Jolene disappeared toward not fifteen minutes ago. I panic. "What do we do?"

"Call her," Bliss orders, and I fumble with my phone to find her number and dial.

Silence.

"It's not working." I try again, but there's not even a dial tone, just a low static buzz. I call my voice mail, just to test, but it won't connect either. "My battery must be low – try yours."

Bliss is already tapping at her tiny pink thing, but she shakes her head. "Me neither. But we can't be out of range."

"No," I groan, suddenly realizing. "That device she got for surveillance must be jamming cell signals too."

Our eyes meet in the rearview mirror.

"We'll just have to go get her, then." Bliss twists her hair up into a makeshift ponytail and then pulls her heels back on, reaching for the door.

"Are you crazy?" I protest. "That guy is parked right out front!"

"Which means he'll catch Jolene the minute she walks out the door," Bliss insists. "She doesn't know he's there. She won't be looking out for anyone."

She wants us to run *toward* the danger?

I shake my head vigorously. "Jolene's the expert in all this, remember? If anyone can look after themself, it's her."

Bliss doesn't listen. She climbs out of the car, looking carefully around before easing the door shut behind her with a silent click. I watch her, bewildered, as all the terrible consequences spin through my mind. I'm not one for worst-case scenarios, but it doesn't take a huge leap of imagination to move from the office security guard to the local police, and from there, it's only another tiny step to interview rooms, lawyers, eternal damnation, and – worst of all – my father.

"Meg, come on." Bliss taps on my window. "She'll rat us out anyway if she gets caught."

I roll it down. "Jolene doesn't want our help," I repeat. "She's said so about a dozen times tonight. We'll only get in the way!"

"So you're just going to sit here?" Bliss demands.

"No..." I search for an excuse, a reason why it's not pathetic to leave her to her own fate. Or, better yet, drive far away. Then I stop. Why should I be the one making excuses? I'm the only one thinking clearly here.

"You know what? Screw Jolene," I tell her, my frustration surging. "She chose to break in there, not me. Why should I be the one to risk everything because of her stupid mistakes?"

Bliss looks at me in shock. "Because you're part of the team."

"What team?" I can't believe her, trying to pull this after everything she's said. "We've spent less than four hours with one another. I bet you both don't even know my last name!"

"So what?" She glares at me, suddenly fierce. "We're in this together, Meg, at least for tonight, so why don't you step up for once and actually do something?" She pauses, giving me a familiar bitchy stare. "That's right, I forgot – you don't actually *do* anything. Hey, good luck with that."

Before I can defend my desire not to acquire a criminal record before I graduate, Bliss turns her back and trots toward the complex. Her white dress flutters like a ghost in the shadows until finally, she's swallowed up by the dark, and I'm left here alone.

Again.

I sit in silence, seething at their utter stupidity. Does Bliss really want to risk her entire future on this stupid stunt? Because I know for certain that getting mixed up in whatever Jolene is doing will wreck our permanent records forever. It's crazy and dangerous, and the kind of thing you don't even ask your best friend to help with, but I'm supposed to jump at the chance when I don't even *like* them?

I get out of the car.

"You're losing your mind," I whisper to myself, hurrying after her down the dark street. My shoes clatter against the pavement, and even the distant sounds of traffic from the highway make me flinch. "Certifiably, undeniably losing your mind." It's one thing to be waiting behind the safety of central locks, but out here, the air is thick and still, and every shadow could be concealing some terrible fate.

But despite every reason I have to turn and flee – put the car into drive, and leave Jolene and Bliss to their much-deserved fates – some new urge is driving me on, forcing me to put one foot in front of the other and bring myself closer to impending doom.

Because Bliss was right. I gave up.

I tried at first. God, I tried. When the grief finally eased a little, and I could make it through the day without wanting to weep, I wanted nothing more than to wrap myself in friendship, in some kind of human warmth. So I went out for those clubs and extracurriculars, stayed late for committee meetings, and signed up for the charity drives. I made awkward conversation with study partners, laughed along with bad jokes and inane lunchroom gossip. But it never stuck. Maybe they could sense my desperation, or maybe I'd spent too long as the miserable loner, but either way, nobody looked me in the eye, no one asked me what I thought, nobody invited me along to their mall trips or movie nights – no matter how hard I tried. Even the memory of it drains me: working so hard, all day, all the time; getting nothing more than a basic acknowledgment of your own existence in return. So I stayed invisible, and slowly, that willpower just ebbed away.

But it wasn't my fault.

At least, that's what I've been telling myself all this time. Bad luck and timing, that's all it was. My life could be so different if only Mom hadn't died, leaving me reeling for that all-important freshman year; if I'd had different classes, been on a different bus route, been assigned a locker next to somebody else...

The possibilities are endless and reassuring, but for the first time, I have to wonder if they're wrong, just a lie I tell myself to make it all feel better. Tonight was something different, after all: the promise of excitement and adventure. But I've done nothing but play chauffeur and drive patiently around while the other girls complete their various plans – and/or insult me. I'm as separate from things as I was lurking in the hallway back at the country club, as detached as the girl at the party. I'm still on the edge, still outside. It's the same as it's always been.

Unless I do something different.

I finally reach the corner, peering carefully around as if the guard will be patrolling, vigilant. But the security car is parked, empty, and the lot is silent, so I steel myself and set out: skirting the buildings, scraping my bare arms on the bricks in my effort to stay back in the shadows. Every step feels like a mistake, but I force myself on, checking each window in turn until I see the pale shape of Bliss's dress, standing in the middle of one of the office lobbies.

I slip through the unlocked door and creep across the room behind her.

"So where is she?" I whisper.

Bliss lets out a yelp.

"Shhh!" I hiss furiously.

"Sorry!" Bliss switches to a quieter voice. "What are you doing here? You scared me half to death."

"I'm part of the team, remember?" I look around, waiting for my heartbeat to return to something resembling normal. The room is shadowed, but I can make out a reception desk, filing cabinets, and couches in the main space, with a fish tank in the far corner, lit up in an eerie blue glow. I turn back to Bliss. "Did you find Jolene yet?"

She shakes her head. "I just got in."

"Right." I try to think like a wild child, hell-bent on vengeance. "She probably headed for the offices, or maybe storage. Do you even know what she's after?"

Bliss nods, but doesn't say anything more.

"Then we'd better—"

The sound of breaking glass suddenly shatters the silence, the loud noise echoing through the room for what feels like forever. We freeze.

"What was that?" Bliss whispers, clutching my arm.

"It was coming from back there." My stomach lurches, just imagining what Jolene is doing. "Do you think anyone heard?"

"They heard that in Alaska!" Bliss's eyes are wide with panic. She looks past me and gasps. "Look, he's coming!"

The dark shadow of the security guard is heading toward the building. My heart stops.

"You cover here." Bliss shoves me toward the door. "Stop him searching the place. I'll get Jolene; we'll try and make it out the back."

"But—"

"Do it!" She trips away down the hallway, stumbling in her heels.

I turn back to the entrance, my mind blank. He's close enough to see clearly now: in his fifties, maybe, wearing a crumpled blue uniform shirt and pants that bulge around the waistband. He's trying to speak into a walkie-talkie device, shaking it in frustration, but it's too late to be relieved that Jolene's remote is still blocking transmissions – he looks up.

"Hey!" The guard pushes through the door, flashing his light in my face. I reel back, squinting. "Who are you? What are you doing in here?"

I gulp.

"Come on, kid. Did you break something?" he

demands, swooping the flashlight around the room. "I heard the noise."

I'm frozen in fear for a terrible second until it registers that his voice has softened. He sounds more confused than angry now, like he was expecting to find a gang of delinquents trashing the place. Instead, there's only me: five foot three, in strappy heels and a floor-length gown.

Thank you, prom dress.

"I ... I'm sorry. " My voice comes out strangled, so I clear my throat and try again. "I knocked some things off the desk. Nothing's damaged, see?" I quickly flip the lights on, flooding the room in a warm glow. Suddenly, it doesn't look suspicious and deserted anymore, just tidy.

The guard pauses, looking around. "But what are you doing in here? These buildings are supposed to be locked tight."

"I ... work here. After school." I swallow, my stomach flipping over in a terrible lurch. "Just ... filing, and answering phones and stuff."

He narrows his eyes suspiciously. "It's kind of late to be sneaking around."

I bob my head eagerly. "I know, I'm sorry, but I wasn't sneaking. I have keys and the alarm code! I let myself in."

"Hmmm..." The guard doesn't seem convinced. "I swear I heard something..."

I watch with horror as he takes a few steps toward the hallway, sweeping his flashlight into the dark. If he goes back there, then it's all over. He'll find the broken glass, and Bliss and Jolene, and all the innocent explanations in the world won't make a difference in our fates.

Do something.

My eyes land on the tank in the corner. "The fish!"

He pauses. "What was that?"

"I came to feed the fish!" I scoot toward the corner, praying the guard follows me. He doesn't move. "They're really rare," I announce, desperate. "A special tropical breed. Look!"

Finally, he clicks off his flashlight and strolls back across the lobby.

"I'm supposed to look after them, you see," I explain loudly, waving at the tank. "Only, I forgot. And it's the weekend, and if I left them all that time without food, they'd die, and my boss would kill me, and..." I take a ragged breath, blood pounding in my ears.

The guard peers through the glass at the whirl of tiny, gold-flecked scales. "Huh. They're special, you say?"

"My boss imported them from ... Brazil," I agree. "I was already at prom when I remembered, so I thought if I came back in, then I could feed them, and nobody would know." I fix him with my best innocent look, wide-eyed and virtuous.

"Prom?" He snaps his fingers, recognition dawning. "East Midlands High, right? My sister's kid goes there. Georgia Hayes. You know her?"

"Yes!" I nod furiously. "We have Lit class together."

Reassured, the guard seems to relax. "Still, it's against the rules to be creeping around so late," he scolds me lightly. "I'm supposed to report anyone I see out here."

"But I'll get fired for sure if they know I forgot!" I try my best to look tragic, quivering my lower lip and blinking in an attempt to muster some tears. Bliss should be the one here; God knows she's the drama queen, but maybe I have some talent after all, because the guard sighs.

"It doesn't seem like there's anything damaged," he agrees, looking around. "And if I make sure you lock up on your way out..."

Lock up? I freeze. I told him I had keys, but how am I supposed to fake that?

"Thanks!" I try, my voice quivering. "That's so nice of you." I stall for time, taking the box of feed from beside the tank and shaking it slowly over the surface of the water while my mind races for an answer.

What on earth am I supposed to do now?

"Do you ... need to go patrol the rest of the complex?" I ask hopefully. "Because I can close up here by myself. I don't want to waste any more of your time," I add.

"No, it's fine." The guard checks his receiver again, but there's nothing but static. "I need to go check the battery on this thing. But we'll get this place locked up nice and tight first."

"Uh-huh," I murmur. Then I catch a glimpse of movement out of the corner of my eye. Jolene. She edges out from the hallway and gestures, waving a set of keys at me. The guard follows my gaze and begins to turn.

"Do you think they look OK?" I squeak. "The fish, I mean!"

He turns back. "What?"

"Because I left them hours without food. Will that be OK, do you think? They seem kind of sluggish..." As I babble about feeding times and whether they're about to go belly-up on me, I see Jolene sneak across the room and place the keys on a table next to the alarm panel. She scurries back, out of sight.

"But you know, I think they'll be fine," I finish abruptly, slamming the lid back into place. "And I need to get home. I don't want my parents worrying."

Scurrying over to the alarm panel, I scoop up the keys. Beside them is a scrap of paper with a scribbled alarm code. I tap in the digits, watching anxiously as the green light turns red and the thing emits a high-pitched beep of confirmation. "See?" I tell the guard, dizzy with relief. "All secure."

I lock up behind us, my hands shaking so much I almost drop the keys, but at last, it's done. "I have to go now. My parents will be waiting." I back away, controlling the urge to simply turn and run.

"You take care now." The guard nods, strolling back toward his car. "And tell Georgia hey from me."

"I will!"

I hurry back down the dark street, but this time, I don't even flinch at the shadows. The panicked knot in my stomach has melted into a glorious exhilaration; every pulse singing in triumph.

I did it.

I stepped up. I saved the day. Meg Rose Zuckerman is a spectator no more.

Bliss

"Hurry!" Jolene yanks my arm, racing down the dark corridor.

"But he's gone," I gasp, stumbling after her. "Meg came through. We're all clear!" I still can't believe it, but somehow the girl flipped a switch and started acting like a different person. Someone awesome.

"Not yet. She set the alarm." Jolene rounds the corner ahead of me, clutching her backpack and that painting of hers, rolled into a thick bundle. "That means we've got two, maybe three minutes to get out before the system goes live."

"Oh, crap."

We run past dark offices and storerooms, fast enough to feel a burn in my chest. I am so not cut out for extreme sports. Or, you know, running.

Jolene throws open one of the heavy metal doors at the end of the hallway. "Back here," she gasps.

"No freaking way." I stop dead. Looming out of the dark are huge stacks of soft toys: rows and rows of oversize, lurid teddy bears and bug-eyed bunny rabbits. "I'm going to have nightmares about these freaks." I shudder, prodding a blue frog. His face is fixed with a manic kind of grin, like he's about to come alive and start sacrificing small children.

"Bliss!" Jolene plunges ahead, her flashlight flickering in the black.

I sigh. We couldn't go sneaking around any bright, warm places in a decent part of town. Nope, with Jolene, it's all creepy warehouses and alarm systems that could go off at any minute. I race down the aisles, my heels echoing on the concrete. There's a loading bay in the back, and – thank God – the pale green glow of an emergency exit sign shimmering above the—

"Locked." Jolene throws down the heavy chain padlock, swearing. She kicks the door angrily.

"That's it?" My panic kicks up a level, but she's already sweeping the back wall for our escape. The beam pauses on a row of narrow windows, closed up tight and way too high to get to. "Oh, no." I shake my head, following her expression. "Are you kidding me!"

Jolene doesn't answer; she just makes straight for the shelves underneath and hoists herself up. "Jolene, stop!" I hiss, but she keeps on climbing, the whole shelving unit quivering with every move. "Get down from there. It's, like, twenty feet high."

"More like fifteen," she corrects me, clambering up the shelves. "And do you see any other way out?"

"No, but do you want us to break our necks?" I gulp. Getting stuck in a brace all summer would wreck my social life way more than Kaitlin and Cameron ever could. I can just imagine it now: them frolicking at every pool party in town, while I stay stuck indoors watching daytime TV and listening to my mom lecture me about the consequences of my actions.

Jolene clearly doesn't share my summer schedule. She reaches the top and heaves the window open, looking down at me, impatient. "Come on, Bliss. Get up here!"

"And then what?" I cry. "Is there even anything on the other side?"

"We don't have time to find out!" Jolene waits another second and then shakes her head. "You know what? Fine. Stay. Get caught!" She starts to squeeze herself out the narrow space, headfirst.

"Jolene!" I yelp, but just like that, she's gone.

The warehouse is silent.

"Perfect," I mutter, gathering my skirts and reaching for the first shelf. "Be that way. I'll just tell the cops you" – I grab for the next railing – "were the one who started all this" – my thigh hits a hard edge, and I let out a yelp – "when they scrape my comatose body off the concrete" – the stack begins to sway; I gulp – "in one great mangled heap!"

At last, I reach the top. The floor is a very, very long way away. I stick my head through the narrow gap. "Jolene?"

"Drop down." I hear her voice coming from outside. In the light from the security lamps, I can see her dusting herself off – way, way below me. "Don't be such a wimp," she hisses. "There are boxes and stuff to break the fall."

Right. Because *break* and *fall* are really words I want to hear so close together. I begin to slowly squeeze through the space.

"Get a move on," Jolene orders, frantic. "The alarm will go on any second now."

With a lurch of fear, I scramble out and lower myself until I'm clinging to the ledge. The window slams shut above me, leaving me with only one way down. I dangle there, feeling only air on my legs.

"Bliss!"

Oh God, oh God, oh God.

I let go.

"OOOOOWWWWW!"

"Shhh!" Jolene clamps a hand over my mouth.

"My ankle!" I let out a strangled yelp. We're in an alley behind the building, surrounded by old packing crates and trash bags. God knows what grime I've fallen into, but all I can register is the pain shooting white-hot all the way through my foot. "I landed wrong; it must be broken."

"I'm sure it's fine." Jolene drags me to my feet. "Don't hang around – we need to find Meg."

"Thanks for the sympathy." I limp after her. "I'm telling you, it hurts."

"And I'm telling you, there's nothing I can do until—"
There are headlights coming toward us. Jolene yanks me
down behind the Dumpsters until the car edges closer and
we can see Meg.

She leans over and opens up the passenger side. "He's
gone to check on the other buildings." Meg's whole face is
lit up with excitement. "Get in, quick!"

I stumble over and throw myself in back. Jolene slides
in the front seat, slams the door, and soon we're speeding
away from the scene of the crime.

"Did you get what you came for?" Meg asks eagerly.
She takes a corner so fast the tires screech.

Jolene pats the canvas roll. "Yup. That was good work,"
she adds quietly. "Covering with the keys and everything."

"Are you kidding?" I pipe up, rubbing my ankle. "It
was amazing! Seriously, Meg, that was awesome back
there. I can't believe it."

"Me neither." She grins, bouncing in her seat. "I was
so scared when you took off and left me. But I didn't have
a choice, in the end. I had to make it work."

I laugh. "You were great. I can't believe you lied so
well. It's like you're a natural."

"I don't know about that." She giggles. "My heart
was racing so fast, I thought he would figure it out at
any minute. And when he went toward the hallway!" She
gasps. "I don't know how you do it, Jolene, I just don't.
Isn't your blood pressure through the roof?"

Jolene shrugs, slumping back. "No."

We drive for a while, heading back toward the

inhabited part of town. Soon, we're crossing through quiet residential streets, the golf course up on the ridge ahead. "So where now?" Meg looks around. "What's next?"

"Umm ... that's it, I think." I pause. "Jolene?" There's no reply, so I reach forward and prod her shoulder. "Jolene?"

"Huh? Oh. I'm done." She rests her head against the glass. "You can drop me up by Union Ave."

"You're sure?" Meg sounds disappointed. "We could go get some food or something. Celebrate?"

"No," Jolene snaps. "I got what I wanted. I'm out."

"OK." Meg is quieter now. "And you're going to Brianna's party, right, Bliss?"

"Umm, I guess." My ankle is still aching, and the pain is only getting worse. I try to ease my sandal back on, but just the pressure of my straps makes me wince in pain. "Does this look right to you guys?" I stretch it out between the two front seats, angling to get a better look.

Meg gasps. "What did you do?"

I gulp. In the dashboard light I can see it's red and swollen, the skin around the bone swollen up in a massive knot. "See?" I tell Jolene. "I told you I broke it!"

"I don't think so." Meg frowns. She pulls over to the side of the road and gently takes my foot in her hands. "Does this hurt?" She presses lightly.

"Yes!" I yelp.

"How about this?"

"Uh-huh." I sniffle, wondering how she's such an expert. "I'm going to need one of those casts, aren't I? And crutches."

"I think it's only sprained." Meg gives me a sympathetic look. "But you need to get it wrapped up properly. We can swing by the hospital. It shouldn't take long."

"Can you drop me first?" Jolene interrupts. "I told you, I'm done."

I can't believe her. "Seriously? I'm injured here!"

"And?" Jolene looks sullen. "There's nothing I can do."

"But, show some moral support," I protest. "I took one for the team."

"You took one because you insist on wearing those stupid shoes," Jolene snaps back. "So I don't get why I need to stand around watching you get an X-ray, or whatever. I did my part of the deal – I got you the diary, and now I have my painting. So, we're quits."

I look at her, confused. She's radiating all this anger, back to being tense and messed-up like she was at her dad's house and the Loft. But we got what she wanted; it's over now. "Why are you being like this? You should be happy; we came through for you!"

"Gee, thanks." Jolene is sarcastic. "What do you want, a gold star?" She sighs. "You know what? Here is fine." She opens the door suddenly, climbing out onto the sidewalk.

"Jolene," Meg calls after her, "it's the middle of the night!"

"And I can take care of myself." Jolene hoists her backpack up. She looks in the car, cold. "What, did you think we were going to sit around painting each other's toenails now? Get a life."

She stops at the end of the street and hops the low fence onto the golf course. Her ruffles get caught on the top, and she yanks at them furiously before disappearing into the night.

"Should we go after her?" Meg asks, worried.

"Why bother?" I can't believe that she's being such a bitch about things, when we risked our lives – well, our good reputations – to go in and save her ass. Some thanks we get. "She wants out, she gets out."

By the time Meg pulls in to the hospital lot, my ankle is the size of a cantaloupe and hurting like hell. "Do you want me to get a wheelchair?" Meg eyes it dubiously.

"I think I can deal," I say, "if I just kind of ... hop."

She helps me out of the car, and we hobble toward the ER. It's not the biggest hospital in the area; the serious stuff goes straight to County, so at this time of night, the waiting room is mostly empty – just a couple of drunks slouched in the far corner, a mother whose kid has half a toy tree shoved up his nose, and a middle-aged man cradling an ice pack in his lap. I don't even want to know.

"Hey, Luann?" Meg taps on the safety glass. "Can we get through?"

"Sure, sweetie." There's a click, and the doors swish open. A pale, red-haired nurse in her twenties is running intake, one of those plastic toy stethoscopes draped around her neck. She looks at us with concern. "It's late for you to be out, Meg. Is your dad OK?"

Meg nods quickly. "Everything's fine. But Bliss here

tripped and hurt her ankle. She just needs a dressing."

Luann relaxes. "Oh, you poor thing." She doesn't flinch at the sight of my gruesome foot, swiveling on her chair to check a chart. "I'll have Patrick come by and wrap you up. You girls just wait in the staff lounge. He won't be long."

"How do they know you here?" I ask, limping down the hall. I'm leaning heavily on Meg, so I can feel her body stiffen at the question.

She shrugs, guiding me down the hallway. "I volunteer every weekend. I want to go to med school," she adds, "and you need things like that on your applications."

"You really do plan ahead," I say, impressed. I wouldn't drag myself here, just for some school I might want to go to four, five years down the line. "I bet you've got everything all figured out."

She looks down, self-conscious, so I quickly add, "No, that's a good thing! I mean, you're making it happen. I bet you'll get into whatever college you want."

Meg gives me a pale smile. "I hope so. Otherwise ... well, I suppose all this will have been for nothing."

I collapse onto one of the couches, propping my foot up. It's a small room, with lockers, a fridge, and an old TV set in the corner. Not exactly luxury, but after all the running around we've done tonight, it's kind of a relief just to stay in one place for a while – without the threat of cops/parents/evil sorority girls chasing us down at any moment.

Meg yawns.

"I know; it's getting late." I try to resist the urge to crash.

"Oh. No." She shakes her head quickly. "I'm fine. It's just, after all that adrenaline, I'm coming back down."

"Relax," I tell her, grinning. "You're allowed to be tired. Tonight's been crazy."

She exhales. "It has, hasn't it? I can't believe you guys talked me into even half that stuff."

I bite my lip. "Maybe we shouldn't have."

She raises her eyebrows.

"I mean, piling on all the pressure." I shift, feeling even more guilty as I remember the way me and Jolene manipulated her. We backed her into a corner, even when she made it clear she didn't want to get involved. I sigh. "I really am sorry. And then I went and said all that stuff…"

Meg seems guarded. "I told you, I was fine."

I roll my eyes. "Yeah, but you didn't mean it."

She breaks a small grin. "Well, no … but I think I needed to hear it, all the same. I mean, you were right," Meg adds quietly. "About some things, at least. The truth is…" She pauses, uncertain.

"Go on."

She looks sad for a second. "The truth is, I have given up. Or, I had; I don't know."

I must look alarmed, because she quickly continues, "Not on life! But, school, you know? Friends. Being happy."

"That's … awful." My voice is soft. She's not kidding around here. I can tell.

Meg shrugs, awkward. "You get used to it. It's scary, just how normal being unhappy can get."

There's silence for a moment, and then a doctor bustles in. "So who took a nasty spill?"

I raise my hand. He's in his forties maybe, and balding on top – less McDreamy than McTeddy, but my foot is aching so much, I really don't care.

"Hmmm…" He feels it for a moment, twisting one way and then the next. "Looks like just a sprain. I can give you something for the pain—"

I nod eagerly. He laughs. "And wrap it up to get the swelling down. Unless you want the practice, Meg?"

"Really?" She brightens.

"Sure." He makes a few checks on a chart and tears off a form. "Hand this to Luann on your way out."

"Thanks," I breathe. "I can walk on it, right?"

He nods. "Careful, though. No leaping off tall buildings, or anything like that."

I catch Meg's eye and have to hide a laugh. If only he knew…

Meg wraps my foot quickly, like she's already a professional. Luann checks it and sets me up with a couple of pills – which I gulp down right away. "No driving," she warns me. I nod obediently. Never mind the medication; I don't think I could even fit my foot on the pedal.

We make our way slowly toward the exit, Meg supporting my arm.

"Won't your parents be freaking out by now?" I ask curiously. "Mine know I'm staying at Brianna's, but you must be way past curfew."

Meg looks sheepish. "Jolene had me tell them I was sleeping over at your place. An all-girl slumber party. Then I was supposed to drive home later and say you'd all started drinking, so I left."

My mouth drops open. "That girl!"

"You have to admit, she's kind of a genius." Meg laughs. "My dad is super-overprotective, but even he agreed it sounded like fun."

"Sure, if it's not your reputation getting wrecked!"

We're nearly at the exit, but she stops in the middle of the hall. I turn, questioning.

"It's not just because I volunteer, how they know me here," she says quietly.

"Oh?"

Meg doesn't reply for a second; she just looks at the waiting room, her face closed off. "I was here all the time, when my mom got sick," she says eventually. "Chemo and treatments." There's another long pause, and then she adds, "She died."

Oh.

I grip her shoulder, and for a moment, I can't tell who is holding the other one up. I feel a lurch of guilt. All those times I wrote off her moping as self-indulgent, or figured she was miserable for no good reason...

As reasons go, this one is pretty freaking good.

"Meg..." I breathe, but she shakes her head, forcing a smile.

"She'd get a kick out of this. Tonight, I mean. She always wanted me to have great adventures, to take more risks." Meg starts walking again, so I follow, out onto the sidewalk. "It's why I kept saying yes to you guys."

"And I thought it was my charm and persuasion," I joke, trying too hard, but I'm rewarded with a smile, genuine this time.

"Sure, those too."

"I..." I stop, awkward. I want to tell her I'm sorry for being such a bitch. I didn't know. I couldn't have known. But she stops me with a look.

"Your ankle's OK?"

I test it with some weight. "The bandages help" – I nod – "and the pills should kick in soon. Good thing Jolene isn't here," I add, still trying to joke. "She'd probably want to sell them on some street corner."

Meg doesn't laugh. She pauses by the car, swinging her keys on one finger. "I hope she's OK. Where do you think she went?"

I sigh. "How would I know? Back home, I hope, or—" I stop, suddenly realizing something.

"What?"

"The golf course. It backs up to her dad's house, remember?" I gulp, remembering just what kind of crappy mood she was in. "Oh, crap."

Meg's eyes widen. "Will she do something, do you think?"

"This is Jolene," I say shortly. "Of course she's going to do something. And in the state she's in right now, it's probably going to be a felony."

God, how stupid can that girl be? I yank the car

door open, frustrated. I was *this* close to getting to Brianna's – back to normalcy and party fun. But no, Jolene has to go back for round two...

"Come on," Meg says, deciding for me. "We'd better go stop her. Like you said, it's a team thing."

JOLENE

I stuff the heels in my backpack and walk barefoot over the golf course lawn, Dante's words stuck in a terrible feedback loop in my mind. For months now, I've managed to forget him, and now his voice is the only thing I can hear – telling me, over and over, all the ways I'm ruining my life. But he's wrong. I'm not the one who wrecked my only shot to get out of this town. I'm not the one breaking promises and being so cavalier with somebody else's future. I didn't choose this. I don't want any part of it. But with each new step, I still hear that note in his voice. Disappointed. Giving up on me, like everyone else.

Screw him.

I stomp onward. It's pitch-black and silent out here, but I've never been scared of the dark. Leave that to girls with faint hearts and weak wills. I know there's nothing out there in the shadows to hurt me. No – the things that cause real pain come with smiles and affection, lulling you into thinking they actually give a damn before they turn so easily and leave.

Screw them all.

I grip the roll of canvas tighter. I'm digging finger-marks into the fabric, but I don't care. He will, though. He cared enough to mount it in that heavy frame, put it in a place of pride behind his desk. I cut it out with my army knife. Not perfect, but good enough. The jagged edges will be waiting come Monday morning, along with that shower of broken glass and the contents of his in-box I couldn't help sweeping to the floor. The plan was invisibility, but plans change. All that sneaking was the wrong idea; I see it now. Why should I be the one to creep around, keeping to my part of town, folding myself into tiny pieces to keep my life away from his? Why should he get to ignore me so easily – just carry on with his perfect job and perfect new family without any inconvenient reminders of everything he's left behind?

He'll have to see me now.

I reach the other side of the fairway too soon, skirting those white picket fences and peaceful backyards until I reach the end of that familiar cul-de-sac and veer off into the road. Lights from every house are bright here, spilling out onto the tree-lined street. So warm and safe, so far away from the rest of my life.

I reach his front yard – neat, flower-trimmed – and stop. My feet won't carry me a single step farther. The hollow ache in my chest is suddenly unbearable.

I breathe in, quick, but it doesn't ease. The rage that's carried me through tonight, through the last few weeks, is twisting back into that same wordless grief that always wells around him when it matters. Ever since I was a kid, he's been my weak spot, and as much as I hate myself for being so pathetic, that bone-deep instinct is betraying me all over again. Sure, I can tell the entirety of East Midlands High exactly what I think of them, but when it comes to my own father? The right words won't make it through my lips. All the reason and logic and heartfelt pleas in the world stay lodged in my throat. Instead, I'm stuck with nothing but the same old screaming and sharp curse-words that let him retreat back into that shell of denial and self-righteousness, as if I'm the one at fault.

I sit down cross-legged on the edge of the damp lawn, staring at the house. It's a pretty lie he's got built for himself in there, and not just the matching dining-room set. I don't think he's once acknowledged – even to himself – that anything he's ever done has caused me pain. No, it was all, "Jolene is acting out. She needs guidance." Guidance. As in, my mom should have just told me to shut the hell up and act nice for those all-too-rare weekend visits where we sat silently in movie theaters and fast-food restaurants, until the allocated hours were up and he left me again. I tried to write him a letter once, when I was sixteen. He slipped a hundred-dollar bill into my birthday card that year and then turned around and threw a huge party for the twins with specially printed invitations on thick card-stock and tiny clowns embossed on every corner. Mom had been laid off as part of the downsizing at her office and was working night shifts at the drugstore to cover the gap; the birthday money went to paying utilities and buying groceries that month.

My RSVP was no.

So I wrote the letter. I didn't ask for more outright – I couldn't bring myself to do that back then. No, I just tried to explain how when he threw money around for them on vacations and a fancy new car, and then didn't even think about how I was getting by, it said he didn't care as much. Care enough. I spent hours getting the words right, trying to show that it wasn't about whatever legal loopholes he'd managed to fix, it was about the fact he was hurting me. They woke up with him every morning, and had dinner with him every night, and if all he could offer me as a parent anymore was money, then he should manage that much, at least.

He called up after and swore at me on the phone, furious as all hell. It wasn't his money – it was hers, too, and he was doing what he could. Stand-up guy, I know. His kid pours her heart out, telling him how much he's hurting her, and all he can do is rant about how I had no right to say those things and be so ungrateful, when he was working so hard to scrape together my college fund...

Oh yeah, the famous college fund.

But I didn't know how all of that would play out, so I bit back the hurt and carried on; tolerated the occasional phone calls and awkward lunch dates. What else was I going to do? For every bright neon sign screaming that he would never give me what I need, I couldn't shake that stupid, tragic ache of hope that he would come through for me. Just once. Finally. It's a fairy tale worse than any of that Disney crap, but it was mine – that one day, he'd own up to what a weak, selfish man he'd been, and try to do better by me.

But here I am. Still waiting.

I've been sitting here five, maybe ten minutes, when the porch light flips on. I stiffen, bracing myself to get this started, but he's not the one to come out. Instead, it's the Blonde who pulls a pretty blue robe tighter and walks down the front steps toward me.

"Jolene," she says, her expression surprisingly calm for someone who's got their hellcat stepdaughter camped out in the front yard at two in the morning. "Is everything OK?"

I set my jaw. "Is he in there?"

She pauses, a few paces away from me. "It's late. Why don't we talk about this in the morning?"

"I'm here now." I sit, determined. She looks older than I remember, or maybe that's just the bare face and tired eyes. Usually, there's makeup and lipstick and perfect newscaster hair, all polished and dripping money and false enthusiasm. Tonight, she looks like a regular woman, worn out.

But I don't care about her. "Aren't you going to invite me in?"

The Blonde gives me a faint kind of smile. "You should get home, honey. Your mom will be worried."

"And he isn't?"

There's silence. She glances back at the house. "We can talk about this another time, I promise. Come for dinner tomorrow," she suggests. "You can see Stephan and Camilla, and he'll be ... he'll be there. I'll make sure of it."

I watch her. She doesn't seem angry or impatient, or anything else I'd expect. Instead, she looks almost sad, her arms wrapped around herself, looking everywhere except at me.

"I came to see him." I hold my ground, that last piece of anger. "I'm not going anywhere."

She's quiet for a minute, then she exhales in a low whoosh. "He won't come out."

The words are simple, but there's a strange note to her voice. I stare at her, confused, until she looks me in the eye and I see it there.

She's ashamed of him.

The truth hits me with a painful twist. This isn't about her – lurking in the background, sniping about his time and money.

This is all on him.

I can't speak for a second. "He knows I'm here?" I manage at last.

She nods, sad.

"And he's up there, hiding from me." I give a flat laugh. My father, the hero.

"I'll talk to him," she promises me, awkward. "We'll figure something out, about college..."

But for once, the money isn't the point. He's never going to be the man I need him to be.

I feel everything drain away. So many years, hoping, and this is how it ends. Out in the front yard of a home he doesn't want me to be a part of.

"OK," I murmur, exhausted. "I ... whatever."

It's not my usual snipe of a word, full of sarcasm, but the truth. Whatever. I can't find it in me to even muster a thought, a plan. "I ... should go."

I pull myself to my feet, staring blankly around. I don't belong here; I always knew that, but instead of being a vengeful invader, I feel detached. Foreign. There's a language here, I don't understand. He's playing out his life by some code I can't grasp, and there's no turning it back.

"Thanks," I tell her, still dazed. "I'm sorry, I got you up—"

"It's fine." She hugs me swiftly, moving back straight after as if that was a step too far. As if it wasn't allowed. "So I'll call? About dinner?"

I shrug uselessly. "I don't know. I'm ... not sure if I can see him." I swallow, already feeling the sting of tears. Something is dead here on the lawn, some last hope, and all I can do is feel the ache of it ringing through me.

"Then maybe lunch, next week. Just us," she adds, hopeful. "I could bring the twins. You should spend some time with them."

"I ... maybe." I give her a helpless look. I can't make decisions now; I can barely keep breathing. "I have to go."

I turn, but she stops me. "Wait – your things."

The painting is still rolled up on the ground beside my bag. I grab them both, stumble backward. She gives me another weak smile, and then I go, racing faster back down that perfect street and onto the next, not slowing up for a second until the suburban blocks blur together, and my legs ache, and my chest burns almost enough to make me forget how much my heart is hurting right now.

I collapse on the empty sidewalk and start to cry.

My body shakes with sobs so harsh they leave me gasping, but it doesn't take long for the tears to be done. People think I act so tough because I can't bear to break down, but the truth is, it's not the collapse that scares me so much as what comes after. Like now. My eyes sting red, and my head aches with a dull throb, and there's nothing but a numb emptiness where all my fury used to be.

It's over.

I sag back, the cold concrete biting into my palms. Dante was right, about this at least. I can't keep holding on. In an awful flash, I see the next years spinning out ahead of me. The same old story, the same damn routine. Every time I think I drag my expectations down to meet him, he finds a way to fall short and break my heart just a little bit more.

I can't do this anymore.

I take a breath, feeling the air slip through my system in a slow wash of calm. I can just let him go.

That's what Dante said, didn't he? Like I have that power. Like I can choose it for myself. I'm not naive enough to think it could ever be that easy, but when has anything in my life come that way? This is how it starts: you make the decision, and the rest comes after.

So I decide. No more.

From now on, he doesn't owe me a single thing. I'll work my way through college, like I would without him. I'll go to State, try for a transfer next year, take on more loans if that's what it takes. I'll get by because I want to; I'll make it out of this damn town on my own – no more fooling around, no more trying to make him care.

But if he doesn't owe me anything, then I don't owe him a damn thing either.

He's not my father anymore. He hasn't earned the right.

I struggle to my feet and stretch, feeling the stiff ache in every limb. I'm so tired I could curl up and sleep right here on the ground, but instead, I take my things and start to walk. Steady, this time.

A car turns onto the block behind me. It slows, drawing level. I tense.

"Jolene!" It's barely stopped before Bliss leaps out and limps over. "Thank God, we've been looking everywhere for you!"

I blink. "I thought … you were going home. Or to that party…" I shake my head, still foggy from tears and tiredness.

"We were, until I figured out what you were going to do." Bliss's eyes are wide with concern. She looks around quickly. "You haven't been there already, have you? 'Cause we swung by your dad's house, but everything looked fine, so…" She pauses, reaching a hand to my shoulder. "Hey. Are you OK?"

I give another awkward shrug, but I don't shake

her off. I don't know why people ask that. What do they expect – for you to spill your soul out right there for them to see? I look past her instead, to where Meg is looking anxiously out from the driver's side, like she actually cares.

They came back for me.

The thought is strangely comforting. I manage a weak smile. "What is this, an intervention?"

"More like a rescue," Bliss answers, taking my bag and pushing me gently toward the car. I don't argue. This time, I'm the one to collapse in the backseat, grateful for the soft seats and warm air. Bliss climbs in up front and twists around. "So you didn't do anything crazy? I was expecting to find, like, every window smashed in, or the pool house burned down or something."

I shake my head.

"But you went there, right?" She frowns.

I nod.

"And you've still got the painting?"

I don't even realize until she says it, but the roll is still clutched in my hand. How stupid. As if a scrap of canvas could ever make a difference, or the smallest dent in his denial.

"I ... I need to get rid of it," I say at last. We're driving slowly, Meg taking us back through the development and up along the dirt road at the edge of the golf course. "It won't make a difference." I try to think clearly. "She's seen me with it, and there's all that mess back at the office. But if they can't find it on me..."

Bliss bites her lip. "Is there anywhere we can stash it for now?"

I shake my head, harder this time. "No, I don't want it back. I need it gone."

There's silence.

"We could burn it," Bliss says cheerfully. "Except we don't have fuel or anything."

"Check my bag," I tell her, slumping back in the corner of the backseat. A moment later, she comes up with the small bottle of lighter fluid I keep stashed in the side pocket. She gives me a careful look.

"Sure, because you should always throw some butane in with your sweater and tampons."

There's a pause, and then all three of us crack a grin at the same time. Mine is weak, sure, but it's something.

"How would you explain that?" Meg asks, laughing. "Oh, no, officer, it's just in case I need to do some spontaneous barbecuing?"

"It's nail-polish remover, honest!"

I don't laugh along, but their giggles soften the harsh ache around my chest. Make me feel less alone.

"Right. Burning it is, then." Bliss still sounds way too breezy, as if this is a trip to the mall we're talking about here. I wait for Meg's objections, but instead, she pulls up on the side of the road. We're on the ridge I trekked up earlier, above the dark valley of the fairway and woods.

"I have matches in my trunk," Meg says, to my surprise. She seems more relaxed somehow, as if the thought of committing felonies doesn't fill her with terror anymore.

But just when I'm wondering what happened to make her so reckless, she can't help adding, "And a fire extinguisher in my emergency pack. Just in case."

That's our girl.

We walk down the hill with our supplies and a blanket Bliss insisted on taking from Meg's trunk. "You'll get it dirty," Meg points out, scooping her sandals up in one hand to walk barefoot like me.

"That's the whole point," Bliss replies, unsteady on her bandaged ankle. "It's machine washable, but my dress isn't."

"And that's the most important thing?"

I let them bicker, walking silently alongside. Soon, the ground levels out and we reach the nearest hole; the flag ripped from the ground and discarded from my first trip through. I carefully pick it up and ease it back into place.

"So. Arson for beginners." Bliss spreads the blanket and sits herself down. "Should this be all ceremonial or something?"

"Light as a feather, stiff as a board," Meg quips, and then looks embarrassed when Bliss laughs. "What?" she says. "*The Craft* is a classic."

"Old school," Bliss agrees.

Their buzz and energy dances around me, just out of range. I'm still wrapped in sadness, too tired to care. I lay the painting out on the ground and douse it with fluid, looking down at the bold brushstrokes that I went through so much drama to get. I thought it held some kind of meaning, but it's just a sheet of canvas and paint.

I light the match, watching as the whole thing flares up and burns, brilliant in the night.

The other girls fall silent, staring at the flames.

This is it; I feel it. This is the end.

Meg

When the painting is nothing but embers and a scorch-mark on the ground, Bliss yawns. "Now that's done, I think it's Meg's turn."

"What do you mean, my turn?" I tilt my head to the side and find her watching me with an unnerving concentration.

"Relax." She smiles, a flash of white teeth in the dark. "I just mean, we've spent the whole night running around for everyone else. It's time we do something for you."

"Like what?" My arms are still spread wide, the grass damp against my skin as I lie, just watching the stars. It's so peaceful here, with the open sky above us and the distant hum of traffic kept at bay by the neat lawn and careful tree line. I take another deep breath, feeling a strange warmth roll through me; not sleepy, but content. Jolene is sprawled, silent, on my other side, but her withdrawal doesn't matter; the wordless companionship is more comforting than they could ever know.

"Anything you want," Bliss says. She flips back onto her stomach and begins to play with the fringe on the edge of the blanket. "I did the diary thing, and Jolene wanted that painting. So, what do you want?"

"Cheeseburgers," I suggest, only half-joking. "I'm hungry."

She throws a handful of grass at me. "I'm serious! What's the one thing you want, more than anything in the world?"

I pause. The one lone wish I do have, these girls could never fulfill, but it touches me that she would even ask. "I don't know…" I stare up at the blackness and those tiny pinpricks of light, so far away. "I wanted the perfect prom. Or, at least, the way it's supposed to be. The dress, the guy, dancing…" I trail off, remembering that excited drive to the country club, and all my naive hope. It feels like a lifetime ago, so much has happened since. "It's stupid, I know," I add softly. "But I wanted to be … normal, just for one night."

"It's not stupid," Bliss insists quickly. "I wanted the exact same thing. I mean, for it all to be perfect," she adds, a teasing note in her voice. "Not normal. Why settle for *normal*?"

I laugh.

"But it's too late now." I prop my head up on one hand, twisting to look at her. In the distance, a car winds its way along the road on the edge of the golf course, its lights glaring through the dark until it turns back out onto the main street. "Prom's finished. The party's over."

"Not all of them," Bliss muses slowly. "Brianna's after-party goes all night. Her parents went into the city for the weekend and left her older sister to chaperone," she explains. "Why don't you come with me?"

"Right," I say wryly. "And in what universe am I actually invited to that party?"

Bliss sighs. It's too dark to see, but I'm pretty sure she rolls her eyes as well. "What was that just there?" she asks in response. "Do you want like, a gold-leaf card or something?"

I shake my head. "Come on, Bliss. It's nice of you to ask, but can you imagine if I actually went? Nobody wants me there." I try to picture the look on Brianna's face if she saw me mingling with the high-school elite. Would she even deign to ask me to leave, or just sit, making bitchy comments with her friends and laughing at me until I slunk off myself?

"So? Make them want you." Bliss bounces up, excited. "Ooh! We could do a makeover!"

There's a snort of disdain from Jolene's general direction, but Bliss ignores her. "I'm serious. If we get you in the right outfit, some makeup, a cute hairstyle... You'll fit in, no problem."

"Really?" I'm not convinced. Hollywood may like to think that all it takes is for the girl to put on some mascara and wear a new pair of jeans, and suddenly the world bends to her every whim, but real life doesn't work that way. At least, mine doesn't.

"Totally," Bliss insists. "Nobody cares, as long as you look the part. And the guys are so shallow, they'll lap it up."

I pause. It's impossible, of course. Even the new, vaguely badass Meg Rose Zuckerman has no place at Brianna's exclusive after-party. Facing down the security guard at the office pales in comparison to the challenge of the East Midlands social scene.

Still, I can't help but casually ask, "Which boys are there, do you know?"

"The usual crowd, I guess." Bliss shrugs. "Kellan, Nico, Tristan..." I must have brightened without realizing, because she stops. "Tristan Carmichael? You have a crush on him?"

"No!" I protest, my cheeks hot. "And I was serious about the cheeseburgers. Let's go find something to eat."

I scramble to my feet, glad it's dark enough to conceal my embarrassment. Jolene lifts her head slowly and speaks for the first time. "The diner on Fifth Street is open twenty-four hours. They do great chili fries."

"There," I say brightly. "We have a plan."

The other girls haul themselves to their feet, pulling on shoes and yanking up the blanket. I walk ahead, barefoot, toward the car, but Bliss catches up with me.

"He is single..." she says, her voice thoughtful.

"Who is?" I pretend I don't know exactly who she's talking about, down to his class schedule and locker location.

Bliss ignores me. "I don't think he's dated anyone since his breakup with Lily over Christmas," she continues, "and he's smart, too. You know, you guys might work."

Just the idea is enough to make me laugh, self-conscious. "You don't have to humor me, Bliss." We reach the car, pulled off the side of the gravel road at the top of the ridge. "I know he's way out of my league."

"Whatever." Bliss is clearly unimpressed by the idea of leagues and hierarchy, but then, she would be. Those at the top don't understand just how rigid the rules really are for those of us not blessed with the sparkling glitter of access or privilege. "If he's what you want, we'll make it happen. Won't we, Jolene?"

She whirls on Jolene, who's slouching along behind us. Jolene makes a noncommittal noise.

"See?" Bliss beams at me. "What do you say?"

I don't believe her. I open the car door instead, flooding us with light. It can't be so easy, to just say she'll deliver the boy of my dreams with a bow on top, as if she's a fairy godmother in designer clothing.

My doubts must show, because Bliss flips her hair impatiently. "Trust me," she insists, and despite everything, I can't help but feel a tiny spark of hope at the confidence in her tone. She wouldn't be doing this to make a fool of me, not after everything.

"OK." My voice comes out hesitant, but I clear my throat and say it louder. Like I know what I'm doing. Perhaps she's crazy, but if there's even the smallest chance

Bliss could come through with this... "Tristan. That's what I want. Who, I mean."

"Awesome!" Bliss beams. "Let's do this."

And then she takes off her dress.

"It still doesn't fit," I say, twisting uncomfortably. We're parked by the knot of SUVs and gleaming cars outside Brianna's, making last-minute adjustments to my new look. The sound of the party is still filtering down the long driveway, every light in the house ablaze.

"That's because you're slouching. You've got to stick your shoulders back." Bliss reaches over and reties the halter neck. I switched into her dress back at the golf course, under the instruction that mine was way too classy – given that it covered most of my available limbs. Now I'm swathed in her white silk designer outfit, while she's happily selected the best of our assorted pajama party heist: striped knee socks to cover her bandage, the giraffe shorts, and, yes, that *snuggly* top.

But Bliss's questionable fashion choices are the last thing on my mind right now. "You can practically see my nipples!" I object, looking down at the folds of white silk draped precariously over my braless chest.

"Not unless it's cold out," Bliss replies, unconcerned. She pulls several thin strips of what looks like tape from her purse and proceeds to stick the dress to my skin, tugging and folding at the fabric until it looks as if it were made to fit me – a miraculous feat, given the fact that I'm three inches shorter than her and at least fifteen pounds heavier, in all the wrong places.

"Voilà!" she declares. "Hot. Very hot. And don't forget the purse to match."

"Very illegal, you mean." I take the beaded clutch she thrusts at me and check myself in the tiny strip of mirror again, my contacts already itching from the amount of mascara and eyeliner Bliss has slicked on my eyelids. I look about two years older and ten times as glamorous as I have in my entire life.

"Do you want Tristan to fall at your feet or not?" she challenges, brandishing a lip-gloss wand at me.

"There." Admiring her handiwork, Bliss secures another strand of hair in the messy ponytail, pulling a few more to frame my face with tiny ringlets. "I am officially a genius. What do you think, Jolene?"

Jolene rises from where she's been laying comatose on the backseat. "You look like a stray Pussycat Doll."

"See?" Bliss grins. "Perfect."

The moment we step past the front door, I'm hit by a wave of music thundering with a bass I can feel vibrate clear through my chest. It's loud and hot, packed with bodies and a whirl of laughter and hollering from every cream-papered room. I pause in the marble-trimmed hallway, hesitant, but Bliss plunges ahead into the crowd. I don't see Jolene, but since Bliss is gripping my wrist in a vicelike hold, I have no choice but to follow.

"None of that sneaking around," Bliss yells in my ear, yanking me through a knot of girls dancing in the living room. Some of them are balanced up on the couch, yelling along to the music as they bounce, barefoot on the brocade cushions. "Remember what I said; you have to look confident, like you belong!"

I nod, wordless. After the college party, I thought I'd be a little more immune to scenes of teen debauchery, but now that I'm here, I realize how different this is: I know these kids. That's gangly Jenny Phillips raising her eyebrows at me as we pass, and Mike Tucker from my Chem lab dropping his mouth open as he does a quick double take. Despite all my grand plans, I begin to retreat into myself, wilting under their gaze.

"I mean it," Bliss scolds me, coming to a stop in the back hallway. Outside, the sound of splashes and squealing filters through the French doors, and I see a tangle of boys hurl themselves into the pool, still in dress shirts and tuxedo pants. "I can only change all this." She gestures from head to toe. "It's up to you to do the rest."

"But—"

"Enough with the freaking *but*s! You're doing this." Bliss gives me a sharp push, and I find myself propelled out onto the back patio, struggling not to fall flat on my newly made-up face.

"Hiya!" I hear Bliss's synthetic squeal ring out even through the noise. I watch as she sashays ahead, greeting kids with bright air-kisses and yells. "No way, I've been here for ages!" she insists, flipping her hair and reaching to take a swig of another girl's drink.

I follow, awkwardly hovering on the edge of the

crowd. It's quieter out here, at least; less soul-shaking music, and more laughter and gossiping. The paved patio area is full of tables bearing crisp cloths and platters of elaborate hors d'oeuvres, with a stone staircase curving down to the pool area and the lawn stretching beyond.

"And then she caught AJ in the foyer with his belt still undone. I mean, can you say cheater?" Nikki is telling her, face flushed. Bliss laughs.

"Like anyone's surprised about that."

"I know!" Courtney interrupts, eager. Like Nikki, she's traded her formal dress for jeans and a tight, belly-skimming shirt. "So what about you, have you been hiding off with Cameron?"

Bliss giggles. "Maaaybe." She winks as if she hasn't spent the last five hours cursing his name. "I don't kiss and tell."

I shift, uncomfortable. Bliss has yet to even look in my direction. It's as if I'm suddenly invisible to her again.

"See?" Nikki nudges Courtney, too hard. "Told you. Kaitlin said you must have gone home, but I knew there's no way you'd bail on us."

"Where is Kaitlin, anyway?" Bliss sounds casual, but I see a slight flicker in her smile.

Nikki shrugs, gesturing drunkenly. "Around. Anyway, come say hi to Brianna; she was looking for you and—"

The girls head down the stone staircase to the pool area, out of earshot. Soon Bliss is swallowed into the crowd, and I'm left, stranded on the balcony, alone.

I watch her go, confused.

That's it? She dolls me up in this outfit, smears on some lip gloss, and then disappears, back to her real friends and their exclusive fun? The confusion shifts to betrayal as I watch her limp over to the crowd and laugh, carefree. The promise to give me Tristan really was nothing more than a shallow, fleeting whim, I realize; some way to make her feel generous and all-powerful. Too quickly, she's back exactly where she started the night, and so am I.

Some fairy godmother.

I wander to the edge of the patio and gaze down at the scene. The A-list has laid claim to the Moroccan-style furniture near the pool house, while the guys joke around, trying to entertain them. None of the girls are braving the water, I note, keeping their careful hairstyles well away from the chlorine. As I watch, Bliss dances over to Brianna and pulls her into an affectionate hug. They tumble back onto a lounger, gossiping happily.

I turn away.

"I heard they tried to book that band, G-link, but it fell through last-minute."

Two girls begin to fill their plates nearby, gossiping about various prom dramas. I feel their eyes on me, acutely self-conscious. This is why I've never tried crashing these parties before. It's one thing getting in, but then what?

"Wait, wasn't Bliss Merino in that exact same outfit?"

I look up. The girls are shooting me glances, whispering loudly. They're dressed in vintage-style dresses, with armfuls of bangles and red lipstick, and while they may not be part of Brianna's clique, they're still seniors, far above me in every way.

I start to blush, but then remember Bliss's rehearsal in the car. Fake everything.

Forcing what I hope is a bored expression, I look over. "She was," I say loudly. They stop whispering. I keep going. "She came in the same thing as me, so she changed."

They pause. "Oh," one says, but there's something new in her voice. "It's a great dress."

"Really great," her friend agrees. They look at me with something like respect in their eyes, as if Bliss submitting to my will suddenly marks me out as somebody significant.

"Thanks," I say, blinking. "I … like yours too."

"Oh my God, you have to try this cake!" The first one is distracted by the food. She takes another bite, licking frosting from her fingers. "Seriously!" They turn to the spread, my supposed fashion showdown forgotten.

But I wonder…

Turning, I make my way back inside to where the party thumps in every room. I stroll slowly through the rooms, aware of eyes on me, but this time, I pay more attention to the looks – the girls who graze my body in a quick head-to-toe glance as I pass, the boys whose eyes seem to zoom straight to my chest. I was too self-conscious to notice properly before, assuming that they were the same dismissive glares I'm so used to, but now, I can see I was wrong. These looks are different: tinted with envy, or lust, or admiration.

Nobody thinks I don't belong.

I stand a little taller, reveling in the attention, when suddenly the music changes, and the room is fuller, packed with people yelling the lyrics as they jump. I slip into the kitchen to escape, knocking into somebody on the way out. "Sorry," I say quickly, stepping aside.

"No problem." The guy laughs. "It's crazy out there!"

I look up and promptly stop breathing.

Tristan.

"Right, crazy," I echo, my mind blank. I'm close enough to feel the heat of his body, to brush against the bare skin of his arm.

"But hey, it's the last big party of the year. Might as well go all-out." He grins down at me, eyes bright and blue. He's still dressed in his button-down shirt, the sleeves rolled up around his elbows, his tie askew. One lock of his hair falls, out of place but perfect.

I exhale in a tiny shiver.

"It's Megan, right?"

I can't speak. I've been gazing at him for three hours every week all year, ever since he walked into AP Calc and collapsed gracefully into a chair directly in my eyeline. He's good with algebra, but shaky on statistical convergence problems. He uses beat-up ball-point pens fished from the depths of a North Face backpack, and prefers those black and red spiral-bound notebooks. I tried using them for a while, in the vain hope that I could strike up a conversation about stationery sometime, but the lines were ruled too wide for my liking, and aside from the same warm smile he gives everyone from lunch ladies to the swooning freshman girls, he's never so much as spoken to me.

Until now.

"Sure, it's a great party," I manage to say, smiling at him. His gaze drifts to my cleavage, for just a split-second, and when he glances back up again, his grin is wider.

Thank you, Bliss.

"Hey, I saw some beers out by the food tables. You want to come hunt them down?"

I nod, and then – to my utter disbelief – he presses a hand against my back and begins to guide me carefully through the room.

My heart sings, and I follow.

Bliss

"And I know the cabin only has like, four bedrooms, but I figure we can double up. Or draw straws for who gets privacy." Brianna gives me a scandalous grin, stretching out on the lounge chair. The whole group is hanging down by the pool house with our own music system and stash of the best desserts: the VIP section for what's already the most exclusive party in town. I relax beside her, finally back where I belong: in the center of things. No angry felons, or dirty parking lots, or humiliating karaoke incidents – just my friends, some great tunes, and a slice of mocha whip truffle cake that the caterer swears is practically fat-free.

Perfection.

Brianna looks out over the party like a princess surveying her kingdom. She's still in her frothy blue prom gown, but considering how much it cost, I don't blame her. "I can't wait for summer vacation. It's going to rock. No school, no work, just partying twenty-four seven."

"Hell yes!" I give her a high five.

"Better hope Bliss and Cameron get one of the suites," Nikki interrupts, taking another gulp straight from her champagne bottle. "'Cause I don't want you rolling around in the next bed like you did over spring break."

"Don't be gross," I complain. "We were only making out!"

"Sure you were." Nikki snorts with laughter, elbowing me. I push her away, and she yelps, sliding down onto the floor with a bump. She looks around, blinking, and then giggles.

"She is so wasted. Shotgun I don't hold her hair back," I tell Courtney, not even bothering to keep my voice down.

Courtney sighs, perched on the edge of the bench. "But last time, she got puke all over my new shoes."

"Don't care!" I say, scooping up some more of the mocha frosting. "Not my problem."

Brianna keeps chatting about summer plans, but I zone her out, sneaking a look around the party for Meg. It was kind of crappy to just cut her loose, but I don't know what else I was supposed to do – keep her hanging at my heels all night? She must have known my invite didn't mean mixing with Brianna and co. Sure, I can work magic with lip gloss and mascara, but that would be more like asking for a miracle. I sigh, not seeing her anywhere around the pool or balcony. She's probably off in a corner somewhere, looking hot, but still too shy to get out and start having fun. It's a shame; she was finally starting to loosen up, like being thrown in the deep end back with that security guard made her stop being such a timid wallflower.

Then I catch sight of her up by the patio doors, and my guilt disappears. She's talking to Tristan, giggling flirtatiously while he stares down her dress, totally smitten. It's the cutest thing: he's teasing her about something, and her whole face is lit up, like she's having the time of her life.

I grin. My work here is done.

"Hey B, where've you been?" An arm snakes around from behind, and I feel Cameron lean down to kiss my forehead. I tense. This is going to be the hard part: acting like nothing's wrong until the news about him and Kaitlin breaks.

"Long story." I force myself to smile, scooting over so there's room beside me. "I've had the craziest night."

"It's been awesome," he agrees, collapsing next to me. "But I missed you." He kisses me lightly on the lips and then drapes an arm on my shoulder.

"Awwww." Courtney giggles on my other side. "So cute!"

But Cameron was always the cute one. Even now as I study him, he looks like an adorable puppy, with his clothes wet through from the pool, and his hair dripping on my bare shoulder. It's why I started liking him, how he was so sweet and genuine when other guys would try and seem cool, like they were serious players or something. Cameron never pulled that crap – I always knew exactly how he felt about me. At least, I thought I did.

"I like the shirt." He grins, tracing the letters.

"And the socks." I stick my feet out, wriggling my toes. "It's all about the socks."

He laughs, and I wonder how he can be like this, so *normal*. It's like nothing has happened, and he wasn't groping Kaitlin in the back of that limo a few hours ago. I start to feel disorientated, as if maybe it never happened at all, and I had some weird hallucination from the pain medication. But I only just took the pills, and I saw them together – too gross to be a dream. It was real.

"I've got to run inside," I say, bobbing up. He grabs my hand and pulls me down to kiss me again.

"Come back soon."

Courtney makes another envious noise, so I smile brightly, ruffling his hair the way I always do. "Sure!"

There's a major line for the bathrooms downstairs, so I head up to Brianna's room on the first floor. She's got an en suite up there, along with every kind of perfume and styling product known to mankind, stacked in neat rows across the wide double sink. I linger by the mirror, checking that everything looks just perfect. Bad enough I've had to cover for where I've been all night; if anything seems even a little off with me, people will start asking questions. And if there's one thing my friends love to do, it's gossip.

"There you are, bitch." I look up as Kaitlin swans in, beaming. She hugs me, checking her own reflection at the same time. "That outfit is the cutest! You should have said you were changing – we could have matched."

She's still wearing her pink dress. The easy-access one.

"Oh, yeah." I try to grin back, even though I'm hit with a sudden urge to leave my handprint on her face. I turn away. "It was a last-minute thing."

I rummage in my purse, not even paying attention until I can't find my lip gloss. Then I realize: I switched bags with Meg. She's got my ultra-juicy gloss, and I'm stuck with ... ChapStick? I sigh.

"Anyway, I was meaning to say, my mom fixed up that spa day." Kaitlin hops up on the counter top.

"What?"

She rolls her eyes. "Remember, that bonding thing? It's set for next weekend. You and me, and our moms, and Brianna and her mom... We have to invite Sonja Ellis too" – she wrinkles her lip – "but they're trying to get her parents on their charity board thing, so I guess it's important."

My heart sinks. Of course, our parents. They're all connected by now – the lunches, tennis games at the club, dinners while us kids are out together. Just another reason I have to bite my lip and give Kaitlin a careless smile.

"Sounds like fun!" I exclaim, slamming my purse shut. "Come on, let's go get some drinks."

Then something makes me stop. "Hey, have you talked to Cameron?" I keep my voice casual.

Kaitlin looks up. "Tonight? Not much, he's been around, though." She raises her eyebrows. "What's up?"

"Oh, nothing..." I sigh. "He's just acting kind of weird."

I sneak a look to check her expression, but Kaitlin doesn't flinch. "Like how?"

"I don't know ... he's being kind of clingy. Really full-on." I wander back out into the bedroom. She follows. "I mean, he was texting all night," I go on, "saying how much he missed me, how he couldn't wait for us to spend some time together."

"Sounds sweet."

Kaitlin's voice is kind of pinched. I feel a swell of satisfaction, the first bit of real emotion I've managed since getting here.

"You're right. I shouldn't bitch about it." I give her a grin. "It's nice, that he isn't afraid to tell me how much he loves me." This time, she definitely looks pissed, so I keep going. "Some guys will just fool around, you know, but Cameron always says how special I am. Don't you think that's great?"

"Great."

We push through the crowd to the kitchen, and Kaitlin grabs the nearest cup of punch from Nico's outstretched hand. "Hey!" he protests, but she chugs it down in one long gulp.

I watch her, wondering why she's so rattled. I would have figured she'd be smug, knowing she'd taken something behind my back, but instead she seems genuinely annoyed at all my stories of Cameron's devotion and love.

Maybe she thought he'd dump me for her.

I almost laugh out loud. That's it! Kaitlin figured she could steal him away – show me up, and get the guy too. No freaking way.

"I got you something." Cameron appears beside me as the rest of the group clusters into the room. I feel Kaitlin's eyes on me, so I slide my arms around his waist and snuggle closer.

"I like presents." I smile at him, but inside I'm cold.

He grins. "I was going to give it to you earlier, but … uh, anyway, here you go." He pulls something from his pocket and drops it in my hand.

I look down. It's a tiny heart-shaped pendant, fixed to a slim gold chain. Did he have it in his pocket while he was groping her, too?

The thought throws me, but then I remember that everyone's watching. I make sure to gasp loudly.

"It's gorgeous!" I say, holding up the necklace. "Look, Kaitlin, isn't this cute?"

She glares at me for a second, then pulls herself together. "So cute!" She squeals, coming closer to admire it. "Cam always has the best taste."

"Not always," I say sweetly, reaching up to kiss his cheek. "But this time, he does."

Cameron flushes, trapped between me and Kaitlin. Now, at least, he's got the decency to look guilty.

"Thanks, sweetie," I coo, pulling him down for another kiss, a real one this time. I count to ten with my tongue in his mouth, hearing the other guys whoop and

Brianna complaining for us to get a room. "Later." I wink, coming up for air.

Kaitlin scowls, stomping out of the room. I step away from Cameron, but he grabs at me. "I said later." I try to laugh, crossing quickly to the fridge to put some space between us.

I pour a glass of water, listening as the gang talks behind me. It's suddenly hot in here – hot, and loud, and way too packed with people. I feel dizzy.

"You OK?"

I jump at the voice. Courtney is looking at me, concerned.

"Yup! Fine!" I realize the machine is still running, spilling water into the overflow. I turn it off and give her a bright grin. "What about you – any new developments?" I nod in Kellan's direction to distract her. He's arm wrestling Nico for the last of the chips, his biceps straining against his shirt. Courtney sighs, getting this glazed look in her eyes, and right away, I'm forgotten.

"No, but we danced together earlier, which has to mean something, right? I mean, it wasn't a slow song or anything, but he was focused on me the whole time. OK, so maybe not the whole time, because I saw him checking out Taryn's butt, but like, it's Taryn's butt – it would be weird if he *didn't* look..."

By four a.m., I'm ready to sleep for twenty hours straight, but somehow, the party is still going strong. Music thumps from the living room, a bunch of football guys are playing table hockey on the formal dining table, and our group has colonized the den to chill out and pick over the gossip of the night. At least, they are: sprawled on the couch with Cameron as my personal pillow, I can barely stay awake to pay attention.

"... in pink instead. Don't you think, B?"

"What?" I yawn, looking around.

Brianna laughs, throwing popcorn at my head. "Don't worry, just planning. Go back to sleep."

"I can take you home, if you want." Cameron leans down, checking that I'm OK. All night, he's been acting like the best boyfriend ever, fetching me drinks and asking if I need a sweater – and ignoring Kaitlin. It's everything a girl could want.

Except that whole cheating part.

"No," I say quietly. "I'm good." As if I'm going to leave early, and risk him coming back here to be with her.

"No freaking way!" Brianna suddenly shrieks, sitting bolt upright. "What the hell is *she* doing here?"

They all look.

"You're kidding me!" Kaitlin's voice is full of scorn. "I mean, showing up at prom is one thing. But this is, like, a private party!"

I pull myself upright to see what's got them so worked up.

It's Jolene.

She's hanging with some senior boys in the hallway, a full beer bottle dangling from one hand. She looks tired, and kind of sad too, but when she hears Kaitlin's loud bitching, her eyes narrow. She turns this way.

"This had better be good." Brianna snorts as Jolene saunters into the room.

"Hey, everybody," she drawls, slow and sarcastic. The badass exterior is back. "What's up?"

"Uh, you mean apart from you gate-crashing?" Brianna doesn't get up; she just lounges there, looking down her nose at Jolene.

"Well, it's not exactly the most exclusive guest list." Jolene looks around the room, her eyes stopping on Kaitlin. She smirks. "Looks like you'll invite just about anyone."

I stiffen. It's one thing to have Jolene knowing the truth when we're out there, away from everyone. But here, in the same room, with all my secrets? I gulp.

"Relax," Jolene adds, as if she can hear my panic. "I'm just having some fun. Getting to know my fellow students."

"Wrong party." Brianna flashes a fake smile. "Your crowd is hanging out by the railroad tracks. You know, down with the bums and druggies."

I catch the flicker in Jolene's expression, but I don't say a word. I just slip lower beside Cameron and hope she walks away.

"Drugs?" Jolene drawls. "Gee, and there I was thinking I'd just have to find your big brother. Didn't he have that problem? You know." She mimes a sniff.

Brianna gets this murderous look on her face. "Like you can judge. What are you, like, some kind of crack baby?"

The gang bursts out laughing. Jolene looks over at me. I let my eyes drift shut, pretending like I'm napping until she looks away.

"Don't worry," Kaitlin coos, "you can't help it. It's like, being born with bad hair or a weird nose or … whoops, I guess you got those too."

There's more laughter, everyone smirking like we're so much better than Jolene.

"What can I say?" Kaitlin beams. "Some people can't get over their genes."

"And some people can't get over being a skanky bitch," Jolene snaps back, but I know her by now, and I can tell she's rattled.

Still, I don't move.

"Whatever." Brianna sighs, acting bored. "Nobody wants you here, so why don't you just head on back to the trailer park, and maybe we'll see you around – working at McDonald's."

"It's Dairy Queen," Courtney pipes up.

Brianna laughs, delighted. "Right! I'll remember to tip you extra next time."

Jolene sends me one last look, as if to say, "*These* are your friends?" I close my eyes again, waiting until she's walked away and Brianna and the girls erupt in a frenzy of post-showdown bitching.

"Can you believe her nerve?"

"I know! You should totally call the cops on her; I bet she's going to steal stuff."

I listen to them, feeling a low flush of shame. But

what am I supposed to say – "Hold up, guys, Jolene is OK; we've been hanging out all night"? Like that would play well with this crowd. No, that would only raise more questions, like what we were off doing together, and why. So I keep quiet, and soon, the girls get tired of bitching over Jolene and her nerve and move on to more important things, like coordinating outfits for the seniors' graduation and how they can convince their parents to let them spend a month backpacking through Europe this summer. But even though the showdown is quickly forgotten to them, I can't shake my guilt. The way Jolene stared at me, it was like I was the worst kind of person – lower than Kaitlin even, because at least she didn't look me in the eye while she had her hands down Cameron's pants.

Cameron. He's still sitting next to me, stroking my hair. I feel something shift inside me. I know the plan was to sit back and look innocent until this thing blew up in their faces, but even the touch of his hand makes me want to break something. Why did I ever think I could pretend like I was OK with all his cheating and lies?

Maybe because I've been pretending so long, I've got it down to an art.

"What do you think?" I nudge Cameron quietly.

"About what?"

"Jolene."

He shrugs, pushing back his damp hair. "I don't know."

"Come on," I press him. "What do you think of her?"

Cameron looks blank. "I guess, she's kind of a freak,

right?" He reaches for the bottle of champagne, offering it to me first with another of those puppy dog grins.

Was it good?

I've been blocking the actual memory of him and Kaitlin all night, but now I can't stop the picture of them together. His hands on her skin, her tongue on his chest.

And it wasn't even the first time.

"Hey B, pass it my way." Kaitlin is propped on some cushions on the floor. She rolls over, giving Cameron a view right down the front of her dress. His eyes slip down, just for a second, but it's enough.

Screw strategy.

"You can have it." I get up, suddenly feeling this roar of blood in my ears. Before I can think twice – hell, before I can even process what I'm about to do – I grab the champagne bottle and upend it, pouring the whole damn thing over her.

Kaitlin screeches, warm alcohol dripping from her head. "What the hell?"

The whole group is staring at me like I've gone insane. Brianna has her mouth dropped wide open, and even Nikki manages to blink through her drunken stupor.

"Have you lost your mind?" Kaitlin is whimpering, wiping at her face. Her hair is hanging in damp clumps, and the booze clings to her dress in wet, sticky patches. She looks ridiculous.

I start to laugh.

"It's not funny!" Kaitlin screeches again. Courtney rushes to her, passing someone's sweater to help dry her off, but the rest of them stay frozen, looking at me in shock. Brianna's face darkens.

This is it, I realize – either I shut the hell up and pretend it's all a joke, or I finish this for good. No going back.

So I don't.

"You know what?" I tell Kaitlin, still sitting there on the floor. "Have everything. I don't want it anymore." Reaching behind me, I undo the clasp on Cameron's pendant and drop it in her lap as I walk past. Despite the limp, the socks, and the fact that I just screwed up my entire social life, I sashay out of that room like I'm strutting on three-inch heels.

I'm done with them.

JOLENE

Their insults slice through me, worse than any slap to the face. I spin quickly and stride out of the room before they can see the damage, hurrying down the fancy hallways to get away. Get the hell out of there. Pushing past drunk guys and giggling girls, I finally slip into the empty cloakroom and sink back, falling behind the layers of coats and jackets until I hit the wall. Something solid.

I take a breath. I shouldn't be so shaken. I shouldn't even care. It's nothing but the same petty bitching I've ignored for the last three years of school, but for some reason, it was different in there. It was Bliss.

An unfamiliar hurt stings in my veins. I feel stupid even realizing it, but after everything we've been through tonight, I counted on some kind of loyalty, the smallest amount of support. But instead, she just sat there, draped over the boyfriend who screwed around on her, laughing along with the friends she's been plotting all night to destroy.

Nothing's changed.

The thought is bitter like metal in my mouth. Tonight wasn't a turning point, or any kind of new beginning. Back at my dad's house, out on that golf course, I had almost convinced myself that these games meant something. That it wasn't just canvas and paint going up in flames, but the past, too. Now I see it's not so easy. Even if I change, everybody else stays the same.

I lurch back out into the party, determined to break this damn haze that's still clouding me. Why should I let them cut me down to size? Why should I even care? Let them play their cruel games with each other – I'll be gone soon enough. The faces blur as I shove my way through, ignoring yelps of protest. They should know by now to get out of my way.

Then I see a flash of someone familiar. Meg's over in the dining room, watching the table hockey game. She looks breathless and happy for some reason, and as the crowd shifts, I see that reason slip his arm around her shoulders, grinning down at her. Tristan.

So, she got her Prin   Charming after all. I watch them for a second, and I can't help but be envious. Not of the status or that preppy jerk, but how damn happy she is. Meg didn't ask the world for a thing, but there she is, granted everything she ever wanted. Sure, it's just the same old high school bullshit – the pretty dress and the cute boy – but everything about her is shimmering with delight. Maybe that's the trick: to expect so little from life, you never feel one ounce of disappointment. Maybe that's my lesson.

I press on. Brianna's stocked the bar, I'll say that at least for her; I pluck a half-full bottle of vodka from the kitchen counter debris and head outside, away from the bright party lights toward the edge of the garden and the silhouettes lurking there. I don't bother saying hey, or even announcing my presence; I just wander right up and plant myself in the center of the knot.

"Jo-lene Nel-son." One of the guys drawls it, exhaling a long plume of smoke from the joint in his hand. "What's up?"

I stare at them all, nonchalant as hell. It's a motley collection of boys from school: some of the party jocks, a few preppy assholes, a couple of guys I recognize from detention. "You tell me." I shrug, taking a gulp from my bottle. The vodka burns the back of my throat, fire all the way to my stomach. I don't shudder, but somewhere inside, I feel a small pang of regret.

I thought I was done with this.

Mikey gives me a sidelong look. He should have graduated last year, but his credits fell short, and the football team was happy to keep him around. "Not your kind of party, I would have thought."

"Want to throw me out?" I reply, enough challenge in my voice to make him hold his hands up in a kind of defeat.

"Whoa, no offense. I was just saying."

"And now you've said it." I look around at the dark

faces, lurking here like they're committing some grave crimes instead of smoking some of Mikey's weak-ass weed. I roll my eyes, not that they'll see it. "Anyone got a cigarette?"

They shake their heads and shrug. Daniel offers me the joint. I pause. "No," I sigh, remembering the last time I mixed alcohol with that stuff. "I need nicotine."

"It's a bad habit," Nico tells me, his lips curling in a smile. I stare back. He's one of the rich, preppy guys that drifts on the edge of Brianna's clique, but it looks like he's slumming it tonight. His white dress shirt is wet through from the pool, and his tuxedo pants droop from a thin leather belt. I offer him the bottle with a flicker of my eyebrow.

He takes it and swallows a gulp straight down. Hands it back. Smiles again.

So this is how it goes.

Suddenly I'm so tired I can barely stand. I lean back against one of the old trees, taking tiny swallows from the vodka as they pass the joint around and murmur idle conversation in hushed tones. The haze is back, still cloaked heavy around me and almost too sad to bear. Anger, I can use, but this aching melancholy? It soaks through my whole system, mixing with alcohol and the sickly sweet smell of the weed until I feel dizzy and too, too hollow.

Dante was right.

"Cool party, huh?" Nico edges a couple of steps closer to me, and I realize that most of the guys have left. Just a few people are still around. A few people, and Nico.

He smiles at me, teeth white in the shadows.

"Sure. If you like this kind of thing." I shrug, still thinking about Dante. I wonder where he even is. Did he go straight home, or out to some party with his new friends? His girlfriend? The idea chills me, so I take another sip. I miss him so much it hurts, but that won't change a thing. It's done. We're finished. The last possibility of him is gone for good, and I've only myself to blame.

He was right. God, he was right about everything.

"You look great in that dress." Nico doesn't notice my fugue, or if he does, he doesn't care. He slides in even closer, so I can feel his body just inches away; lets his gaze drift over the tight bodice and ruffled skirt. "It's cute."

I roll my eyes at his weak line, but I don't pull away when he leans in and kisses me unceremoniously on the lips. His mouth is soft and hot, and for a moment I think there could be a way to forget everything after all.

Hands and teeth and the tree, hard against my back; just make it all go away.

We're both breathing heavier by the time Nico grabs my arm and begins to lead me out toward somewhere. "C'mon," he says. "Let's go."

"Where?"

He shrugs. "Does it matter?"

No. It never does. A backseat, a dark alley; it's all the same. I know where he's leading; I know it too damn well. But what's wrong with that?

And then I hear my own words, echoing back in my head.

You're better than this. Than him.

What I told Bliss there in the dorm room, about throwing herself away on stupid guys and stupid lies. I know now that it wasn't even true – she's not better than this.

But I am.

I pull away.

"What?" He blinks at me, confused. "It's cool. Nobody's going to see."

"How sweet." I feel myself slip back together, a handful of broken pieces finding some kind of shape and order. The edges hurt like hell, but it's something. Something whole. "Look at you, so worried about *my* reputation."

Nico just reaches for me again, so I duck around him. "You know what? You're right. A girl can't be too careful about these things."

I keep it light, joking even. I'm not looking for another fight, even though it's clear I could lay him out in five seconds flat if it went that way. Nico clearly realizes it too; he scowls at me like a boy who's lost his toy, but doesn't try and stop me as I yank my dress straps up and walk away from him, back through the garden. I pass other couples, intertwined in the shadows, but they don't look up. Everybody is caught up in their own drama. Everybody is just out for themselves. Sure, the barrier came down for a while tonight, in the buzz of those pranks, and the unexpected friendship of Bliss and Meg. But they've returned to their rightful places, and I'm still stuck on the outside, where I belong.

It's time to go home.

• • •

"There you are!"

I'm barely ten steps away from him when Bliss comes charging toward me. She skirts the pool, looking like a slumber-party exile in that pajama outfit. "I've been looking everywhere for you."

"And?" I take in her anxious expression and want to laugh. Sure, *now* I get the apology, when none of her precious friends are around to see. "I don't want to hear it, OK?" I start to walk away, but Bliss won't quit so easy. She trots at my heels, and for a moment I flash back to the start of all of this: back at the country club, getting roped into the whole deal to begin with. I figured it would be so, so simple. Never again.

"Jolene, wait." Bliss grabs my arm. I fix her with a glare, but I guess she's immune by now. "I really need to—"

"What, apologize?" I cut her off, shaking. "No need. I got the message, back inside. You know, with all your *friends*?"

I was wrong. I'm not completely numb – there's still a slice of anger left in me for this. For her.

Bliss blushes like she's actually ashamed. Or maybe she's just worried about being seen with me. The pool area is quiet, lights reflecting in the dark water, but there are people still up on the balcony, and stragglers making out among the trees. "I know, I should have said something, but…" She trails off, biting her lip.

"But you didn't." I finish for her. "You didn't do a damn thing."

"I *know*!" She quivers. "You don't think I get how bad that was? I felt like the worst person ever."

"Aww," I drawl, ignoring how distressed she actually looks. "You poor thing. You feel bad for acting like a total bitch. Hang on while I weep for you." I'm tight-lipped, my hands clenched, mad at myself for even caring how this shallow, rich waste of space treats me. Bliss Merino has been and will always be one of *them*, and a few hours of acting buddy-buddy was never going to change that. "Are we done yet?" I glare.

"Will you just listen?" Bliss cries. Sure, because it's all about what she wants. "I said I'm sorry!"

"You didn't, actually," I correct her, feeling the anger kick, like it never left. Maybe it never will. "You've said plenty about how bad you feel, and what a terrible person you are, but you haven't gotten around to, you know, trying to make *me* feel better."

Bliss blinks. "Why are you making this so hard?"

I gape. "Seriously? You're the one sitting back while they tear me to pieces, and it's my fault?"

"No." She backtracks, her face anxious. "That isn't—"

"And what are you even doing out here, where they can see?" I jerk my head over at the patio, where her clique is gathering. "I mean, I'm the lowest of the lows on your grand hierarchy. Will you have to go grovel to them too, after? Say what a trashy slut I am, just to keep your place?"

"Jolene," Bliss pleads, her eyes filling with tears. But I'm unmoved. God forbid she smear her mascara over someone as worthless as me.

"What?" I reply, fierce. "What do you want from me? I got you that stupid diary, made sure it went where you needed it. I came through for you!"

"And so did I!" Bliss whips back. "Or are you forgetting that whole warehouse cop thing?"

I snort. "You think just because you act like a real human being out in the world, it gives you the right to be a bitch back here? That's not how it works. Friends don't take that crap. They stick up for each other, no matter what." I stop dead, realizing what I've just said.

Friends?

But before I can take it back, Kaitlin marches down the steps, planting herself down in front of Bliss. "What the hell was that about?" Kaitlin demands, a murderous expression on her face. Up close, I can see her dress is stained with liquid, and her hair is matted against her face. "Have you gone totally insane?"

Bliss looks at her blankly.

"Yeah, what's going on, B?" That bitch Brianna and a pack of clique girls arrive a few beats after, circling like the audience in an arena. Ready for blood. "You left booze stains all over the carpet. My parents are going to kill me." Brianna stops, seeing me here. She curls her lip in a sneer. "Uh, shouldn't you be gone already?"

I give a bitter laugh. "I wish."

"Leave it, Bree." Bliss sighs.

"Ex-cuuse me?" Brianna whirls around.

"You heard me." Her eyes narrow. "Shut up and stop being such a bitch."

Brianna's mouth drops open in shock. "What are you doing even talking to her?"

"Yeah!" Kaitlin elbows her way in again. "What's with you tonight? You ruined my dress!"

I'm ready to bail and leave these girls to their stupid drama, but then Bliss sets her face in a fierce glare and announces, "Well, you hooked up with Cameron, so I guess we're even now."

I stop. The clique gasps.

Kaitlin turns a bright shade of pink, spluttering. "That's, like, ridiculous!"

"No," Bliss says loudly. "What's ridiculous is thinking I wouldn't find out. Are you totally stupid, or just a total skank?"

Kaitlin's mouth drops open. The other girls stare at her, scandalized, and for a moment, it looks like Bliss will come out the victor in this showdown. Then Kaitlin launches herself at Bliss with an almighty screech. "You're lying!"

"Eugh ... Get off me!" Bliss backs up, trying to ward off Kaitlin's attack. "Owww!"

I watch them, amazed. Kaitlin's pulling at Bliss's hair with one hand, while the other swats away at her body, while Bliss struggles to push her away.

"You take it back!"

"I saw you with him, in the limo!" Their shrieks fill the yard, but neither girl manages a single decent punch. Nope, it's all girly scratching and hair-tugging as they reel back, dangerously close to the water.

God, these girls can't fight for anything.

I stay on the sidelines, wondering if I should step in, but finally, a guy pushes through the crowd and tries to separate them. "Kaitlin, let her go!" He drags her away, still kicking. "What are you doing? Get a grip!"

"On what?" Bliss recovers. "Your dick?"

I can't help it – I burst out laughing. But I'm the only one.

Cameron looks back and forth between them. His face changes, as slowly he realizes what's going on.

"B—" he starts, guilty, but Bliss just yanks her tank top back into place.

"Don't even try. You deserve each other." Bliss looks past him, at Brianna and all the other vultures, watching wide-eyed. "Hell, you all do."

For a second, it looks as if she's about to stalk off with her head held high, but then she pauses, and a wicked smile comes over her face. Two quick steps, and she's in front of Cameron, her hands planted firmly in the middle of his chest. She shoves him, hard.

He lands in the pool with an almighty splash.

She turns to Kaitlin.

"No way!" she screeches, but Bliss is already moving. They tussle for a moment, knocking into me, and then Kaitlin loses her footing. She grabs at Bliss, who yanks at my arm for balance.

For a moment, we're all teetering on the edge of the pool, then gravity takes over, and we fall.

Meg

"I'm thinking law, or maybe poli-sci, so that means Harvard – of course – and then Yale, Cornell, Columbia…" Tristan ticks them off. "My dad is pushing Duke, so we'll take a trip out to visit in the fall, but I don't know … I think I can do better."

"Mmmhmm," I murmur happily, perched just inches away from him. The party is winding down now – or at least, the music is – and people have split off into groups to laze around, talk, and even sleep; sprawled in piles of blankets in the darker corners of the house. Tristan drapes one arm over the back of the couch, his fingertips brushing my bare shoulder. The touch sends shivers through me, and in my breathless haze, it takes everything I have to even focus on a single word he says.

"It's the extracurriculars that kill you – you better look out for that," he's telling me helpfully, "but I've been packing my résumé with all that volunteering stuff since I was, like, in preschool. The only thing I'm not sure about is sports." He frowns, the light behind him shining through his hair in a perfect blond halo. "I've been on the swim team, but do you think that's enough?"

"I don't know, it should be." I lean forward to take a sip of my soda and then sit back, this time close enough for my whole left arm to press against his body. My thoughts scatter at the contact, but I recover. "I, umm, don't have any sports, and the guidance counselor said—"

"But it's kind of late to start anything," Tristan interrupts, still pondering his future applications. "They always can tell if you join stuff senior year. Maybe I should do another internship this summer. I'm already lined up at my dad's office, but I could throw in some time teaching, like, disadvantaged kids how to play softball. Two hits in one!"

"Right." I look up at his face: tanned, and perfect, and looking straight at me, as if there's nobody else around. I smile back at him. "That sounds like a great idea."

We stay in the den for a while, chatting about college applications and his plans for summer vacation, until a group of seniors arrives armed with pillows and claims the room as a designated sleep area.

"Who are you looking for?" Tristan asks as we wander back through the house.

"Oh, nobody." I take time to glance in every room, but I

haven't seen Jolene all night, and even Bliss has disappeared. She's probably camped out in Brianna's suite, back with all her real friends. Not that I can really blame her now – everything worked the way she promised. I turn to Tristan with an encouraging grin. "What were you saying, about Mexico?"

"Oh, yeah." Tristan brightens. "Everyone always just sticks to the beach, but I want to go trekking, out in the mountains. Maybe stay in one of the villages..."

He keeps talking for a while, but I let my attention drift, enjoying the envious looks from people as we pass, and the weight of his arm on my shoulder. This is what Bliss must take for granted every day: the sense of belonging, as if you have a place in the world carved just for you. No worries that nobody will talk to you, or that they'll turn away and laugh behind your back; this is what it's like on the inside. To be someone who matters.

"Amit, wait a sec." Tristan pauses to talk to one of his student government buddies, and I wait, patiently exchanging smiles with the other boy's girlfriend. Girlfriend. For the first time since he spoke to me, it occurs to me that I could make this last, make it become something *real*.

The thought blossoms in my mind, full of possibility.

Will tonight be my Cinderella story before everything shifts back to normal, or is this the start of a whole new life for me? Dating Tristan, getting invites to their parties and trips, making friends with the other girlfriends, actually showing up to the school events and organizing committees. I can see it now, unfolding ahead of me in a glitter of friendship and activity. Not just one, perfect prom night, but dozens more.

All senior year.

"Right, Meg?"

I realize Tristan is looking at me expectantly, so I give a grin and nod, even though I haven't followed a word of the conversation. It doesn't seem to matter; the boys barely pause before continuing, something about planning a fundraiser for next year.

"You're the other Meg, aren't you?" The other girl moves closer. It's the petite redhead I saw outside the country club, the one who rushed to be a part of the group photo. "I've seen you around, in school."

"That's right." I smile. "I think we have gym together."

She makes a face. "Volleyball, ack. I've only just figured out how to spike the ball, and we finish next week!"

We both laugh. "Anything's better than cross-country running," I confide. "I pretend to get my period so often, they're going to think I have weird health problems soon."

"Eww, girl talk." Her boyfriend catches my last words and grimaces, as if we're discussing something gross. "You two need some space?"

"Grow up!" The other Meg elbows him lightly, laughing. I watch them joke, wondering if I'll ever be so comfortable with a boy. Even now, I'm hyper-aware of Tristan's every move – whether he seems relaxed, if he's still smiling at me, or if his attention has drifted elsewhere. I see his eyes slip past me, so I tuck my arm through his.

"I could use another soda," I suggest, nodding toward

the kitchen. "Let's go see who's still awake."

He grins, pulls me closer. "You read my mind."

I exhale with relief.

We find his friend Kellan in the kitchen, surrounded by an avalanche of party debris. He's stacking empty cups into a tower on the counter top, slowly, as if it's a serious undertaking.

"What's up?" The boys exchange fist bumps and back-slaps; the rituals of popularity.

Kellan shrugs. "Nothing much. Things are winding down. Oh, wait, did you see what happened with Kaitlin?"

Tristan shakes his head, handing me a beer. I wait until he's turned away, and then casually switch it for a carton of juice.

"It was crazy." Kellan laughs. "B flipped out and, like, smashed a bottle over her head. Kaitlin went into total meltdown, ran out in tears."

I stop. Does he mean Bliss?

"Those girls, it's always drama, drama." Tristan rolls his eyes, unconcerned, as one of the other boys – Nico, I think – wanders in. I melt back against the fridge, making room for him to saunter past. Tristan slaps his back. "Hey, man, where you been?"

"Around." Nico begins shaking the cans of Pringles in turn, trying to find some remnants. He looks up, noticing me for the first time. "Hey, who's this?"

Tristan laughs. "It's Meg, from school. You know, Meg Zuckerman?"

I give an awkward wave.

Nico blinks. "No way."

"See, man, I told you she could be cute." Kellan looks back at me. "You know, if you lost those glasses and some weight. Right, dude?" He tosses one of the cups at Tristan. The tower wobbles.

"Right." Tristan grins, ruffling my hair affectionately. "Now look at you. The belle of the ball."

I stare at him, the warm haze of breathlessness parting for just a second as their words sink in.

"You want to head outside for a minute?" Tristan's breath is warm against my ear. He doesn't wait for a reply before taking my hand and tugging me gently out of the room. Nico and Kellan let him go without a word, now both deeply fascinated by the ever-growing stack of cups. I follow.

"I'm sorry about the guys. They can be kind of blunt." Tristan squeezes my hand as we slip out a side door. It's silent here, shaded from the backyard by trees and a canopy of vines strung up on an elaborate trellis. There's a winding paved path and even the low bubble of a fountain – the perfect romantic retreat. I look around, my stomach already fluttering with nerves. A cute boy, a secluded spot, moonlight – well, the glow from inside the house – I know what this means. My pulse jumps; my legs feel numb. He's going to kiss me.

And not just any kiss. My first.

"It's just kind of a surprise, that's all." Tristan is still talking. "You know, one minute you're just Meg, and the next, you're … wow." He smiles at me with that charming half grin I've been pining over all year.

I catch my breath. This is it.

He knows it, too. Taking both my hands in his, he pulls me closer. Everything is in slow motion now – the scene that's played over in my mind dozens of times. I've felt foolish, being so inexperienced when other girls my age are off doing, well, all kinds of things, but right now it feels worth it. Perfect.

His head dips to mine and I close my eyes, feel the warmth of his face brush mine. Then it happens: Tristan Carmichael kisses me. It's soft, and gentle, and everything I could ever want.

One minute you're just Meg...

The voice pops out of nowhere. I try to ignore it, to focus on Tristan's lips instead, and the hand he's placed against my cheek. I don't want to get this part wrong, so I press closer against that swim team chest. The kiss deepens.

Now look at you, the belle of the ball.

Tristan's words from before break my concentration, but this time, I feel myself snap out of the moment, as if I'm separating from my body. The magic dissolves. His lips are just lips; his hands, just hands. We're not so much kissing as pressing parts of our bodies together, like complete strangers.

The delicious flutter turns to frustration. Here I am, in the middle of a moment I'll remember for the rest of my life, and all I can think about is a random comment. What's wrong with me?

Tristan clearly isn't so distracted: his hands are

roaming across my back and hips, tongue exploring my mouth. I pull away, breaking for air.

"It's, umm, really pretty out here!" I say, feeling like an awkward kid. I've ruined it now; I can tell.

But Tristan doesn't seem to think so. He just gives me that smile again and leans back in. "I know," he whispers, pushing a tendril of hair from my face. "It's really pretty right here, too."

I duck away. "I like the way they've done the garden!" I babble. "To make it look natural like this? I hate it when it's just neat rows of flowers, and—"

A frown flickers across his face. "Is something wrong?"

I blink. "No," I say quickly, "everything's … great."

"Good." Tristan steps toward me, placing me lightly back against the wall. I close my eyes and feel him kiss me again, but my mind won't stop now; something has been triggered, and now all I can hear is the wave of rebellious thoughts.

Since when should I have to cover myself in make-up and bare half my body just to get noticed by these people?

Tristan is still up against me, but I barely register him. Instead, I finally realize what's wrong with this perfect picture.

I pull free from his embrace.

"What's the matter now?" He sighs impatiently but quickly covers it with another encouraging grin. "It's OK. Nobody's going to find us. They're all off asleep now."

But that's not the point. I take another step away from

him, away from everything I thought I wanted. I can't believe I'm doing this. After all this time, all those math classes spent daydreaming about his arms around me, and here I am turning him down? I swallow, wondering how on earth I can explain. "I'm sorry," I manage to say. "This was a mistake."

Tristan blinks. "But I thought ... I mean, you like me."

He says it with such certainty that any last doubt I have disappears.

"I did," I admit, blushing. "So much. But you didn't like me. Not at all, not until all this."

I gesture at the hair, the dress, the shiny, sexy costume that somehow caught his attention in a way that "just Meg" never did. Because the fact is, he's looked right past me all year. Even in my old gown, I didn't register – like I don't exist unless I fit their weird category of hotness. I suppose that's what they don't tell you about makeovers in the movies – that maybe the people who gasp with grand double takes aren't worth the effort. Because if I don't deserve his attention when I'm myself, then what good is he?

"Thanks for tonight," I tell him quietly. "I had fun."

"I don't understand." Tristan can't seem to process the fact of me turning him down. He pushes his hair back, staring at me in frustration. "I thought this was what you wanted!"

I give him a faint smile, turning to go.

"I changed my mind."

• • •

I slip back through the house, retrieving my purse from where I hid it under a pile of coats in the hallway. I feel a pang, just leaving like this, but I suppose if Bliss and Jolene wanted to say good-bye, they would have by now. Perhaps they've already gone. I take one last look at the party – my prom night over, at last – and then hurry out of the front door.

It's not until I'm halfway down the steps that I remember: Bliss switched purses with me to match the dress; there's nothing in her bag but lip gloss, tape, and a wedge of photocopies, folded over to fit. My car keys are nowhere to be found.

Perfect.

Collapsing on the steps, I stare blankly at the dark lawn. I'm worn out, my contacts itch, and all I want is to curl up in bed at home, but now I have to search the house for her – and that's if she hasn't left already. So much for an airtight alibi; arriving home in a cab or calling to get picked up here might be the smallest hint to my dad that I haven't spent the night at an innocent all-girl slumber party. My gaze falls on the papers, the reason all of this even began. It seems like a lifetime ago that Bliss was so determined to make Kaitlin and Cameron pay. Well, was it worth it?

Skimming the first pages, I begin to read. Page after page of Kaitlin's immature whining, about Bliss and Brianna and Cameron, and then—

I stop, horrified.

Oh, God, what have we done?

Leaping up, I sprint back into the house and search

every room in turn. There's no sign of Bliss anywhere, so I head out to the back patio, scanning the yard. People are grouped around, laughing at something down by the pool, so I trip down the steps, jostling in the crowd until I see them. Jolene and Bliss hauling are themselves out of the water, completely soaked.

"Hey, guys, I need to talk to you." Finally, I break through the onlookers.

"I can't believe you just did that!" Another girl – Kaitlin, I think – is still splashing around in the water, but I don't have time to figure this out. "Bliss, Jolene, come on!"

They ignore me. "Couldn't you keep me out of it?" Jolene shakes water from her hair. The ruffles are hanging in damp clumps from her chest, the fabric almost transparent.

"You were the one who got in the way!" Bliss wipes water from her eyes. "You should have just stayed back."

"Listen!" I grab an arm from each of them and drag them a safe distance away from the crowd. "We've got a serious problem!"

"You mean besides Bliss's unresolved anger issues?" Jolene smirks.

"*I'm* the angry one? You—"

"Shut up!" I interrupt. "We don't have time for this." I pick a page and begin to read. "'I can't believe anyone would have sex with her, and now the sad bitch is pregnant!'"

Bliss looks confused. "What is that?"

"Kaitlin's diary," I tell them grimly. "Miranda Jones

had an abortion. Uma Pearson cheated on her SATs. Kenji Anede spent a month in rehab last summer for an eating disorder – it goes on and on." I look between them, trying to make them understand just how bad it is. "This isn't just about Kaitlin's secrets; don't you see? She found out all kinds of dirt on everyone else. And we gave it away."

Bliss

Oh, crap.

Right away, I forget about the pool and the fight and the cold water dripping down my body. I snatch the Xeroxed pages from Meg, frantically scanning through the scrawled print. But she's right; the secrets are all there, laid out in Kaitlin's stupid curly writing for anyone to see.

Jolene sighs at me. "God, did you even read it?"

"Not everything!" I protest. "I was just finding parts about Kaitlin and the boys she was hooking up with." But now that I'm looking for it, I can see the names of the other girls buried in sections about Kaitlin's fat thighs and how much she hates Nikki. I groan. "She must have been keeping this stuff as blackmail, or some weird power trip. How was I supposed to know?"

"Right," Jolene snipes, sarcastic. "Because why would you pay attention to anything that isn't all about you?"

"It doesn't matter how it happened," Meg tells her before I can answer. "What matters is what we do now."

Jolene shrugs, scrunching water from her dress. "Why do we have to do anything at all?"

"Are you serious?" Meg glares at her. "Can you just imagine what will happen to them if that information gets spread around? All it would take is one mention on the school network, or for Jason to pass the diary on to someone else…"

I shiver at the thought. Those girls don't deserve it. God, even Kaitlin wasn't cruel enough for that. No, this was all my doing. I didn't mean to, but that doesn't make a difference when it comes to gossip and rumors. All their darkest secrets, and now I've let them loose. How could I miss this stuff?

"Meg, let it go." Jolene shrugs. "We left the diary in his room hours ago."

"Exactly." Meg stands firm. "And now we've got to get it back."

"Back?" Jolene looks up. "It's four thirty in the morning!"

"So what?" Meg is riled up now, her face totally serious. "We don't have a choice. Right, Bliss?" She appeals to me, but I don't need convincing.

"She's right," I say, already sick with guilt. "Kenji, Miranda – they're good people. We've got to make this right. All of us," I add, before she can pull a tantrum and bail again.

Meg and I stare at her, determined: two against one. Jolene shifts and sighs, but finally she rolls her eyes. "Fine, whatever. But this is it. Nothing else."

"Good."

We squelch along behind her as Meg leads us back through the house. Nearly everyone's crashed out now, but I don't even want to think about how I look. The pajama outfit that was sweet and adorable is now clinging to my skin like I'm an extra in some X-rated rap video.

"If we're lucky, he drank so much he's still passed out somewhere," I tell them, trying to focus on a plan. "We can snatch the diary back, and it'll be like we were never even there."

"Aren't you going to say good-bye to all your friends?" Jolene can't resist digging at me as I find Meg's purse and pass her the car keys. "Or you can go out a different exit, so they don't see us together."

"It's kind of late for that," I mutter. And it's true. As we head to the hall, I see Kaitlin come through the side door, wrapped in a bathrobe, with her damp hair scraped back. She catches sight of me and glares, then Courtney and Brianna appear behind her, all stopping dead the moment they see me. My friends. Or, at least they used to be, but now they're lined up like some kind of firing squad, ready to throw me out for crimes against the social order. Any chance at all I could smooth things over with them dies with the ice-queen looks they all shoot my way.

Never mind the scene with Kaitlin; leaving with Jolene and Meg is definitely going to get me exiled from their group forever.

It's too late to take it back, even if I wanted to. I keep walking.

Nobody says much as we pile into the car and take the exit out of town – again. Meg hums softly along with the radio, while Jolene kicks her bare feet up on the dashboard. At least now I've got her in a confined space, without any water nearby. Or weapons. All the same, I check that her backpack is stashed out of her reach before leaning forward.

"Jolene," I try. "Jolene, would you just listen to me? You heard me back there. I told them all where to go! You can't still be mad."

Jolene messes with her hair, ignoring me.

"I know I should have said something before, in the living room. I just wimped out, OK? But I made it right in the end."

She looks out the window.

"OK." I sink back onto the damp seat. "Be like that." I turn to Meg instead. "How did it go with Tristan? Did he mind your leaving?"

She meets my eyes in the mirror. "No, he was fine with it."

I begin to get a bad feeling. Another one. "But it all worked out, right?" I ask, anxious. After everything, I wanted Meg to get the night of her dreams. "I saw you together. You looked like you were having a great time."

"Yes." She gives this quiet grin. "It was all perfect. For a while, anyway."

"So what happened? I don't understand."

Meg shrugs, her hair falling in a dark wave. "I'm not that girl. And I don't want to be."

She doesn't seem sad about it, just calm – content, even – so I give up trying to make conversation and just let the dark highway speed by. None of us got what we wanted tonight, I realize. Jolene wound up burning that painting to ash, Meg isn't snuggling happily-ever-after with Tristan, and as for my grand secret revenge ... not so secret anymore.

It was worth it, though, all of it. I pull the blanket around my damp clothes, surprised to feel relief wash through my whole body as I think of their icy stares. I'm done with them now. Kaitlin's backstabbing, Brianna's power plays. The gossip, the drama, all that effort to stay part of the loop and on top of things. I can stay in bed all weekend if I want instead of trekking to the mall with the girls. I can roll out of bed without spending twenty minutes blow-drying my hair in the morning. I can eat carbs.

I'm done with them.

But almost as soon as it comes, the relief slips into panic. What am I supposed to do now? I think of telling Mom that the spa days are off, that all her friends' daughters hate my guts. And summer's coming now – months without a single party invite or girl to hang out with. The worst-case scenario I've been fighting all night to avoid is looming ahead of me; only it turns out, I chose it for myself.

Way to go, Bliss.

I'm still running through ways to avoid total social leper status (go emo, join band, become one of those drama kids) when I realize the car is making a weird clunking noise. "Uh, Meg?" I sit up. "What's that noise?"

"I don't know!" She slows down as we all listen to the splutter.

"And why is the warning light flashing?" Jolene looks over. "Are we out of gas?"

"We can't be." Meg checks the dashboard, worried. "I filled up on our way back, remember?"

The car lurches suddenly. Meg swears under her breath and then yanks the wheel, pulling off onto the side of the road just as the engine cuts out entirely and we roll to a stop.

For a second, there's silence. It's still pretty dark outside, with no light from houses or anything along the highway. And, I realize with a sinking heart, no other cars around either.

"I'll go see what's wrong." Meg unbuckles her seat belt and gets out of the car. I watch through the windshield as she yanks up the hood. A hiss of steam billows up, and she jumps back.

"That can't be good," I mutter, scrambling to follow. Jolene doesn't reply, but she pulls her shoes back on and soon, all three of us are staring into the mess of cables and metal.

"I don't suppose either of you took auto shop?" I say hopefully. They don't reply. I was tempted for a while – I mean, a whole class of guys – but Kaitlin convinced me that getting engine grease under our manicures was going too far in pursuit of hot guys. Right now, I wish I'd held out: bad nails seem like a way better option than getting stranded on the side of the highway in the middle of the night.

"I better go call triple A," Meg says at last, heading back to the passenger side. She retrieves some papers from the glove compartment and begins to dial. Jolene wanders away from the car, wrapping her arms around herself, her wet dress still sticking to her skin.

"Are you cold?" I ask, offering the blanket. She turns away. "Aw, come on." I sigh. This whole martyr act is getting old. She's stalking around like I committed the worst crimes ever, but even if I did let her down – for five whole minutes – I'm trying to make up for it now. Not that she'll let me. "Can you just give it up already? I've said I'm sorry. Let's just go back to being" – I pause – "well, whatever we were before."

It wasn't friends, exactly, but it wasn't this either.

"No." Jolene folds her arms. She looks at me with disdain – not the snooty looks Kaitlin and co. were shooting at me, but something colder, like I'm just dead to her. It's so blank, I have to take a step back, but I won't let her just block me out like this.

"What's your problem?" I break. "Do you have any idea what I gave up back there? My friends are never going to speak to me again!"

Jolene snorts, kicking gravel along the road. "Great friends."

"Because you'd know all about that," I shoot back.

"Seeing as you don't have any!"

"Better that than putting up with those dumb bitches all day. *Ooh, Brianna, what do you think of this lip gloss? I don't know; does it match my bra?* For God's sake, get a freaking brain!"

"And you sit around debating politics or whatever?" I yell. "At least I won't end up in jail before the end of summer!"

"Only because your rich-bitch parents will pull enough strings to get you out!"

"That's enough!" Meg suddenly steps between us. She glares. "Both of you, over there."

"What?" Jolene stares.

"Line up, against the car."

I blink, but there's something kind of terrifying in her voice, so I shuffle over to where she's pointing. Jolene doesn't budge.

"NOW!"

She moves.

"What's going on?" I ask when we're both up against the side of the car like this is a police raid. The highway is empty and dark, nothing but our headlights for miles around. "Did you get through to triple A?"

"Yes, but they won't be able to come pick us up for hours. And I'm not going to stand here, listening to you two bitch at each other." Meg folds her arms, glaring at us. "So, Bliss, apologize."

"I already did," I complain, "like, a hundred times." I'm surprised by how *bossy* she's being. I'm beginning to understand how Frankenstein must have felt: I've created a monster here.

Meg stands her ground. "Yes, but the point of an apology is to make the other person feel better. And since Jolene clearly doesn't, you need to do it again." She waits, standing tall, a lifetime away from that girl who used to flinch when I looked her in the eyes. But now, she means business, so I sigh.

"I'm sorry I blew you off at the party," I say for what feels like the hundredth time. I shoot Jolene a sideways look. "I ... I was a bitch. And wrong. But I made up for it!"

She shrugs, still avoiding my eyes. "Too little, too late. Just because you made a scene with Kaitlin, it doesn't undo being a bitch to me."

"See?" I appeal to Meg, since she's apparently the one in charge here. "I tried!"

Meg sighs. "Jolene, let it go. She's not your father."

"Uh, what?" We both look up.

"Well, obviously she's not your father," Meg tells Jolene. "But you're acting like she is. You're so angry at him, you're putting all that pain on everyone else. Bliss and Dante, too. Classic transference."

Jolene clenches her fists beside me, and for a second I wonder if she's going to lunge right at Meg. We're stranded way out in the middle of nowhere here, and it would be a while before the ambulance could get to us... "What makes you the psychological expert?" she growls.

Meg shrugs, like she doesn't realize just how close she is to a full-body cast. "Nothing but a couple years of therapy. I get it, Jolene; I do. They both messed up, and you've got a right to be mad at them."

"Thanks for validating my feelings," Jolene mutters, sarcastic.

"But in case you haven't noticed, they're trying to make it right. Bliss apologized, Dante showed up." Meg sighs. "So are you really going to keep punishing them, just because your dad is the one who's still letting you down?"

There's silence.

I wait, expecting some kind of carnage – literally. I can't believe Meg has the nerve to say all of this, and more than that, I can't believe Jolene is even letting her.

Then Jolene exhales, and it's like all the fight goes out of her body. "Fine," she murmurs, sagging back against the car. "You're sorry. I get it. We're cool."

I blink. Is she serious? "Umm, OK." I look carefully, but she doesn't seem angry anymore, just worn out. I guess carrying all that anger around can really take it out of you.

Meg claps her hands together in triumph. "There you go. Now, hug."

"What?" I blink. "Come on, what is this, a Lifetime movie?"

But she insists. "Hug!"

Jolene and I look at each other, rolling our eyes, but Meg is waiting, so I awkwardly reach out and pat her shoulder. Her body is stiff, like she's not used to the contact. "Well, come on." Jolene sighs, holding an arm out to Meg. "Since we're doing this whole girly bonding thing."

She bounces over to us, and for a moment, we hug.

Then Jolene detaches herself, brushing her body down like she might have caught something from the brief show of intimacy. "So, what's the plan? We hang out here until the tow truck comes?"

"But what about the diary?" I panic. "We can't leave it until tomorrow – he might read it before then!"

"We can't call our parents," Meg adds. "They think we're all tucked safe asleep somewhere. If my dad knows I lied about staying over with Bliss…"

I think fast. And then the answer arrives – a way to solve two problems in one. "I know who we can call," I say, smiling.

"Who?" Meg asks, but I don't reply. My phone is nestled by the front seat where I left it, so I scan through to find that number he gave me when we were at the Loft. Just in case, he told me. I edge a safe distance away from the others and dial. It takes a few rings, but finally someone picks up.

"Hey," I say, crossing my fingers. "This is Bliss. Remember, we met earlier?"

There's a pause, and then, "What's happened? Is Jolene OK?"

I knew it. His voice is anxious, and nobody gets that worked up over just a friend. I can't help but smile. Despite all her ice-queen bitching at him, Dante is still totally hung up on Jolene.

"Yes, she's fine," I reassure him, sneaking a look at where she's lighting up another cigarette. She doesn't know it, but I'm doing her a major favor here. "The thing is, we're kind of stuck. Can you come give us a ride?"

JOLENE

I sit on the trunk of Meg's car, idly swinging my legs as we wait for Bliss's mystery friend to come pick us up. It's a warm night, but my dress is still wet through, and every breeze sends a shiver right through me.

"Will you take the blanket?" Bliss sighs, leaning against the car. "Catching a chill isn't, like, some moral victory."

I finally take it. "Thanks."

"No problem." She beams. "It was worth it though, right? I can still picture Kaitlin's face, when she came up for air..."

"It was a treat," I agree. There's a pause. "So, you really won't be going back to them?"

"Who? Brianna and that group? No." Bliss lets out a bitter laugh. "That's pretty much done. You're looking at the latest outcast of East Midlands High." She strikes a pose, but I can tell from the flicker in her expression that this is no joke. That was her life back there she just destroyed, I realize. It may have been shallow and false, and built on a foundation of bitching and unstable foot-wear, but that doesn't mean it didn't matter.

"You'll be OK," I tell her quietly. "I mean, sure, it's not going to be easy, but you'll do fine without them."

"I know, but…" Bliss exhales, giving me a rueful smile as she admits, "I've never been that good on my own."

"So, you won't be," I tell her, gazing out at the black highway. "You've got Meg for next year – she's going to need someone to stop her from slipping back into wall-flower mode." We both grin. "And," I add cautiously, "I'm going to be stuck around town. For the summer, at least. We could, I don't know, hang out. Maybe."

"Really?" She looks up at me, hopeful. With all that makeup and the fancy hairstyle washed away, she looks like a real person for a change; not that overdone, syn-thetic girl she used to be. Who knows? She might just be a good influence on me – all that normal teenage fun. My mom would be so proud.

"Yeah, well, you can be OK, if you try." I remember that look of hers just before she began hurling people into the pool. That Bliss, I can deal with.

"You're not too bad, either." Bliss grins.

Meg comes around, depositing our purses and clothes in a heap on the asphalt. She's taken her contacts out and pulled a gray zip-up hoodie over that white flouncy dress. "I've locked everything up and left a note for the tow truck," she says, twisting some hair around her finger in thought. "What am I forgetting?"

"Nothing," Bliss says. She straightens as a pair of headlights approaches on the horizon, drawing closer. "And here's our ride."

I pause, watching as the beat-up Camaro slows and pulls up alongside. My heart skips, but it's not until the driver climbs out and saunters toward us that I realize why.

Dante.

"You know that nice stuff I was just saying about you?" I tell Bliss through gritted teeth. "I take it all back."

"Come on," she says. "Don't tell me you're not happy to see him."

Not happy so much as sick with sudden nerves. But before I can reply, she dances over and throws her arms around him, gushing thanks for helping us out. He's still wearing that leather jacket, his eyes dark in the shadows of the headlights. But I don't need to see: I know that boy by heart.

"We only need a ride to the campus and back," she promises. "It's an emergency, I swear."

"Sure, no problem." He steps into the light, giving a lazy grin. It widens as he looks her up and down. "Do I, uh, need to ask what happened to you guys?"

I fold my arms defensively, but Bliss just laughs. "Just a thing with my ex and a pool. Hope you don't mind damp spots!"

"In this old thing?" Dante grins good-naturedly. "She's seen worse, I promise."

The other girls climb in the car, already telling him about the dorm we need, and where would be best to park, but I hang back, reluctant. He hasn't said a word to me yet. He hasn't so much as looked in my direction. After that fight we had back at the warehouse, I can't say I'm surprised, but his indifference stings more than any angry glare ever could.

"Jolene, come on!" Meg instructs, hanging out the front passenger door. I brace myself. Means to an end, I tell myself; he's just the means to a necessary end. Clambering in the backseat, I slam the door, and we go.

Meg and Bliss chat the whole way, giving him an edited version of our diary quest. They laugh and joke, happy about our rescue, but I curl up, silent as the dark streets speed by. After everything that's happened, my defenses are down and Dante's presence is overwhelming. He hasn't looked my way since that glance, but I can feel him all the same – every smile and nod of his head, every idle finger-drum on the steering wheel. I watch his profile, lit up in the glare of passing cars, eyes fixed on the road. It would be a comfort to be near him again, if it wasn't for the ugly things we said just a few hours ago. The yelling, the frustration in his eyes.

He's out of reach now.

"I'll go," Bliss says when we arrive on campus. The quad is empty, the earlier partiers all safe asleep – or passed out somewhere. "Shouldn't be long. Third floor, right?"

"Yup." Meg nods. "Good luck!"

We watch her hurry over to the front entrance. It's

locked tight, but, after a moment, a security guard comes to the door.

"I am going to sleep sooo late tomorrow." Meg yawns. "I mean, today."

Dante laughs. "Not a natural party animal, huh?"

"Um, no," she admits.

"Jolene should give you some tips," he says casually, still not looking back at me. "She's gone days straight on nothing but caffeine and bagels."

The memory is sharp: me and Dante in this car, with nothing but open roads and Lyle Lovett on the radio. "My seventeenth birthday," I answer, my voice sounding like it belongs to someone else. "We drove to Philly for that Thermals show, and then just kept going to make the date in New York."

Meg twists around to look at me. "You went cross-country?"

I shrug. "Sure, it was fun." We planned to go abroad, too, one of those days. Europe. South America. Dante had an itch; he used to want to see it all. Maybe he still does.

"My dad won't even let me leave the state. Not without him and Stella," Meg says wistfully.

"We'll work on that," I tell her, managing a smile. "Who knows; maybe by the end of summer, we'll get you as far as DC."

She looks at me, and then her face breaks out into a brilliant grin. "Maybe we will."

"Here's your girl." Dante nods. Bliss is hurrying back from the dorm. She climbs into the backseat next to me, already shaking her head.

"No go. It's a different guard now – he won't let me up. They shut the party down hours ago, and now he's only letting in residents with ID."

We all exhale.

"Didn't you try to make an excuse or something?" I ask, frustrated.

Bliss looks insulted. "What do you think? I said I was his sister, visiting from out of town. But he didn't budge. He's kind of an ass," she adds, frowning. "I mean, imagine if it was true – where does he think I'm going to sleep?"

I slump back. "So, what now?"

"We can't just give up," Meg insists. "Remember what's in that diary – we've got to get it back. Tonight."

"But how?" Bliss asks. "I mean, I tried everything in there. I even cried!"

We're silent. Then Dante speaks. "What's the setup in there? Do you sign in, or what?"

Bliss thinks, "Umm, there's a card swipe on the main door. But even if we get someone to let us in, they're not allowed to sign in guests after midnight. And this guy doesn't leave his desk."

"Huh..." Dante pauses, and I just know his mind is ticking over something. Give him long enough, and he could steal the Declaration of Independence. "Jolene, you still got that hack from Eli?"

He's speaking to me.

"Uh, yeah." I manage to recover. My heart pounds as I finally meet his eyes. "It's in my bag."

"OK." He nods, beginning to curl his lips in a smile. "And do you think you guys could find an ID? It doesn't have to be from this dorm, just a college one."

"You mean we jam the entry system and then bluff our way in?" Meg brightens, way ahead of me. "That could work. The library should be open all night, and I could try and borrow someone's card…"

"Perfect." Bliss bounces out of the car. "You go take care of that, and I'll go back and work on the guard, in case he breaks."

They slam the doors. It's just me and Dante now. Silent.

"Wait a minute." I scramble out and hurry after them. "What do I do? I should go with you, Meg, to help out."

"Nope." Bliss stops and gives me that grin again, the devious one. "She's the one with the access there, and we don't want to draw attention to ourselves, do we?"

"But—" I look back at the car. At Dante. "You can't leave me alone with him," I whisper.

"You'll be fine." Meg looks amused. "He won't bite."

"Unless you're lucky," Bliss adds, giggling.

"Guys!" I cry. They don't understand; this isn't a joke. "Please…"

"Try starting with an apology," Meg advises, already backing away. Then she pauses and gives me a curious smile. "He came, you know. To prom. I saw him outside, all dressed up. I'm guessing that was for you."

And then they split off in different directions and leave me here to my fate.

. . .

He showed up.

I don't go back to the car. The thought of sitting there in icy silence with Dante is worse than the night chill, so I wander down the sidewalk a ways until I reach one of the benches overlooking the quad. Not that there's much to overlook: a dark patch of grass and the looming ugly concrete buildings all around. Ivy League, this isn't. A lone neon lamp washes me in a thin pool of light. Hugging my knees to my chest, I wait.

He showed up to prom. After all this time, he remembered too – found a tux, came back down from college. That has to mean something. And even though I screwed everything up with my stupid, blind quest to even the score with my dad, Meg's revelation still fills me with the smallest bit of hope.

If he gets out of the car, there's still a chance for me.

I repeat it like a mantra, watching groups of drunken stragglers stumble back to the dorms. The minutes stretch out, but still I hope. If he gets out of the car, maybe this can be mended, somehow. If he comes to talk to me, then he still cares. Part of me wants to march right up to him and demand forgiveness – I'm not the kind of girl to ever wait around for a guy to make his move – but some instinct tells me that I can't force this.

Five minutes turn into ten, and soon my butt is numb from the hard seat and I've got goose bumps all over my body. And he hasn't gotten out of the car.

I'm surprised to feel a sob well, stinging in the back of

my throat. I've been fooling myself all year into thinking I'm better off without him – better without a friend who could just bail like that. But it's a lie. He went because I pushed him. I pushed them all. Hell, I've been sabotaging any chance I have of being happy – too angry to see past my dad, and the sneers around town, and all the ways this world is stacked against people like me. But what can that anger change, in the end?

Not one damn thing, except to prove them right.

I sink back, miserable. It's ironic, I know. Now, when I finally understand what he's been trying to tell me all this time, I can't do anything to change it.

"Are you trying to catch your death?"

His voice jolts me back with a lurch. Dante is standing a few paces away, hands in his pockets and hair in his eyes. He's casual and irritated, sure, but he's here.

I stop breathing.

"You sound like my mom," I tell him, trying to stay cool.

"Your mom's got the right idea." He sighs, peeling off his jacket. "Here, you're turning blue."

"Better than the pink," I quip softly.

Dante drapes it over my shoulders, still warm from his body. I snuggle down, breathing in leather and tobacco and the unmistakable scent of him. He hovers for a moment, tapping a cigarette against his thigh.

"You haven't quit yet?"

He gives me a twisted smile and then sits. "Clearly, my willpower needs some work."

"I should give it up too," I say quietly. "All my bad habits."

"Oh, yeah?" Dante laughs, dubious.

"Really."

There's silence. I try to find the words to say anything at all, but my tongue is thick with panic. I can't even look at him.

"Those two have come around." Dante relaxes back, stretching. "Bliss, and that Meg girl. You whipped them into shape, huh?"

I swallow. "More like the other way around, I think."

"Oh?"

I run my fingers over the jagged edge of the zipper, more nervous than I think I've ever been in my life. Even opening those college letters, I had my defenses up – expecting the worst. Now it feels like my chest is cranked wide open, and my heart is beating and bloody for him to see.

"You were right." My voice almost breaks with effort to get the words out, but then it's done, and they're sitting heavy in the air between us. "What you said back at the office. About me, about everything." I inhale a shaky breath, and then give him the one thing I've got left. The only thing I can.

"I'm sorry."

Pulling some last store of hope, I move my hand until it's touching his. A breath, and then I curl my fingers around his palm.

He doesn't respond for the longest time; I can't even tell if he moves. But staring out into the dark, his hand warm beneath mine, I feel my nerves slips away. Instead, I feel a wash of calm. So he forgives me, or he doesn't – that part is out of my control. But the rest of my life? That's stretching ahead of me, warm with a new kind of possibility. College, some attempt at new friendships maybe, try to let that fury ebb away. The world won't wipe my slate clean so easily, but I can do it, for myself.

I can do this.

And then Dante pulls away.

"No." He gets to his feet, not looking at me. His shoulders are tense, his body tall and stiff. "It's too late for this, Jolene. It's all too late."

I stop breathing.

"I'll be in the car. Let me know when the others get back." With an awkward shrug, he turns to go.

"Wait!" I call, but he keeps walking. "Dante!" I sprint after him, desperate. Suddenly, all that zen resignation falls to nothing. Screw waiting for him to forgive me, screw not forcing anything at all. I can't let him walk away this time. "Dante, listen to me!"

I grab his arm, pulling him to a stop.

"What?" He snatches away from me. "Don't you get it? There's nothing you can say."

"But…"

"I gave you chances. I've been waiting all year!" Dante exclaims. "But you didn't apologize. You didn't see you had anything to be sorry for!"

I stare at him, paralyzed.

"See?" Dante exhales, the fight suddenly going out of

him. He gives me a smile, faint. Sad. "You know I'm right, Jolene. We could have been something, but … it's time we just moved on." He backs away and then leaves, a silhouette in the dark.

I watch him go, stricken.

"But I love you!"

My voice echoes out across the dark quad.

He stops.

"I love you." I yell it again, loud and certain. It sounds crazy, a last-ditch fight to make him stay, but every word of it is true. I catch up with Dante, moving so I block his way.

"Jolene—" His face twists, but I don't wait to let him tell me no again. With my blood pounding in my ears, I take two quick steps toward him and reach up, kissing him with everything I have.

He freezes, motionless against me.

Nothing.

Slowly, my courage fades, and in its place, I just feel a deep flush of embarrassment.

What the hell am I thinking?

"I … I'm sorry." I reel back, looking anywhere but at him. "I get it. You don't—"

And then his mouth is on mine, arms locked tight around my waist. He kisses me hard, like it's the end of the world, and there's nothing left but us: lips and hands and hot breath against my cheek. I feel my whole body relax against him, overcome with relief.

"You mean it?" he says, finally breaking for air. He looks at me with an intensity that sets fire, bright in my chest. "You're done with this bullshit? Because I swear, Jolene, I can't watch you do this anymore. I just can't."

"I promise. It's over." I meet his eyes, trying to make him see that I mean it. "I don't want to screw this up again. It's not just you," I add, hesitant. I don't want to sound like I'm making any less of what he means to me, but this has never just been about him. "It's ... my life. I need to make it different this time."

But Dante doesn't take it wrong; he just breaks into a grin. "About time."

He lifts me suddenly, swinging me around in a circle. I laugh, clutching at him in surprise. "Dante!" I swat his head. "Put me down!"

"OK." He sets me down with my back hard against the car, and suddenly my laughter fades. I look at him, breathless.

"So we're doing this?" I ask, still nervous. How is it even going to work? Just the summer before he's back at college, trying to paste over the raw gaps we both left behind. There'll be no hiding here: it's all or nothing.

He leans close, touches his lips gently to my forehead. "Hell yes," he whispers, and then that grin is back, and he's kissing me hard enough to make me believe everything's going to be just fine.

Meg

The library is almost deserted now, and even the security guard just waves me in with a yawn, barely moving from his seat by the front entrance. The building is eerily still: fluorescent lights bright overhead, and not even the usual hushed murmurs to be heard among the tall stacks. I try not to shiver. Quiet is good, especially when you're about to "obtain" official identification cards, but I can't help wishing for more than a few sleeping bodies slumped over their books for company. Although...

Slipping silently past the empty tables, I creep up behind one of the students – facedown in a large textbook, unmoving. I can't believe I'm doing this, but I carefully scope his desk: highlighters, note cards, and – yes! – the pale edge of his student ID card, peeking out from under his right elbow. I hover there for a moment, just to be sure, but he lets out a snuffle and then settles again, his breathing steady and slow. Perfect.

Leaning in, I reach for the card, easing it out from under him with the very tips of my fingers. Slowly, slowly … I hold my breath, tugging it closer until—

"Meg!"

I startle at the noise, knocking into the sleeping boy. He jerks awake under me, making a grunt of confusion. I leap back.

"Hey, I thought it was you!"

I whirl around. The boy from before, Scott, is hurrying down the stairs toward me. He looks tired but happy, his T-shirt wrinkled and his sandy hair all messed up. He comes to a stop in front of me, breathless. "You switched outfits again; I nearly didn't recognize you. What are you?" He grins. "Some kind of secret agent?"

I gulp, glancing back at my target. He's frowning, still sleepy, but beginning to register the noise.

"Whas goin' on?" The boy yawns, looking around. I panic.

"Nothing!" I squeak, backing away. Scott opens his mouth, so I pull him after me, dashing into the library stacks until we're out of sight, surrounded by tall rows of books and abandoned stepladders.

I catch my breath, leaning against a section of ancient philosophy. "Sorry," I manage to say. "I was, umm, in the middle of something."

"Should I even ask, or is this top secret too?" Scott raises his eyebrows. He peers around a shelf and scans the floor, hand above his eyes in an exaggerated gesture. He ducks back. "All clear. He's napping again."

"Thanks." I relax. Then I think of the last time I saw him – and my less than polite exit. "Did it go all right, with those sorority girls?" I bite my lip, remembering their wrath. "Sorry I had to bail like that, but..."

"But they were pretty mad," he agrees. "It's OK. I threw down gossip magazines to distract them, and eventually they went looking for easier prey."

I blink, but then the edge of his lip tugs in a grin, and I realize that he's joking.

"Oh." I laugh. "Good move. Although, maybe you should keep a spare *US Weekly* on you, just in case they come back. Or some diet snack bars."

"Not that, you know, we're making shallow assumptions about those fine members of the college community," he adds, mock-serious.

"Of course not." I grin.

There's a pause. Scott tilts his head to look at me. I shift slightly under his gaze, but I'm surprised to find I don't feel self-conscious in this dress anymore. I stand a little straighter. "There was this party," I say, waving my hand vaguely. "I was ... trying to impress someone."

He nods. "So, what's is latest mission you're on?"

"I'm not sure I'm at liberty to tell you..." I reply, but my voice comes out more teasing than I meant.

He laughs. "Well, if you need any help, I just finished up here for the night."

"This late? Ouch."

"Finals," he agrees, looking briefly woeful. "So if you

can give me any distraction at all..."

"Well." I pause, but it doesn't just seem like an empty offer; Scott hoists up his book bag and waits expectantly. "I need to borrow an ID to break into Westville dorm." I tell him matter-of-factly. "In the next ten minutes or so."

He stops. "Wait, you're serious?" He laughs. "You really are a little criminal, aren't you?"

I give a private smile, well aware of the irony. "That's me," I quip lightly. "Woman of mystery. So" – I stick my hands in my hoodie pockets and give him a cautious look – "can you help?"

"Sure," he says immediately. "Use mine."

"Great." I let out a breath, relieved at the plan – and the fact that he doesn't seem outraged by my proposal of minor fraud and deception. "You're the best."

"Can you put that on a sticker, maybe? Or a cap." He grins, eyes crinkling behind those square, retro glasses. "Or just keep repeating it for the rest of my life."

Oh.

I glance away, thrown by the sudden twist in my stomach and the bright look in his eyes. But that's ridiculous; he's a college student. He can't...

I peek back. He's lounged against the book case, and even with mussed-up hair and a faded old T-shirt, he's still older and cute and a hundred times cooler than I'll ever be.

That's enough of that.

This time, it's my own voice drowning out those insecurities, stern enough to make me giggle.

Scott raises an eyebrow.

"Nothing," I tell him, trying not to blush. "So, let's see this ID of yours."

Once I explain everything, Scott insists on coming with me, even though I could just take the ID and return it later. "It's fine," he promises, strolling beside me. "I was planning to have some coffee and study straight through. Besides" – he gives me a look – "I kind of want to see if you pull this off."

"We'd better." I walk quicker. "That diary is too dangerous to leave laying around."

"And then what, you'll destroy it?"

"Somehow. Although, we used up all the lighter fluid already..." I giggle.

"Uh-oh." Scott elbows me lightly, just a nudge. "You're going to be trouble; I can tell."

The idea that I, Meg Rose Zuckerman, could ever be trouble – let alone a woman of mystery and intrigue – would have been laughable even a day ago. But now I smile to myself, hugging my arms around me as we walk.

We round the last corner. "Is your exam first thing, or—?" The words fade from my lips as I look up and see Jolene and Dante making out against the car. Seriously making out. He's pressed her right up against the driver's side, and his hands are slipped so high inside her jacket that I blush, just looking at them.

"Ummm, guys?" I start, hesitant. There's no change. "Jolene?"

He brings his hands down to her thighs and then lifts

her up; she wraps her legs around his waist, but before things can get R-rated, there's a piercing whistle. We all look over. Scott lowers two fingers from his mouth. "Hey." He gives them a casual wave. "We, uh, got the card."

Jolene slips to the ground again, untangling herself from Dante's arms. "Great," she says, breathless. "That's awesome!"

"Good work." Dante gives me a sheepish grin.

"OK." I'm trying not to laugh, but they look so dizzy it's hard to keep a straight face. "How about we go ahead and break in, while you ... umm, keep watch here."

"It's a plan," Dante says immediately. He wraps his arms around Jolene's waist, leaning his chin down on her shoulder; she relaxes back against his chest. "We'll be, uh, vigilant."

"I'm sure you will." I smirk. Jolene looks happy, if such a thing were possible. Dante whispers something in her ear, and she swats him good-naturedly.

"I'll turn the jammer on." Jolene looks over as an afterthought. "So you – and Scott?—can take your time." She holds up the remote control as evidence.

"I guess we're up." Scott grins, turning back to me. "You ready?"

I nod, determined.

There's a wide walkway leading up to the dorm, but we approach from the side, skirting along the front wall to stay out of sight. I peer around, through the walled glass entrance. The old security guard is at his desk inside, watching something on the computer screen as he munches on a slice of pizza. Bliss is watching from her perch on a file cabinet behind him, slurping at a soda. I risk a wave. She glances up and catches my eye; I gesture. She nods.

"Let's go," I whisper to Scott, even though there's nobody around to hear us. Taking a breath, we stroll around and approach the door in full view. Scott swipes his card. Nothing. He swipes again, miming in a big gesture. I step up beside him and knock loudly on the door.

The guard looks up. Scott waves his card and points to the scanner. Reluctantly, the guard puts down his pizza and comes to let us in.

"I don't know what's wrong," I say, heart beating quicker. "It won't even beep."

He frowns, swiping his own card through the machine, but there's no response. "Come on," he says with a sigh, waving us inside. I make it halfway to the elevator before he adds, "I'll still need to see—"

"Quick, Brazil is about to score!" Bliss cries. From this angle, I can see that he's streaming a soccer match on one of the computer screens. The guard glances back, torn.

"Here!" Scott takes the opportunity to wave his card in the guard's face. He glances at it for a split second.

"Oooh!" Bliss cries out with excitement. "That was so a foul!"

With a quick nod at us, the guard hurries back to his station. "What did I miss?" he demands, as Scott hustles me into the elevator. I hit the button, and finally the doors slide shut.

"Oh my God." I cling to him, breathless. "That was close!"

"He barely looked at it!" Scott exclaims. He looks down at me, laughing, and I suddenly realize I'm still holding on to him, pressed warm against his chest.

"Right." I quickly let go, blushing. "I, umm..."

The doors open.

I step out into the hallway ahead of him, forcing myself to take a deep breath. *You're not clear yet,* I remind myself. There's still the matter of Jason to navigate – who could be poring over the diary at this very minute.

"Which way now?" Scott gets his bearings. There's mess from the party still scattered all around: garbage bags littering the lobby, and bottles stacked in recycling boxes outside every door.

I check the map on the wall. "Room 318, that-a-way."

"Lead on."

With the dorm so quiet now, there's nobody to stop us from making our way quickly through the hallways to Jason's room. I stop outside and assess: the door is shut, no light coming from inside.

"Do we knock?" I wonder.

"And ask politely for it back?" Scott asks, pressing his ear against the door to check for noise.

"Good point."

Besides, aren't I past the point of asking politely — standing back and waiting for something to be given to me? Isn't it time I reach out and take what I want myself?

Putting my hand to the doorknob, I carefully turn. It's open. "Shh," I tell Scott softly, easing the door wide enough to slip into the room.

It's pitch-black inside, with the drapes pulled shut and nothing but dark shadows all around. I feel Scott edge in behind me, closing the door behind him to block the hall light. We stand silently in the black for a moment, until my heartbeat slows again and my eyes adjust to the dim.

The sound of light snores is coming from the corner.

"Here." Scott's voice is quiet in my ear, and then there's a pale flicker as he takes out his cell phone. "Do you know where it is?"

I nod, before realizing he can't see it. "They said they left it on the bedside table," I whisper back. His arm brushes mine, and I shiver.

Scott takes his phone and sweeps the room, casting a bluish glow over objects in turn until he lands on Jason's body, slumped unconscious over his bed with a paper party crown crumpled on his head.

"I don't think we need to worry about him waking up anytime soon." Scott laughs, his voice returning to normal, but then there's a sound from the far corner. We freeze.

"Jase?" a male voice slurs from the floor. A head pops up on the other side of the room, adorned with his own crown. "Isthatyou?"

I gulp, lunging for the dark, squarish shape beside Jason's bed. My hands grope in the dark, feeling my way for something hard and booklike.

"Yup," Scott says behind me, trying not to laugh. "Just go back to sleep, buddy."

"Mneughh." The body slumps back down, just as my fingers close around pages and a leathery cover.

"I think, maybe...?" I hold the book out to Scott, anxious. He shines his phone over the pages, and in the faint light, I can just about decipher a girlish scrawl. "Yes!" I breathe, full of relief.

"Come on!" he whispers, grabbing my free hand and pulling me out of the room. I barely have time to shut the door behind us before he pushes me down the hallway, sprinting toward the elevator. We collapse laughing against the back wall, and then I realize. He's holding my hand.

This time, I don't let go.

"The outfit..." Scott begins, when we've both caught our breath. "You said you were trying to impress someone." He looks straight ahead as the elevator slowly descends. "Did it work?"

"Yes," I say quietly.

"Oh." His hand loosens in mine.

"But it turns out he wasn't worth impressing," I add.

"Oh." The grip tightens again.

I grin.

And then, because adrenaline is still sparkling in my veins, because tonight I've done things I never thought I'd have the courage to do, and because – most important of all – I suddenly want it so badly I forget how to breathe, I turn around and kiss him.

My lips bump awkwardly against his at first, but before I can feel clumsy or embarrassed at all, Scott pulls me closer, kissing me properly. His lips are warm against mine, hands gentle on my cheeks. I fall against him, giddy.

Now *this* is perfect.

Bliss

We meet back at the car – Jolene and Meg both grinning like cats who got the cream. Or, you know, the cute boys.

"Great." I sigh, looking between the happy couples. "Now I'm the third wheel. Or is that fifth?"

Meg blushes, shyly holding that Scott boy's hand. I size him up for a moment, but he's gazing at Meg with such clear adoration, I can't even hold those indie sideburns against him.

Jolene isn't so coy. "Get over it," she tells me, one hand in Dante's back pocket. "You're the one mourning your lost love, remember?"

I stare at her blankly.

"Uh, Cameron, remember him?"

"Oh, right." I pause, thrown. After everything tonight, he feels like a stranger – someone from a different life.

"So, we've got the diary back." Jolene yawns. "What's left?"

"Food," Meg announces immediately. I laugh. "What?" she protests. "Theft and deception is hungry work!"

"There's a diner just off campus," Scott suggests, looking around for approval. Meg bats her eyes up at him, lost, while Jolene shrugs, Dante still wrapped around her. Clearly, they need someone to take control before they all melt into a sickening pool of hormones.

"Let's go!" I declare, shooing them into the car. "Dante, get your hands off her for, like, two minutes. You're the only one who can drive this old thing."

We make it to the diner without any more public displays of affection, piling into a huge red leather booth in the corner. The place is bright, full of early-morning truckers and students recovering from the night before.

"Hash browns, and waffles, and sausage, and maple syrup," Meg tells the waitress, practically swooning over the menu. Scott grins, still holding fast to her hand.

"Need any help with that?"

Meg shakes her head so fast, her hair spins out. "Get your own!"

"Just coffee for me, black," Dante says. He slips out of his seat and heads for the corner jukebox. A second later, the twang of an old country song begins to play. *"Jolene, Jolene..."*

Smooth.

"If I'd known you were so easy to crack, I'd have

called him in a long time ago," I tell her.

"Shut up!" she protests, but there's no bite in her tone. Jolene nods at the small book on the table between us. "You know what you're going to do with it yet?"

"I was thinking a ceremonial shredding." I decide. "Every last page."

"But there's still Kaitlin's dirt in there," Meg points out. "You could keep that."

I shake my head. "I'm done with her. All this stupid bitching ... I'm better than that."

"And so modest, too," Jolene elbows me. I yelp.

"Just for that, I'm stealing all your bacon," I inform her, sending a longing look at the kitchen. Then I stop. "No way!"

I blink, staring at the group of goth girls crammed into a table by the door. But I'm right: it's her. My cousin, Selena, in thick black eye makeup and a black strappy corset, her hair twisted into sharp spirals. All this time I've spent trying to be as perfect as her, and it turns out, my sorority cousin isn't so image-perfect after all.

I laugh, waving across the room. She looks confused, and then worried, and then finally she raises her hand and gives me a tiny wave back.

"What?" Meg cranes her neck around.

"Nothing." I turn back to my table with a grin. Maybe my mom won't be freaking out so much about the feud with Kaitlin. At least I don't have a metal bar spiked through my nose.

"Did you see the flyers by the door?" Dante returns,

pushing all of us tighter together. "Okkervil River is playing out by the lake tomorrow night."

"You mean tonight," Jolene corrects him. He rolls his eyes at her, she sticks her tongue out, he leans forward, and then I interrupt before it all descends into make-out city again.

"Let's go," I suggest as the waitress begins to dispense vast piles of food in front of us. I inhale the carbs. Heaven. "After we've had, like, ten hours' sleep I mean."

"Sounds good to me." Scott reaches for the home fries. "My last final will be done."

"I don't know." Meg bites her lip. "My dad—"

"Leave him to me," I promise.

"And my mom…" Jolene adds, looking up from her bacon.

"Trust me," I insist, snatching a piece from her plate and settling back in the booth. I look around, happy. "This is going to be an awesome summer."

Acknowledgments

Thanks as always to my wonderful agent, Rosemary Stimola, and the fabulous team at Candlewick: Liz Bicknell, Kaylan Adair, and Tracy Miracle, and everyone else who worked to make this book possible.

Thanks also to my mum and dad, and the friends who offered ceaseless enthusiasm and advice: Veronique Watt, Elisabeth Donnelly, Darinka Aleksic, and Narmada Thiranagama. Thanks to Tyler Ruggeri for the support, and Will Sheff for writing "Unless It's Kicks."